Talking with the Dead

Surrounded by death, a man with a terrible gift reaches for life.

A horrific tragedy blasted open a door in young Michael O'Rourke's mind—cursing him with the ability to talk with the Dead. Nearly two decades later, Michael has moved from victim to survivor, using his abilities to seek out those who would go unjudged.

With his gift, he talks to those who've died violently and seeks out their killers. Only once he's found the murderer, can the victims be at rest. After his last case, the only thing he wants is peace and he hopes to find it in the small town of Mitchell, Indiana.

But something is horribly wrong—the dead are waiting for him there, as well.

Small town sheriff Daisy Crandall is frustrated. The murder investigation she's leading is going nowhere, the few leads she's had haven't panned out. She needs a break—this case is personal and when a stranger arrives, turning up where he shouldn't be, she's suspicious. Finding out that he is more than what he appears to be should shock her but doesn't. The fact she's highly attracted to him at the worst possible time is a hindrance.

Unfortunately, teaming up with Michael is the only way.

Now it's a race against time before the killer destroys the life of his next victim...

Warning, this title contains the following: explicit sex, graphic language, violence.

Vicious Vixen

He's given one chance at redemption—hers and his.

Hired killer Vixen Markham doesn't have any illusions about life or love. Unable to trust even the one man she lets into her heart, she makes a decision that she'll regret for the rest of her life—which won't be much longer by the looks of things. Loaded with vengeance and a small arsenal of weapons, she's ready to face up to her past and say goodbye to her future, until she's confronted by a pair of eyes she could never forget.

Graeme Mackenzie Lawson lived a hard life. Hard on himself and harder on those who got in his way. Betrayed and murdered, he's given one chance at redemption—but not for himself—for the woman he loved, the woman who killed him.

Can he keep Vixen safe, when she seems determined to lose her life—and her soul?

Warning: the following contains violence, hot sex and one vicious vixen.

Look for these titles by
Shiloh Walker

Now Available:

The Hunters Series:
The Huntress
Hunter's Pride
Malachi
Legends: Hunters and Heroes
Hunter's Edge

Always Yours
Talking with the Dead
Playing for Keeps
For the Love of Jazz
Beautiful Girl
Vicious Vixen
My Lady

Taking Chances

Shiloh Walker

A SAMHAIN PUBLISHING, LTD. publication.

Samhain Publishing, Ltd.
577 Mulberry Street, Suite 1520
Macon, GA 31201
www.samhainpublishing.com

Taking Chances
Print ISBN: 978-1-60504-400-2
Talking with the Dead Copyright © 2009 by Shiloh Walker
Vicious Vixen Copyright © 2009 by Shiloh Walker

Editing by Heidi Moore
Cover by Scott Carpenter

Talking with the Dead, ISBN 1-59998-384-2
First Samhain Publishing, Ltd. electronic publication: November 2006
Vicious Vixen, ISBN 1-59998-946-8
First Samhain Publishing, Ltd. electronic publication: August 2008
First Samhain Publishing, Ltd. print publication: October 2009

Contents

Talking with the Dead

Prologue

Although Lucas never mentioned it, and neither did Mom, Michael O'Rourke was a disappointment and he knew it.

Lucas, now, Lucas was everything their charlatan mother could ever hope for. She'd taught him well, teaching him how to run scams, how to pick pockets and how to evade cops and social workers. Yeah, she'd taught him well, all right—maybe too well. Lucas was sixteen. Strong. Smart. He wasn't going to hang around and keep helping his mother run her scams.

She called herself Lavonne, but her birth name was Rachel O'Rourke. Her great gift in life was in the grift. She could run a scam like nothing Michael had ever seen. Even Lucas couldn't sucker them in the way Mama could.

But Lucas had gifts, *real* gifts, the kind Mama liked to pretend she had. He saw things.

The "sight" Mama called it. Ran in her family, she liked to say, although Michael didn't think she had ever seen anything that he couldn't see with his own two eyes. Lucas once told Mike that their mama couldn't see a spirit if it bit her on the ass. They'd laughed themselves sick, thinking about it.

Lucas could see, though. He *knew* things. He had known when it was time to leave New Orleans and he had known when it was time to leave Memphis and he had warned her about going to Nashville. She'd pissed people off there, but Lavonne was stupid. Plain and simple. She was going to do what she wanted to do.

She got herself embroiled in shit and then slid away before it was time to pay the piper. Her luck wouldn't last forever. Lucas just hoped it would hold a little while longer. He was going to get the hell away from her. One night, while she was screwing some dude for drug money, Lucas and Mike were going to disappear. It was going to have to be soon. Mike wasn't safe around Lavonne. Last night, Lucas had overheard Lavonne talking to a major freak—she'd offered the guy an hour alone with Mike for a grand. Of course, the man wanted to see Mike first. Too bad too. The guy was mean enough, if he had paid Lavonne upfront and then they couldn't find Mike, he might have killed her.

Lucas wanted her dead. More than anything, he wanted their mother dead. That had been the eighth time he had saved Mike from being raped. Mike knew about that one—he'd been with Lucas when Lavonne was trying to pimp the twelve-year-old out. He had been there three other times, too. But he knew nothing about all the other times and Lucas planned on keeping it that way.

They had to get out of there. Sooner or later, Lavonne would try to set it up when Lucas wasn't around.

Lucas was pissed off. He'd been mad ever since last night and Mike knew why. His gut had been twisted into slimy, sick knots all night but today, he wasn't so worried about it. Lucas had gotten him away. Lucas had protected him. Again. Lucas was always there—even though he was smart enough, looked old enough, he could get away from Lavonne whenever he wanted. He didn't though.

Mike knew why.

No, he didn't have any special sight and he couldn't see inside a person's mind. But he did have a bond, a close one, with his big brother. They could talk. Carry on entire conversations all without even moving their lips.

"She's been drinking again," Michael said. He didn't have to tell Lucas that. The older boy would have seen it long before Michael did. Still, being able to talk this way with Lucas made him feel special. Lucas made him feel special. Lucas made him feel wanted.

Didn't make him feel like he was some useless baby that he had to lug around, or worse—like some worthless piece of crap that shouldn't have ever been born.

"Gee—ya think?" Lucas said. Even his mental voice had a sardonic tone to it and the smile on his mouth was a bitter one. His blue eyes met Michael's in the mirror for the briefest of seconds before he went back to pretending to focus on the book

in his hands.

Lucas loved reading. Neither of them had ever spent any serious time in school unless a social worker arrived on the scene. Then their mother would pretend to get all weepy, begging for forgiveness and understanding. No matter how times it happened, Lavonne managed to convince the effing government that she was ready to change. She'd do it this time. She loved her babies and just couldn't make it without them. She really would get sober and straight and blah blah blah. Mike knew all that garbage by heart, just like he knew every last bit of it was a lie.

She might love Lucas but that was because he was her meal ticket. But she didn't give a damn about Mike. Anybody with eyes should have seen it, Mike figured. But he was tired of hoping that they would take him away. She suckered them all. They'd go to whatever school was close by for a few days and then they'd disappear, moving on to another city where the process would start all over again. Two years ago, their mother had finally gotten smart.

If she moved around enough, no social worker could keep track of her.

So they rarely stopped moving. Since then, Michael and Lucas hadn't slept in the same place for more than a week. It sucked, but it was better than dealing with the shit they had to put up with when their mother went all ballistic the second the social worker left.

But school or no, Lucas loved to read and he had passed that passion onto his kid brother. As long as Michael kept his books hidden from her, of course. She liked to take them away and burn them, right in front of him. He learned pretty damn quick that he had to hide them from her. Lucas, though, he didn't have to worry about that. Lucas didn't have to dodge her fists, he didn't ever go hungry, and he could read as much as he wanted, as long as he got his work done.

Michael didn't mind. It wasn't like it was Lucas' fault that Lavonne loved Lucas, but hated Michael. It wasn't like her love was some big prize. Her love was almost as revolting as her hate—Mike had seen the way she liked to cuddle up to Lucas, petting him like he was some teddy bear. The bigger and older Lucas got, the more attentive she became. She looked at him with greed in her eyes and Mike knew what that look meant. So did Lucas.

Mike sighed and rested his head against the window. She'd dragged them out of bed before sunrise this time and he was worn out. He wanted to sleep, but he didn't dare sleep if she was driving. Later, she'd get in the back seat and get stoned. Once she passed out and Lucas was driving, Mike would feel safe enough to sleep. The streetlights sped by in a blur and Mike glanced toward the front seat. She was edging up over ninety as she weaved in and out of traffic.

"She don't slow down, we'll get pulled over."

Michael felt Lucas' mental laughter, the kind that wasn't really laughing at anything. *"We should be so lucky."* But Lucas looked up, and from the rearview mirror, Mike saw the thoughtful way his eyes narrowed, saw the distant, off focus look form there. "Lavonne, I think you might want to slow down," Lucas said levelly.

They couldn't call her Mama. Or Mom. Nothing like that. She didn't like it. She blew out some smoke before drawing once more on the cigarette in her mouth, her voice low and rough from years of smoking. "Why would I want to do that?" she rasped.

"Cops," Lucas replied, shrugging one shoulder.

She scowled and slammed on the brake so hard that Michael went flying into the seat in front of them and the car behind them laid on the horn for a good thirty seconds. Mike glanced over his shoulder as he eased back onto the seat. The driver of the black sedan flipped them off.

"What in the hell are you looking back there for?" Lavonne snapped. "Bastard was tailgating me. Ain't my fault."

"Yes, Lavonne," he said automatically. She sent him a dirty look. Michael could see the hatred in her eyes. Then it was gone and she looked at Lucas, her expression irritated. "Damn it. You feel cops around and you're just now telling me?"

She hated him. She always had. She always would.

But Michael didn't care. He had Lucas. That was all that mattered. He stared out the window, eyes searching for patrol cars. He saw nothing.

But if Lucas said there was cops, then there was cops.

Funny, though, how Michael had thought it...and then Lucas mentioned it.

CRSO

"You can't take my boy!"

Michael hid in the attic, huddled in a tight little ball, frozen with shock and fear. He stared through the tiny crack, watching as the big guy busted Lucas in the mouth again.

Help him. He had to go help Lucas. They were going to kill him. Whatever Lavonne had done this time, she had done it to the wrong people and they were going to kill Lucas because of it.

No. I can't let them. He started to get up, for probably the fifth time. And just like the past four times, Lucas did something to him. Michael felt his muscles freeze, felt his body shut down. His arms and legs refused to obey him, following the silent commands from his brother as Michael sank back into his hiding place.

"Now didn't I tell you not to come back here without my money, Rachel?" It was a big, mean looking guy. Mike had seen him before. His head was bald on top, long on the sides and back. He always wore it slicked back in a ponytail and he spoke with an accent like the guys in that movie, *The Godfather.*

Her eyes were red with tears but she forced a smile at him. "That's why I came back, baby. I got some money and I got a line in to get more."

"Yeah. I bet you do. You think you can find enough johns to cover the 5k?" He curled his lip and gave Lavonne a very long slow once-over. "Not with that used up snatch."

Her face turned an ugly red, but she didn't say anything other than, "I got a plan, Mitch. Promise."

Mitch just laughed. "Sure." He looked around the small space and demanded, "Where's the brat?"

"Leave Lucas alone and I'll tell you," Lavonne said, crying.

Michael flinched. If Lavonne knew where to find him, then she *would* trade him for Lucas. Not that Michael wouldn't do the same—he'd walk through fire for Lucas, sell his soul to the devil for him.

Pretty damn clear that was what the old lady wanted to do. Even though she'd tried to do it before, hearing it all over again really sucked.

"You fucking bitch," Lucas seethed. Hatred blazed in Lucas'

eyes and he snarled at Lavonne. He struggled against the men holding him, determined to get his hands on his mother. "I'd rather die now then let them get their hands on my brother."

Lavonne ignored him, moving to one of the men in the apartment, stroking her hands down his arm as she whispered, "Mikey's young. You're bound to know somebody who'd like a boy like him. People that would pay five grand, easy. More. Just leave Lucas...I need him—"

"*Bitch!*" Lucas roared, trying to break free of the two men holding him.

Michael's belly pitched and rolled from all the emotions he felt flooding off of Lucas, and through Lucas, he felt the emotions of the others. Hatred, greed, boredom... He buried his face in his hands, wishing he could just disappear. For good. Forever.

"He's just a worthless brat. Not like you, baby," Lavonne said, forcing a shaking smile at her son before looking back at the guy who looked like he was in charge. "So what do you say? You can get some good money. A trade, the kid for whatever I owed you."

The man laughed as he backhanded Lavonne with casual ease. "No. I'd rather take the one you want the most," he responded. Standing aside, he jerked his head toward the door.

From the attic, Michael watched in horror as they dragged his brother away.

It seemed like hours passed as Michael lay frozen in shock. He couldn't move until the old lady was gone. If he did, she was going to take this out on him. And Michael knew he wouldn't survive the beating this time around. Lucas wasn't there to save him.

Lucas...

Oh, God. Raw pain ripped through him, followed by terror, guilt and too many other emotions for him to understand. Lucas might never be there again. The way that guy had looked at Lavonne as his boys dragged Lucas away—he had *smiled.* Lavonne screamed.

He was going to...to... *No. You can't think like that. Get moving. Save him.*

But he couldn't get moving. Not until Lavonne was gone. It didn't take long, though. She screamed and cried for a few minutes after they dragged Lucas away, but in typical Lavonne fashion, she was more interested in saving her ass than anybody else's. Even Lucas'.

She packed in a hurry, throwing her stuff into a sack and leaving behind everything else. When she walked out, she had a bag full of clothes in one hand, a bottle of whiskey in the other and she never once looked back.

Now that she was finally gone, he could sneak down and take the money Lucas had been hoarding, get some food—then Michael was going to find his brother and they were going to get the hell out of there, as far away from Lavonne and her crap as they could.

Michael wasn't thinking of her as Mama any more. Not Mom. Not anything. She was no relation to him.

She was no blood. She was no family.

She was scum, less than that. The shit she had got herself into was why Lucas was in trouble. The man had come looking for money she owed him and Lucas was the one paying the price. She'd been willing to give away her own son to pay off her trouble.

Gingerly, he climbed down from the attic, still listening, well aware she might be waiting out in the hall to see if he came out. But he figured she was probably long gone. The bastards who took Lucas may decide to come back and she wouldn't want to be anywhere close, just in case.

She sure as hell hadn't been concerned about leaving him behind, had she?

No. "Not my blood, not any more," he whispered furiously, working open the tiny slit in the mattress he and Lucas shared. There was money there. A lot of it. More than Lavonne could even imagine having her hands on. Lucas was careful, and he was smart.

They were going to be okay. Unaware of the tears that rolled down his cheeks, Michael jerked out the little bag that held the money, tucking it inside the waistband of his shorts and using duct tape to make sure it stayed in place. They would be just fine.

He crept out the window in the bedroom after he grabbed a pack of crackers, some peanut butter and the stash of candy bars Lucas had hidden from Lavonne. It wasn't much food but it would have to do. Michael had to get out of there.

His young, twelve-year-old mind never questioned the

urgency that filled him. He just knew he had to *go*.

Night had fallen and he stayed in the shadows as he moved out of the alley. Had to stay away from everybody. Both the dealers on the streets and the cops who cruised through the streets of Nashville. Had to get out. Get away.

But Lucas first.

The bond between them hadn't ever been closed off before. Michael needed to be able to feel Lucas to find him. But it was like Lucas was hiding from him.

Finally he was able to reach out and touch his brother's mind and he could have cried with relief. Huddled in the back of the old garage, he rubbed at his gritty eyes and called out to Lucas.

But Lucas shoved him back. *"Get away, Mikey. Now."*

Although he didn't know the reason, Michael heard the panic in Lucas' voice, panic and a fear he hadn't ever heard from Lucas before. *"Where are you? We got to get out of here."*

"You go, Mikey. Go now—"

The scream that tore through Lucas echoed from Michael as well. And suddenly, Michael wasn't in the old garage any more. He was in a cold room with gray walls and he *hurt*.

Terror flooded Michael and he flinched as Lucas' voice filled his head and sounded off the walls in the room. *"Mikey, go!"*

The people who surrounded them stared all around, looking at each other before looking back at Michael...no, Lucas. They were looking at Lucas. Michael was just feeling the same damn things, seeing the same things as Lucas.

The hot metallic taste of fear filled his mouth and he tried to break away, but he couldn't.

"Mikey..."

There was a gun pointing at him.

"Lucas!"

"I'm sorry, Mikey. We were going to..."

The horrendous crack filled the air, and then there was darkness.

Michael came screaming out of the darkness, struggling against the arms that held him. But he was alone.

Alone in the garage.

And Lucas was gone. Dead.

Chapter One

The scent of blood, gore and earth wasn't a scent that a man forgot easily. Gun drawn, Special Agent Michael O'Rourke breathed through his mouth and tried not to pay attention to the smell. It was hard, but he had done this often enough that he could block it out a little.

A few of the less experienced agents were feeling pretty squeamish. That was more a distraction than the smell—at least for Mike. Their nausea hit him like a sucker punch, right in the gut, and he had to battle back the same bile that they were fighting to contain.

None of them had the luxury to get sick right now. Samuel Watkins had killed six times and his seventh victim was running out of time. Michael could feel her too. He could feel her terror, her pain. She wanted her mama, but she didn't dare cry out. Brave little thing.

I'll get you to your mama, sweetheart. I promise. Not one more child would die because of this bastard.

It was darker than midnight down there and descending the steps was like a descent straight into hell. Dark, ugly, and terrifying. Mike wasn't afraid of Watkins. The worst thing Watkins could do to him was kill him and Mike would go happily if it meant taking the monster with him. No. He was afraid that Watkins would find the girl and finish what he had started.

But Watkins was preoccupied. As Mike reached the bottomof the stairs, his booted feet hit the dirt floor and he went still, staring at the sight before him. Faint greenish lights hovered around Watkins and the short, stout man was flailing at the air with fisted hands. He was also screaming.

"What the..."

Destin Mortin came to a dead stop just at Mike's shoulder. A new agent in Oz's little motley crew, Destin couldn't see ghosts. Her skill was a little odd, even to Mike. She fit in well, though, on this case. Officially, Destin was still in training. Unofficially, she was ready to take to the streets and kick some ass. Oz was worried that Destin would get to Watkins first and take out several pounds of flesh. That morning, Mike would have agreed with Oz. It was completely possible that Destin might find Watkins first and seek some good old-fashioned vigilante justice.

Wasn't going to happen though.

Samuel Watkins wasn't going to leave this basement alive.

He was already a little gray in the face, although it was hard to really judge his color well with the ghostly lights flashing around him. As one of the spirits moved closer, it solidified and a girl's face became visible. Mike recognized her from the missing person's file. Misty Brighton had disappeared on her tenth birthday. She had been Watkins' first victim. She'd been dead for eight years.

She looked toward him. A mean little smile curled her lips and Mike said softly, "It's time, Misty. You can go on now."

Misty shook her head. *"Not yet."* Her voice was wispy and insubstantial, but it had an underscore of rage. It burned with a blistering intensity that stung Mike's skin. She reached out and Mike winced as she stuck a ghostly hand inside Watkins' chest. The man screamed. It was a high-pitched, terrified sound. It ended abruptly and then Watkins collapsed, falling forward.

Mike stood there, staring at the man who had raped and murdered six girls. He lay face down in the dirt, still as death.

Misty lifted her head and Mike waited, apprehension drawing his skin tight. Would she go? Or would the rage bind her here?

"Your mom is waiting for you," he said gently.

Misty's eyes closed and her form became more and more insubstantial. *"I'm scared, Michael."*

He smiled at her. "I know. But there's nothing to be afraid of, not now. Not any more."

At least, not for her.

CR80

Death did ugly things to a person.

Tanya had been so pretty. The body on the ground couldn't possibly be one of Daisy's friends. It just wasn't possible. Death had turned her pretty, sweet face into a macabre mask and her toned body had long since gone through rigor, her limbs limp and flaccid.

Just like the others, she'd been raped, beaten, strangled. But she'd bled out. That was what had killed her. There was no pooling of fluids, no mottling. The coroner would find very little, if any, blood left in Tanya's corpse. So far, Daisy had counted more than twenty shallow little slices. It would have been very, very slow.

"Ten minutes."

Daisy looked over her shoulder at Deputy Wyatt Lock. Lock was staring at Tanya with a mixture of grief, horror and disbelief. "Wyatt?"

He turned his head and met Daisy's gaze. His normally mild hazel eyes were burning with fury and his voice throbbed with intensity as he said, "I want ten minutes alone with him, Daisy."

Get in line. When she managed to get her hands on the killer, if she didn't kill him herself, she was going to have her hands full keeping him safe while he awaited trial. The thought of a trial made Daisy get her ass in gear. They had a crime scene to secure and there couldn't be a single mistake. Everything had to be done perfect and legal, because this bastard wasn't going to get off due to a lack of evidence or some damned legal loophole.

He was going to pay for what he was doing and he was going to pay dearly.

She stepped aside and beckoned for the crime scene photographer to get to work. It was a grim and thankless task and by the time it was over, Daisy was hovering between wanting to scream bloody murder and breaking down into tears. She would have settled for a nice, stiff drink but she wasn't going to get that either.

A man was standing at the very edge of the crime scene and only the four volunteer firefighters were keeping him from running up to Tanya's body. "Hurry it up," she said in a low voice as she passed Wyatt. "He can't see her like that."

Daisy approached Tom Dourant and said the words that every cop hated.

CR&O

It took two more days to finish up the paperwork. By the time he had fulfilled that particular pain in the ass obligation, he was ready to leave Philadelphia behind and never, ever return.

Whether or not that would happen, Mike had no idea.

He left a message on Oz's machine and told her that he'd be out of contact for a while and then he turned off his pager. If she needed him badly enough, she'd find him anyway.

But he had to get away. Had to clear his head and hopefully get away from the ghosts that chased him. He doubted it would work, but he was going to give it a shot. There were other problems in Philly, but somebody else was going to have to handle them.

Destin had to stay in the City of Brotherly Love and she had a decent partner in Caleb Durand. Those two could handle the bad vibes that were keeping the agents awake at night, and they could do it without Mike's help. His grip on sanity often seemed pretty slippery, but never as much as it did now.

If he didn't get away and get a break, they might as well lock him up now and throw the keys in the Delaware. He wouldn't be good for anything else. He didn't bother checking out of the hotel. The Bureau would handle his tab. They also would have paid for the cab he called, but since he didn't want them tracking his every step, he paid the driver in cash.

The driver left him in the drop off zone without a thank you for the five dollar tip. Mike hoped the guy would go and buy some deodorant and an air freshener. The guy reeked to high heaven. He could still smell the oily stink of unwashed body ten minutes later as he waited in line for a rental car.

It meant using a credit card and ID, but he would have to show ID to get a flight out of the city anyway. Losing one's self was a lot harder since 9/11. Normally, Mike wouldn't care. Normally, he was of the mind that there wasn't enough being done to make the country secure. But this one time, he really,

really wished he could just disappear and nobody be able to find him.

CR80

Michael's appetite for food was dead.

He'd come in here, starving. After nothing but fast food for the past couple months, a decent home cooked meal sounded like heaven. But five seconds after sitting down, all thoughts of food had fled his mind. He sat staring at the Formica table top while dread, anger and disgust formed a leaden ball in the pit of his belly.

Am I ever going to get a break? he wondered bleakly. There was no answer and he didn't really expect one.

Too tired for this mess, he almost climbed off the chair and walked back to his car. He could put the top down on the powerful little convertible, hit the gas and be miles away before dark. He could put two or three states between himself and this darkness, and just maybe, he could forget about it.

But even though he was tired and dancing on the edge of depression, he couldn't make himself leave. The darkness in the air was too thick, and the violence too recent. It sat on the back of his tongue like something gone sour. He lowered his shields and opened himself up to the darkness hovering.

It was more than just darkness though. It was something bloody. Something evil.

This small town in Indiana was quiet, damn it. He had found the little bitty dot on the map at the rest area right inside the state's border and figured it was as good a place as any to get some rest. A good a place as any to get away from the darkness, the death.

The ghosts.

As always, Mike had been wrong. In a major way. The ghosts were here, just like they had been everywhere he had gone for the past two decades. They followed him. Why in the hell he'd thought he could get away from them here, now, he'd never know. These ghosts were his only companions in life and for as long as he lived, they'd find him.

After twenty years, he was even used to it. The company of ghosts was a sight better than being left alone with his thoughts. But he didn't like the darkness he felt here. Not at all. He didn't even have to ask around to know that something very, very bad was going on.

Something bad seemed to be his reason for existing. Like a moth drawn to flame, he was drawn unconsciously to places just like this, places where an evil lived, an evil that he would have to hunt down. He hadn't felt any inkling of wrong as he drove here. Nothing as he entered the small town. Mike had actually thought, finally, for once, he had gotten away from them at least for a while.

It wasn't that he thought he could leave them behind forever, although he sure as hell wouldn't mind it. But after the last job, he needed some peace. Some silence. Just a little bit of time to pretend that he was normal.

Mike hadn't ever been normal, even before he picked up his bizarre little talent. When it first came on him, he had run away from it. Half out of his mind from fear and slowly going insane as he tried to get away from the people that few others saw.

The counselor who had finally helped him to understand what was going on was gone now. Michael had been close to sixteen before he made sense of the things and voices and sights crowding his mind. Even Lucas had no idea what had been done to him that night when Michael had shared in his brother's death.

Elizabeth Ransome had looked at the child lying in the hospital bed and she had understood. She saw a boy who was nearly a man, one who was terrified and tormented, but not insane. More, she helped Michael understand.

She saw somebody with a gift. A terrible, unpleasant gift, but a gift nonetheless. *You can let this gift rule you and drive you crazy, or you can learn to use it. Save others from dying like your brother did, Michael. Let me help you. Then we can help them.*

She had helped him make sense of the people he saw that others couldn't see, the voices he heard that nobody else could hear.

Yeah, if Elizabeth hadn't come along, he would have gone insane. Sooner or later, he'd have even managed to succeed when he attempted suicide.

He knew that.

It was getting to him again, though. He was losing his

distance, losing his focus. Mike was walking too damned close to the brink again, too much death, too many voices that had been silenced long before their time. Michael had to learn how to block them out again.

This last case had damned near destroyed him.

Baby killer.

That was what Samuel Watkins had been. He hadn't died a painful enough death. His heart had stopped. The official report was heart attack, but unofficially, he had been scared to death by one of his first victims. Too damned easy—he had taken six young lives. Six sweet, innocent young lives in a way so brutal, so horrifying and perverted that it had taken everything Mike had just to stay on the case.

Those little faces haunted him at night. Not their ghosts— no, they had passed on once their killer saw justice. Even Misty had finally let go, leaving this earth to go on to what waited beyond.

But the knowledge that he hadn't been quick enough to save them filled him with bitter, tired anger. Six lives lost, forever gone. Their leaving had left gaping, raw wounds in the lives of their parents and siblings. And inside of Michael. Although he didn't know them until after they had died, he felt their absence acutely.

Too late. He was always too late. This was the story of his life. He came in after the horrors happened and tried to piece things back together again.

It was destroying him.

The tiny chiming of a bell over the door intruded on his brooding and he glanced up automatically before returning his attention to the plate in front of him. It held no appeal for him, but he knew if he didn't eat, he'd never rebuild the strength he had drained tracking down Watkins.

Energy crackled through the room as a cool breeze from the outdoors came gusting through the door just before it closed. Like static electricity, the energy danced down his skin, shocking him, sizzling under his flesh, bursting through his mind like fireworks on the Fourth of July.

Slowly, he raised his eyes from the unappetizing food and found himself staring at a snug little backside covered in khaki as a woman boosted herself onto a stool at the café counter. Her hair was golden brown, caught in a thick braid that hung more than halfway down her back. As he watched her shrug out of the rather official looking jacket, Michael cursed the blood that was suddenly running hot through his veins.

This was a distraction that he didn't want and didn't need.

First the dark cloud that had taken hold of his mind and now all he could smell was the faint tropical fragrance that drifted from the woman's hair and the soft vanilla of her skin.

And the purpose that filled her entire being. It was like she was walking around wrapped with neon, but only Mike could see it.

Anger.

Frustration.

Rage.

Bingo. The woman was all but a walking, talking cry for help and Mike just didn't know if he could take any more on right now. Then he blew out a breath and muttered, "You can handle it. You always do."

Rolling his eyes skyward, he thought silently, *But it would be so nice to actually be able to have a relaxing vacation.*

A soft, familiar voice echoed in his mind, *"Then maybe you should try some remote cabin in Alaska. Might be a few less unsolved murders out in the middle of nowhere."*

Years of practice had taught him not to flinch, not to jump, not to even look directly at the man speaking to him. Nobody else would see him. He had been dead for twenty years. *"How's the afterlife, Lucas?"* he asked dryly, arching a brow as he nonchalantly turned his gaze to stare at his brother.

"Ever the smart ass, Mikey." A slow smile tugged up Lucas' lips in a grin that haunted Michael's sleep. *"You know, you could move into one of those glacier caves. I bet not too many people have been murdered in one of those. You can get some peace there."*

Lucas' face was forever young. Some movies painted ghosts as grisly images, but it had been Michael's experience that a ghost was an echo of what the ghost remembered seeing in life. Lucas looked exactly as he had the last time he'd seen himself, standing in the bathroom, running his hands through his hair. Wavy brown hair, a little too long, blue eyes surrounded by spiky lashes that both of the brothers had inherited—and hated. Thin to the point of being bony, with big hands, big shoulders. Exactly as Michael had looked at that age. Mike had grown into his body—Lucas hadn't been given the chance.

Forever young. Forever handsome.

"You're becoming pretty damned moody, Mikey."

A tiny smile lit his face. Nobody but Lucas had ever called him Mikey. And even though he had most likely passed the age where Mikey was an acceptable name, hearing it from Lucas was oddly comforting. Just like seeing him was comforting. But at the same time, Mike hated seeing him.

He interacted with ghosts on a regular basis and they only hung around the living for as long as they had to. Once their business was finished, they passed on.

Lucas had been waiting for twenty years to finish his business and he didn't seem to be in any hurry to move on now, either.

"When are you going to move on, Luc?"

"When I make sure I keep a promise. Promise is a promise, Mike. I told you I'd make sure you were happy. That's when I'll move on."

With a sigh, Michael shoved a hand through his hair. This was an old conversation, one they'd had a hundred times. *"There is something wrong here."*

Lucas lifted one shoulder in a restless shrug. *"I know. I felt it this morning. Young people. A lot of blood. Some old. Some fresh. But something is definitely not right in Smalltown America."*

Michael suspected the lady sitting on the stool in front of him had answers. He could see it in her weary, bitter eyes and the way she sat. Although she sat tall and straight with her shoulders pulled back, there was an invisible weight bearing down on her.

He didn't need to see the shiny brass badge on her jacket to know what he was looking at.

Cop.

From under the fringe of his lashes, he sat back and studied her. It was there in the purposefulness of her walk, the way she held herself, in the tense frustration he felt rolling off of her. *"Go ask her,"* Lucas suggested.

"Stranger in town, asking if there's something odd going on in her town. Oh, yes, excellent way to not attract attention." Michael shot that idea down as he shoved the sandwich on his

plate around.

"If you don't eat that, you're going to be sorry later."

Michael curled up his lip and slowly lifted the sandwich, trying to tune his brother out as he bit into the pile of meat, cheese and bread. It had about as much flavor and appeal as a sawdust sandwich would, but he knew he needed it.

"That's a good boy," Lucas teased, reaching out to pat Michael's head.

Michael felt the touch like a cool wind on his scalp. It didn't bother him anymore when the dead touched him. But he still slid Lucas a look and silently said, *"Fuck off, man."*

Lucas might be dead, but he was still Michael's brother.

Dasynda Crandall saw the guy sitting at the far end of counter and summed him up with a fairly quick glance as she crossed the café. Built, handsome, and something about the look in his eyes added *not to be messed with* to her list.

He made her back itch, but she couldn't exactly say she felt something off about him. Not that she could really trust her instincts much any more. Her first guess would be that this was a decent guy for the most part, even if he did look a little too big and a little too scary to set the mind at ease.

But Daisy's instincts just plain sucked, as far as she was concerned. She had a damned killer in her town and she wasn't getting so much as an inkling on who it was.

Her instincts had always served her well, but they had four bodies now, and no clue about the killer. Daisy was frustrated beyond all belief. Why in the hell had murders started *after* she had taken office?

This was why she had left the Louisville Metro Police Department. The instincts she had lived her life by seemed to be failing her. Women she had known all her life were being killed and Daisy didn't even know where to start.

She watched the stranger from the mirror that had hung over Elsa's cash register for a good twenty years. Even though Elsa had finally given up the fifties and the beehive hairdo, she still kept that mirror and checked her cardinal red coiffure rather regularly. Daisy watched as the man glanced to his right on a regular basis. Like he would if he was talking to somebody.

But his lips never moved. And there was nobody there. The food on his plate didn't seem to interest him much, but she did see him finally eat some of it. He had some of Elsa's world famous pot roast on that sandwich, but he might as well have been chewing bark for all the enjoyment he showed as he took yet another bite.

Forcing her attention back to her own food, she started to eat. To think. She didn't want to think about the killer. Thinking about it reminded her just how incompetent she had become. But she hadn't ever been one to run from her problems and she sure as hell couldn't run from this one.

There had to be something somewhere. No killer could come and go without a trace like this.

But what in the hell was going on in her town?

The image of Tanya's body danced before her eyes and her stomach pitched. Tanya hadn't just been killed. She had been tortured. Raped repeatedly. Strangled so brutally it had damned near crushed her throat. When death had finally come, it had come slowly, her blood trickling out so she was aware of exactly what was coming. Her death had been slow and horrific.

Daisy's fondest wish in life was to mete out that same brutal death to the man who had killed Tanya. Dropping the sandwich, she shoved the plate away and propped her arms on the counter.

"I'm going to find you," she whispered harshly. "Just wait."

Chapter Two

Somebody was having fantasies at that moment.

Oh, he was going to have fun with her. The young ones were always the best. She didn't know him—he would miss out on that initial shock, the denial, when they came swimming up out of sleep and saw him for the first time. He did enjoy seeing that look on their face. Enjoyed listening to them beg and plead...*why are you doing this to me?* Then they'd try to bargain. *I have kids—babies. They need me. You know they need me.*

Yeah, that was fun. But a young girl was even more fun. Pretty little runaway had no idea what she had gotten into when she climbed into his car. As he took his time tying her up, he smiled and ran his hand through her platinum blonde hair from time to time. He had her restrained at the wrists, the elbows, the ankle and knee, legs spread wide, straining the crotch of her cotton jersey pants.

The hair was silky, soft, straight as could be. She wasn't a real blonde—he'd already checked. The wispy little curls between her legs were a dark brown. But the blonde locks did look good on her.

As her eyes finally started to flutter open, he rested a hand on her belly and crouched down by her side. He propped his chin on the bed so that his face was next to hers. He wanted to be the first thing she saw when she came to.

Appropriate, since he planned on being the last thing she ever saw as well.

First there was confusion. The nerves and anxiety. As she started trying to move her arms and legs, she realized she was tied down, and that was when the fun began. As the terror entered her eyes, a pleased smile spread across his face.

"Morning, sweetheart. Didn't anybody ever tell you not to go hitchhiking?"

She opened her mouth to scream and he just laughed.

"Nobody close enough to hear you, sweetie. They never heard the others. They won't hear you," he told her, leaning close so that his nose brushed against hers.

She recoiled into the mattress and screamed, the sound high and terrified. Pleased, he sat back on his heels to listen and watch.

CR&O

Mike felt the cool brush of the woman's body against his own as he hugged her. He never knew what to say to them, never understood if what he did was the right thing. But so far, this time, it seemed to be the right thing.

"I'll try to help her," he said.

She smiled up at him.

"Who is he?" he asked quietly. "Can you tell me?"

That was when she retreated. The minute he mentioned the man who had killed her, the ghost faded away. Fear crowded her mind and she fled.

Shoving a hand through his hair, he spun away, kicking a rock. Lucas was watching him from a distance. *"She's young."* Anger colored his voice, turned it into a thunderous crash that boomed through his mind as he spoke to Michael.

Sourly, Mike muttered, "Too many of them are."

"You can't keep doing this, Mikey. Looking for killers, talking to ghosts." Lucas looked at Mike, his eyes concerned, his mouth turned down in a familiar scowl. Mike had heard this song and dance before and it would end the same way it always did. Stopping wasn't an option.

Just like leaving wasn't an option for Lucas.

"Then why don't you give me a break—you talk to me nonstop."

Lucas grinned. *"I'm an exception. We're family."*

Slanting him an evil look, Mike started to prowl the grounds. He'd seen the yellow police tape but he'd also seen too many cases where small things had been missed. He needed something small—something the killer had brushed up against could lead him right to the bastard.

It wouldn't take much. Hell, a rock that the killer had kicked as he dumped the body. Mike could lift a psychic impression as easily as a crime scene unit lifted fingerprints. But nearly an hour later—he had to admit, the whole place was virtually null. The killer had been very, very careful.

There wasn't a single thing that Mike could see to trace him.

At least not here. There would be something, though. There always was. All Mike had to do was wait. He just hoped it happened before another woman was killed.

CRISO

Daisy had to stifle the urge to snarl in pure frustration as the last possible lead she had on the killer who had killed four women in her town came up empty. Nothing. Yes, Kelsey Morrow told her, she *had* seen a car that night before she called her. But it was so dark...and she couldn't tell a Trans Am from a Camry, Kelsey relayed mournfully. She thought it was a four door—maybe. And the color was dark. But dark blue, dark green, gray...black...

Damn it. Daisy suspected it could have been a Pinto painted with black and white pinstripes, and Kelsey wouldn't have remembered. It could have been a vintage Mustang convertible in pristine condition, and Kelsey wouldn't have noticed.

Why, on earth, did the one woman who had seen the probable killer have to be Kelsey?

She was a sweet enough girl, and Daisy loved her dearly—after all, they were stepsisters.

But Kelsey was an airhead. Talking to her made Daisy as dizzy as a whirlwind. Daisy tugged on her braid in a gesture born of nervous habit as she muttered to herself, lowering her gaze back to the papers, reports and pictures spread out in front of her.

An hour later, she had poured through the scant file on Tanya Dourant and she came back to the conclusion that she had already reached.

Taken from her home, late at night, no signs of struggle in

the house—and on the one night that her husband had been out bowling like he did every Wednesday.

She had known her killer.

Of course, they lived in Mitchell, for crying out loud. The small town in Indiana had less than a thousand who lived inside the city limits. Several hundred more in the county, outside the city limits. Almost everybody knew the other, at least at a glance. And Tanya was a nurse for the town's sole pediatrician. So she knew almost everybody. Damn it all.

Thirty-three, sweet, funny, good with kids...and dead.

Some son of a bitch had bled her like a damned pig.

Rubbing her thumb along one of the pictures, she studied it. That bright, happy grin made her heart hurt. Thinking about those little kids, asking for Mama day after day, and Daddy having to explain she wasn't ever coming home again.

Fury pulsed through her and she shoved back from the chair, pacing the small office and turning it over in her mind.

"Something. Has to be something," she muttered. Gritting her teeth, she lowered herself back into the chair and grabbed the first thing that came to hand. It was a crime scene photo of the empty field where Tanya's body had been dumped.

"Waste of time, going out there again." Then she shrugged and stood, grabbing her jacket on her way out the door.

Not that staying in the office was terribly productive right now.

The road was paved up until about a mile from the field. Tanya had been found by some hunters, a week after being reported missing. The hunters had known who it was. Daisy had seen the knowledge, the fury, the shock, in their eyes as they led her back out there.

As Daisy had expected, the official cause of death was hypovolemic shock, caused by massive blood loss. There had been thirty-six cuts, all inflicted by the same blade. Most likely the same knife that had been used on the other victims. They had all been cut thirty-six times as well. There was nothing careless or uncontrolled. The victims hadn't been stabbed violently, but cut with a careful precision.

Also like the others, Tanya had been raped. He had also spent some time strangling her. He'd squeezed her throat until she blacked out from the lack of oxygen and then he'd let her go. Let her wake up. And then he'd start all over again.

All of that, and he hadn't left a single sign of himself. Not a hair follicle, not a bit of skin under the fingernails, not a drop of semen or blood. He left nothing and Daisy had come up with nothing.

The instincts that had helped her nab some of the biggest drug runners in Louisville had deserted her. Not even a quiver as she walked the trail back to the field. Her gut had been playing tricks on her for a while, but now it was like she was working blind. No gut urges, no hunches to follow.

Just four dead bodies...and a stranger standing in the meadow where the last body was found.

It was the guy from the diner. He stood there, facing away from her, staring down at the ground. There was a knapsack slung over one big shoulder. It had a worn look to it, like it had been used a lot. Other than the bag, his hands were empty. But his clothes were dusty, like he had been kicking around the field for quite a while.

Twilight was starting to gleam gold on the horizon as Daisy calmly shifted the gun she wore inside her jacket. Hadn't ever gotten used to wearing a holster at her waist the way her predecessor had. Too many years working in narcotics, she supposed.

"You're on private property, pal," she said levelly.

The blue eyes that cut her way were the color of the sky just before sunrise. Deep, dark blue. And cool. Very cool. She hadn't noticed the color of his eyes back at the diner. Neither had she realized just how very...*large* he was.

Six feet four, easy. Shoulders that would have done a linebacker proud. High cheekbones and a chiseled chin. The only things that saved him from being too pretty were his hard, unsmiling mouth and his eyes. He had the saddest eyes that Daisy had ever seen.

"I'm sorry," he said, his voice a low, easy drawl that spoke of the South. "Just out seeing the sights. Saw the road. I wanted to take a look around."

"Look for...what, exactly?" she asked, suspicion in her gut. Sad eyes or not, there was no way he had just happened upon this place. The field was too damn far out for somebody to stumble on to it. The path to it was overgrown and unless somebody knew it was there, it wasn't going to be easy to find.

He lifted the bag at his side and smiled, but it wasn't a real smile. It wasn't reflected in his eyes, or on his face. Just a polite little smile to set people at ease, she suspected. But she wasn't put at ease. Not at all.

"Scenery. I'm an amateur photographer. On vacation, wanted to find someplace quiet." His voice was soothing, the kind of voice that tended to reassure people.

Daisy wasn't looking for reassurance. She was looking for answers and she wanted to know what in the hell he was doing standing in the middle of her crime scene.

For a brief second, she entertained the possibility that this was her guy. It wasn't unusual for killers to revisit crime scenes—could explain why he was at the site where they'd found Tanya. He definitely had the weird, mysterious vibe to him. But it wasn't him. She didn't know why he was here, but it wasn't because he wanted to see if his victim had been found yet.

So instead of calling for back up, she just said, "Mitchell has plenty of nice places. And a lot of them aren't on private property. Maybe you should find of one of them."

That same polite little smile, and he nodded. "Of course. Hope I didn't cause trouble, Sheriff," he said. And then he was gone, moving past her on incredibly silent feet.

Daisy fought not to scowl as he headed for the trees, that black bag slung over his shoulders, his hands tucked into his pockets, broad shoulders straining at the seams of his worn denim shirt.

Nice ass.

Then she mentally slapped herself across the head, turning back to study the field with narrowed eyes.

She slid her gaze back in the direction where that sexy stranger had disappeared. Blowing a breath out, she started to jog across the field, catching sight of that faded blue denim. "Hey...hold up a minute."

Michael stopped in his tracks and raised his eyes heavenward as the woman's voice drifted to him.

"Should have split when ya had the chance," Lucas said, a grin curving up his mouth. He was standing in the middle of the path. The lower half of his body was lost to sight. A big oak had fallen down some time ago and was blocking a lot of the path. Lucas looked like he was standing inside the oak. His

upper body was transparent but it took on a more solid look every time he spoke. As he winked at Michael, he could have almost passed for something other than a ghost. *"I will tell ya, she is a looker."*

"Hmmm," Michael murmured. He turned around and watched the pretty sheriff approach. Nope, he couldn't disagree. She had a head full of riotous golden brown curls and a direct hazel stare that was kind of uncommon in a woman. Of course, since she was a cop, that direct stare shouldn't be a surprise. She had a small, straight nose, high cheekbones and her eyebrows were so dark a brown they appeared black.

Her body was a compact, deadly package of curves and muscles. She looked incredibly soft and incredibly strong. Definitely a lethal package. As she moved, he caught a quick glimpse of the shoulder holster under her jacket and he imagined she was every bit as competent with that gun as she looked.

Michael had always had a weakness for women like her—confident, composed, strong and sexy as all get out. She wouldn't mind if a man opened the door for her but at the same time, she probably handled a weapon better than most men did.

He heard Lucas snickering and he gave his brother a silent warning. The last thing he needed was to make the pretty sheriff think he was just a little too strange. That sort of thing could land him in jail, considering the shit they had going on here.

He met her eyes, arching a brow, keeping his expression blank, forcing his mouth into a curious smile. "Ma'am?"

"Just occurred to me. I haven't seen you around before," she said. "Well, at the diner. But eh...other than that, well, you know, Mitchell doesn't see too much in the way of tourists or travelers. Been in town long?"

He shrugged, keeping his gaze from cutting to his brother as Lucas murmured, *"She's onto us, pal."*

Michael said, "I drove in yesterday. Slept at the Spring's Inn. Was planning on heading out today, but then I decided to wait a few days. It's quiet here. I like the quiet."

"Yes. I do too. I work real hard to keep it quiet. I'm Daisy Crandall. The sheriff here. We've been having some trouble lately. Strangers in town probably aren't going to help people rest easier. Care to give me your name? What you've been doing the past few days?"

"Michael," he sighed out, rubbing his hand across his eyes. "Michael O'Rourke. And until four days ago, I was in Philadelphia. I'm on vacation for the next few weeks."

"Taking...pictures?" she supplied, arching a skeptical brow.

"If I feel the need," he said shortly.

"And what is it you do in Philadelphia? You don't exactly sound like a Yankee to me. Lived there long?"

Damn. Cops. He wasn't in the mood to lie to her, although he could fabricate a very believable, very plausible story. Still, if he thought she'd believe him, he would have done it. But she wouldn't believe him.

She'd know he was lying and that would just make more trouble. So instead, he hedged a little, telling her the truth without really telling her anything. "I don't live there. I was there for a job," he said, clenching his jaw.

"A job, huh?" She propped her hands on her waist—a move that was intended to let him see the gun tucked into its holster, and the shiny badge on her belt. She had her intimidation tactics down pretty well. "What kind of job?"

Michael debated on what to tell her. Finally, he blew out a sigh and shook his head. Oz was going to shoot him. His boss wasn't very fond of having people outside the unit know about any of the agents. Of course, if this cop started running his name, she was going to find him in areas where all sorts of bad things happened.

When he stayed silent, she glanced at the black strap hanging from his shoulder. "Let me guess...photography?"

That little smirk of a smile on her lips probably did all sorts of things to piss people off. And he was sure that was exactly the point. "No." He tapped his fingers against the wallet he kept in his front pocket. "Mind?"

"That depends on what you have in your pocket," she replied drolly.

"ID."

Her eyes narrowed and she said, "Why do I have the feeling you already know the drill? One hand only...use two fingers."

"Well, you are quick," he drawled, drawing the wallet from his pocket and handing it over before letting his hand fall back to his side.

"FBI?" she said, that brow inching up higher, her voice thick with doubt.

"Sort of. A division. I was there on assignment, finished it. Now I'm on vacation," he said.

"Says you're from Tennessee. It's been my experience that most Southerners are a little more talkative than you," the sheriff said, still holding his ID in her hand as she studied him with very cynical eyes. "Don't suppose there is somebody I can call to verify this information?"

Behind him, he heard Lucas snickering. *"I can verify,"* his brother said. *"Lot of help that will be though."*

"Will you just shut up?" Michael thought sourly. Lucas just continued to grin at him. His brother had always had a weird sense of humor. Being dead twenty years had only made it more so.

Michael ran a hand through his hair and muttered, "Oz is going to kill me."

"Oz?"

Okay, so she was expecting either a drugged out rock and roll singer, or an actor with a quirky smile that just liked to shape shift into a werewolf. *I watch too much TV.* The low, smooth contralto on the other end of the line was definitely not what Daisy had expected when Michael scrawled out the number and agreed to ride with her into town.

"Yes," Elise Oswald said levelly. "O'Rourke is one of my men. I'm kind of curious as why you are calling me. My people generally are rather closed mouthed."

"Oh, he's closed mouthed, all right. But he happened into a town in Indiana where we've been having some kind of serious problems," Daisy said. As she spoke, she tapped her pen on a pad of paper, then circled the woman's name, the phone number, drawing a line under it. She doodled a little more, adding a triangle under the name, then jotting the sexy agent's name down as well.

"Indiana." Oswald repeated it slowly, like she was speaking a foreign language. Then she made a little humming noise and murmured, "So that's where he disappeared to."

"You been looking for him?" Daisy asked, giving him a wary glance. She shifted in her seat a little, making sure she could grab her weapon if she needed it. He watched her the entire time, with that little half smile on his mouth.

"Not exactly. O'Rourke made it clear he wasn't interested in being found any time soon. Please let him know that he is officially on a leave of absence for the next month, so if he would turn his pager back on, I'd be most appreciative."

"Riiigggghhhttt..." Daisy drawled. "Why don't you tell me a little more about him, Ms. Oswald."

On the other end of the phone, Elise laughed. "Call me Elise or Oz. I rarely respond to Ms." She made that little humming sound again and murmured, "Now let me see. About O'Rourke. There's not too much that I can share, but O'Rourke has a habit of happening into places where all sorts of trouble is going on. That's one of the reasons he's with me." She sounded just a little amused as she said it.

"You like troublemakers?" Daisy asked curiously.

With a laugh, Oswald said, "Hardly. What I like is the fact that he always ends up where he is needed. There's a problem, he finds it, solves it, moves on to another."

Dryly, Daisy said, "How nice for you. But I don't need a problem solver. I just need you to verify he was in Philadelphia...like for last week?"

"I can verify that."

Eyeing the silent stranger in front of her, Daisy scowled. "Can you expand on that a little? Some more detail?"

"No, Sheriff. I can't. You asked for verification, not detail."

Elise Oswald spoke with a cool amusement that only added to Daisy's irritation. Patience and professionalism took a quick leap out the window. "Look, lady," she snapped. "I've got four dead bodies and I just found your boy standing in a very remote area where the latest one was found. That's a little strange, don't you think?"

Elise Oswald's evasiveness sure as hell wasn't helping Daisy's mindset either. Oddly, though, the lack of answers didn't matter. Michael O'Rourke wasn't a killer. She knew it with a certainty that went clear down to her bones.

Oswald started to laugh. "Not if you know O'Rourke. You have absolutely no idea how many strange places with all sorts of bad things that he just happens to walk into. And if you have O'Rourke there, you should know, he's not a boy, mine or otherwise."

Daisy fell silent, staring at the ID in front of her. Instincts, long since fallen silent, started to scream at her and the hair on the back of her neck stood on end. "Exactly what does that mean?"

On the other end of the line, Oswald simply said, "Could mean a lot of things—could mean he just has a habit of ending up in weird places. Could be something else. But like I said, he was here, on assignment, last week. And every week before for the past several months."

"Doing what?"

"Now that...I can't answer." And the line went dead.

Slowly, Daisy hung up the phone and sat back in the chair. Looking up, she stared at Michael O'Rourke. She did have to agree with Oswald on one thing—Michael O'Rourke was no boy.

Dark, broody looks, lean powerful body and a mouth that looked like it had been made for kissing. Sleepy looking blue eyes, that deep slow voice with its faint Southern accent—the man was a walking, talking dream. Sure as hell nothing boy-like about him.

He sat in the chair across from her desk, his hands resting on his thighs. His bag was sitting at the desk out front where he'd surrendered it without protest. He didn't fidget, didn't do anything that portrayed any kind of nerves, guilt or a need to intimidate.

There was nothing he had done that shouted *threat*.

Yet, everything about him made Daisy aware of just that. He wasn't a man to be tangled with.

Meeting those dark blue eyes, she pushed his wallet back across the desk. With a polite, professional smile, Daisy said, "You're clear. But you might not want to hang around town, Agent O'Rourke. People are getting antsy. Having a stranger around isn't going to help any."

She arched a brow at him, angled her head toward the door. "You can go."

Without comment, he stood and tucked away his wallet. He turned to the door but instead of leaving, he just stood there. When he turned back around to look at her, his eyes were hooded. "Curious. What's going on around here? People are edgy. Even for uptight Yankees," he said with a twist of his lips.

"None of your concern, Agent O'Rourke. Especially if you were just in the field for the scenery," she said, tongue in cheek.

"Don't, man."

Michael ignored Lucas' intense voice as he picked up the heavy rock that sat on Sheriff Dasynda Crandall's desk. It was an amethyst. The purple spikes that stood out from the inside caught the light as he shifted it back and forth.

"Don't do this, Mike. If she doesn't believe you, you're going to find your ass thrown in jail."

Focusing his mind toward Lucas, he replied, *"And if I don't, somebody else dies. I can't let that happen. That woman in the field asked for help—I can't walk away."*

Mike blocked his brother from his thoughts and concentrated on the crystal in his hands as he started to speak. "A woman was found in that field," he said softly. The images rolled in his mind like a silent movie, her body being dragged out of the trunk, thrown on the ground...a wood cabin, a hand closing around her throat, the silver flash as a knife lifted and descended, over and over. The slow trickle of blood. The eventual weakness.

"But she wasn't killed there."

Daisy sat up and he watched as the flat, blank look entered her eyes. Cop look. He knew one, had practiced and perfected his own, even though he wasn't exactly a cop. At least, Mike didn't think of himself as one.

"Okay. Care to tell me how you know any of that?" she asked tightly.

"There was a cabin," he said distantly, hardly even aware of her question. He continued to stare down at the amethyst but instead of the pretty purple spikes, he saw wooden plank floors and wooden walls, a narrow bed, rusty bloodstains on the floor. "He killed her there. She knew him."

Daisy stood up so quick her chair toppled over. Her eyes flashed with fury, the professional cop gone in the heat of anger. "All right, slick, I don't give a damn if you do have an alibi, if you don't tell me how you know that, you can look forward to spending some time behind bars," she snapped.

The jagged points of the amethyst pressed into his palm as he murmured, "Your dad gave you this. He was a cop too, wasn't he? Died in the line of duty—drug deal. You almost left your badge behind when that happened."

Blood roared in his ears as he felt the surge of emotions rolling from her. Confusion, the first wink of understanding, smashed out by her disbelief. They never wanted to believe. Lifting his head, he stared into her wide, angry eyes.

"How in the hell do you know that?" she demanded.

The smile that curved his lips now was a real one, cynical, just a slight twist of his lips, as he shrugged. "I think you already know."

Daisy felt the knowledge slam into her like an uppercut, shock and disbelief warring in her mind for supremacy. This wasn't possible. Not possible.

"He has another."

Slowly, she leaned forward and planted her hands on the table. "What?"

"A girl."

"Not possible. If a girl was missing in Mitchell, especially with this going on, her family would have already called," Daisy said flatly. One of the nice things about small towns.

"She isn't from here. A girl. Walking down the highway," Michael O'Rourke said, staring into her eyes. "Long blonde hair—not her real color. She's...she's not well. Bad heart."

She watched him with disbelief as his lashes lowered, hiding his eyes for a minute. When he looked back at her, she felt the power of that gaze like a punch in the solar plexus. That mild blue gaze was no longer quite so mild.

His eyes seemed to glow.

Daisy blew out a shaky breath and turned away from him for a minute while she tried to calm her rattled emotions. The deep breath didn't help and neither did staring out the plate glass window that took up most of the back wall of her little office. She was too aware of him. She could feel his eyes boring into her back, waiting to see what she did. How she reacted.

But Daisy wasn't sure how to react to this. Suddenly, this case had become a whole different ball game.

CRSO

Whoever the killer was knew small town life, knew when to play his cards and when to hold his hand. He also knew how to hide his tracks. How to blend in. He lived here. She knew it in her gut.

It was somebody that she knew, probably somebody she'd grown up with. Most serial killers were men, usually under the age of forty, which put him right in her age bracket.

Son of a bitch.

Lowering her eyes, she looked at the gruesome pictures one last time and silently promised yet again, *I will find you.*

"How many?" Michael asked quietly.

Cutting the man at her side a narrow look, she said sarcastically, "Don't you know?"

"Doesn't work that way," he said, lifting one shoulder.

"How does it work?" she asked, crossing her arms over her stomach.

"Ever seen *The Sixth Sense?*"

Her nose wrinkled. Images of animated corpses walking around filled her head. "Ewww..." Then she looked back at the pictures of the dead victims. "Dead people?"

"My gift. They don't look like that—they look however they last see themselves. They usually know they are dead and if they don't, they figure it out pretty quick. That doesn't always help though," Michael said. His voice was expressionless, his blue eyes blank, and just blue now, no longer glowing. "They talk to me. The woman who was in the field..." His gaze drifted over her shoulder and she shivered. He was looking at somebody. "She sees the girl. But she's confused. Still doesn't understand what happened. She knows somebody killed her, and she's scared. Hurt."

"Sees what girl?" Daisy asked warily. This all felt surreal. But not for a moment did she think he was lying. She hadn't ever met a person she believed more.

"The one he has now. She's blonde, young...pale," Michael murmured. "I can see her through your friend's eyes...Tanya...yes, Tanya. I can see her through Tanya's eyes."

A shiver raced down Daisy's back as he lifted his head, turning it to stare to Daisy's right, at a point by the window. His eyes seemed to lock with something, but the room was empty, save for them.

"Are you...talking to Tanya now?"

A smile edged up the corners of his mouth and he shook his head. "No. She can't come here. She's trapped there, in the field. And in the cabin where he killed her."

"I need to know more about this cabin."

Michael's eyes closed and she watched as he sighed, his shoulders slumping just a little. "I can't tell you more...she only saw the inside of it. She never saw a clock, never saw the sun shining through the window. Pine...she could smell pine trees. She's blocked out his face."

"What do you mean blocked it out?" Daisy asked, scowling.

"Blocked it. She's too afraid of him, what he did—she won't think about it. And I can't make her do it until she's ready." His voice trailed off. Then he shook his head and looked at her, his eyes blank and empty. "I can't tell you anything that could help. Not right now, not yet. When she's ready, she'll help us. But right now's too afraid."

Tears burned her eyes. *God...Tanya...*

A hand came up, squeezing her shoulder. "I'm sorry."

Shrugging away from him, she closed her eyes. "I thought once a person died, they were beyond that," she said, forcing the words past the knot in her throat. God, she prayed, she hoped.

God, how she could face any of these families knowing that the poor victims might be stuck here...

"A lot of the time, they can move on. Sometimes they can't." Michael's gaze flickered back to the window and she frowned, looking at the window then at him.

"What stops them?"

"Life. Sometimes they see or feel right before they die—" his voice broke off.

"And what's keeping Tanya here?" she demanded. "Damn it, you don't have any idea what he did to her!"

He lifted haunted eyes to her face. "Yes, I do. You don't. You saw her body. You didn't feel it. She can't talk to you. You can't feel her fear. You aren't trapped inside that cabin. She is. And she's terrified she won't be able to keep him from hurting the girl who's there now."

Chapter Three

Daisy tried to dismiss it.

Tried very hard.

But she couldn't even find it in her to *doubt* him, much less totally dismiss him. Over the next hour, she flipped through the flyers, studying them, looking for a young, pale blonde.

There were a number of them. Had he taken one of them?

She sifted out the five blondes who had disappeared recently, tossing the rest into a basket on her desk, rubbing her temple as she read the names. Should be easy. Bad heart. Hair wasn't the natural color.

A breeze blew through the room and she absently rubbed her arms, not noticing as one of the flyers in the basket drifted to the floor.

A young girl, teenaged, pale skinned, her brunette hair waving around her narrow face, stared up from the grainy photo. The words *urgent* right below her picture would have caught Daisy's eye if she had seen it.

When somebody called into her office fifteen minutes later, she pushed the flyers aside, scowling as Deputy Jake Morris grinned at her from the doorway. "This is the third time Myrtle has called the office. She'll only talk to you, Daisy," he said, laughter dancing in his eyes.

"I can't help that some stray dogs are shitting in her petunias," Daisy muttered, smoothing a hand across her hair, tucking a stray lock behind her ear.

"Roses. It's her rose bushes this time," he said helpfully. "You going to talk to her?"

Sourly, Daisy muttered, "Why in the hell should I? She'll just keep calling until I go out there."

"Should I tell her that you're on your way?"

"Yes." Lifting her eyes skyward, she murmured, "Give me patience."

CR&D

Twenty minutes later, Daisy repeated, for the fifth time, "Mrs. Morrow, please, if you will tell me what the dog looked like, maybe we can figure out if it has an owner. But unless you *see* the dog, there's not much I can do."

Daisy covered her nose as Myrtle Morrow waved a blue plastic grocery bag in front of her, the stench of the dog poop inside the bag drifting out to flood her nose. "You're telling me you won't help me?" Mrs. Morrow demanded in strident tones.

"I'm saying I can't—not unless you can at least tell me what the dog looks like," Daisy said, trying not to grit her teeth. She didn't know if she had succeeded though.

"It's a *dog!*"

Daisy rubbed her temple and said, "Listen. We have more than three hundred and thirty-three dogs in the town limits. I checked. And more strays than I care to think about. So unless you have an idea to figure out which of those three hundred plus pooches crapped in the rose bushes, I don't know what I can do."

A chill ran down her spine, making her shiver. The skin on the back of her neck prickled, and the feeling of being watched settled within her. Blinking, she forced herself to focus on Myrtle, taking her arm and guiding her back to her porch. She made the appropriate sympathetic noises as the old woman brandished the poop bag and gestured wildly toward her roses.

"I'll find the dog. I'll stay up night and day if I have to," Myrtle muttered, staring at the bag and sulking.

"And as soon as you can tell me what it looks like, I'll do what I can," Daisy promised.

Which wouldn't be much, because Myrtle would most likely describe a dog that matched the description of half the strays and registered pets in town. But at least Daisy was able to walk away from her house. Sliding into her car, she checked the rearview mirror. Nobody around that she could see. But somebody was watching her. She could feel it.

It felt like somebody was trying to puzzle her out.

But there was nobody even around, that she could see. Myrtle lived at the end of a cul-de-sac and there was only one other house on her street. The Busseys were out of town on vacation and Myrtle had most likely gone inside to sulk some more over her roses.

With a sigh, she started the car and headed back to town. "I'm losing my mind."

CR80

"She's a good cop."

Michael closed his eyes as Lucas wavered into view.

"Leave her alone, Lucas," he said tiredly. It was a waste of time. Lucas was feeling the need to investigate, which meant he was going to do everything *but* leave her alone.

Not good.

He sensed something about Daisy Crandall that made his skin itch. She had believed him all too easily. Cops didn't do that. And it didn't matter that her badge said *County Sheriff.* Still a cop.

She should have been a lot more skeptical.

The only reason that made sence as to why she didn't scoff at him...she knew he wasn't lying.

Some people had that knowledge, the ability to look at somebody and know whether that person was telling them lies—or truth. She had known. Plain and simple. And if she could sense truth, she could possibly sense other things. He'd rather she not know about the ghost that followed him.

"I like her."

Now Michael frowned. Staring at Lucas, he cocked a brow, waiting. Lucas hadn't ever said that about anybody before. He wouldn't like somebody he couldn't trust. He'd been very cautious in life about who he cared for—death had only enhanced that.

Lucas shrugged as he met his brother's stare. It was an odd gesture, one that made his mostly solid image ripple for a moment and Michael saw the outline of the dresser behind Lucas for the briefest second. *"She's...solid,"* Lucas finally said. *"And sad. There's something broken inside her."*

Michael felt his heart clench at Lucas' words. Yes, he had sensed the grief inside the pretty, hazel-eyed woman. It had left an urge inside him, to go to her and cuddle her against him, stroke away the bleak look in her pretty hazel eyes. "Nothing I can do about that," he murmured. He wished he had just moved on. There were complications here that he didn't need—complications that went beyond the ghost of a murdered woman and a missing runaway.

But she pulled at him...not just the ghost.

The sheriff.

Too often, the only people who could hold his interest were the dead. They whispered to him at night, surrounded him during the day. But the living, they rarely held any interest for him.

He felt her determination to find the murderer, a deep, steady intent that all but colored the air around her. Solid. Yes...true blue. Loyal, determined, steady, through and through.

Michael couldn't walk away until he knew there would be no more ghosts behind him when he left. Which meant stopping the killer.

Running his tongue along his teeth, he studied the articles in front of him, sifting through to find the earliest one. Six dead women. Going back a year and half. The last two had both been killed within the past four months. The killer was escalating. They developed a taste for it, a need. Time passed and they had to kill more often, more frequently.

More violently.

Were there only the four? Or had he hidden some of the victims?

Areas like this were thick with woods and valleys, easy places to hide bodies. These four had been local. But Michael knew there was one out there that wasn't from around here. A runaway...somebody barely more than a child. If he had taken one runaway, he'd likely taken others.

So possibly more murders than they knew about.

Rubbing his thumb across his chin, he contemplated the grainy picture in the paper. Pretty. Young...in her twenties. But the second one was in her early forties. And then a college coed who'd been home on summer break. The fourth one, the nurse, the ghost he had met earlier—twenty-eight, married, mom with kids. Only thing they really had in common...they were female and white.

No pattern. That made it harder to pin things down.

There was something else that had to link them.

"What's the damned link?" he muttered, shoving a hand through his hair.

"You know, some people just like to kill."

"Yeah, but they usually have a preferred sort of victim," Mike said absently.

"You've become too much like a cop."

Mike smiled. "I don't know what else there is left for me to be, Lucas."

A cool breeze drifted through the room.

Feeling the heavy weight of emotion that seemed to roll from Lucas, he looked up. "It's not your fault," he said quietly. "And this isn't a bad rap, you know."

"You wade through the shittiest type of scum known to man, Mikey. You've put yourself inside the heads of monsters—I see how sick it makes you. I know how angry it makes you. I know it hurts. And you want me to buy that it's not a bad rap." Lucas shook his head. His eyes were so full of grief, it hurt to even look at his brother, but Mike wouldn't look away.

"Yeah. I want you to believe it." Scrubbing his hands over his face, he sighed. Pushing back from the small desk, Mike started to pace the tight confines of the hotel room. "Yeah. I've had to deal with shit. But you and me...we've been doing that all our lives. It's not like I don't know how to handle it."

"I should have tried harder. We should have left sooner."

"Neither of us could have known how low she would have stooped. Or what kind of messes she had gotten involved in," Mike said quietly.

Lucas spun away. The force of rage flooding him had made his image wavery and Mike could barely see him. *"I should have. I knew her—I knew what kind of scum she was involved in, knew better than you what she was capable of. I was supposed to protect you, Mikey. I failed. I shouldn't have let this happen to you."*

"It happened to *you*," Mike said.

"It happened to us both."

That stopped him in mid-stride. He turned around, looking

across the room at his brother. "Guess it did. And it happened for a reason. If it hadn't..." Grisly images, things he'd rather forget, rolled through his mind. No, he didn't want to remember many things that he'd seen in the past ten or fifteen years of his life. But lives had been saved because of it, killers had been stopped. "There's a man sitting in jail right now because of what happened to me. His last victim didn't die. We got to him before he could hurt her. You know what? I couldn't have stopped him if I was your everyday average Jones, Lucas. It may not be the easiest thing to live with, but I'd rather have some bad nights and know that bastard will never kill anybody again, then to change it."

"Don't you think you've done enough, Mike?"

Focusing on the papers in front of him, he blew out a breath. "No. There's a girl out there, Lucas. A kid. He has a kid. And I'm not going to stop until I've stopped him."

"And then there will be another. And another...and another. When will it ever be enough?"

"That's the way it works."

As Lucas' presence faded away, Mike focused again on the information in front of him.

You hurt that girl, you son of a bitch, and you're going to die.

ભ૪૪

Tanya felt it in her heart when the girl died.

The blackness that surrounded the cabin expanded and she wanted to flee, but at the same time, her own anger kept her chained. She had hoped...had prayed...the man, she'd thought he would help. He hadn't, though.

Tanya waited and waited but he never came and now it was too late.

Terror welled inside. Only one thing caused that. *Him*—the killer. The killer was coming. *Her* killer. *"My killer,"* she whispered.

Her throat felt tight. It was weird. She could still feel things. When Michael had touched her earlier, she had felt it. His arms had felt bizarrely hot, like he'd had a fever. It had been like getting a shock, all over her body and it left her skin buzzing and burning, in a very, very painful way.

Did she feel cold to him?

She wanted to run. But the only place she could go was the field. She already knew that. And that was just as bad as here. Every time she ended up there, she kept remembering what she had seen. She'd run there the first time. Because *he* had come here. To clean up after he had killed her. She ran, and she found herself. She saw what he did to her. Seeing it was just as bad as feeling it, in a different way.

Tanya had watched as two childhood friends led the police to her body. She was stuck there, watching as Daisy and her deputies searched for clues that would lead to him. Deep inside, Tanya knew that she knew who he was. But it was like she'd closed the door on his memory, on his face. She couldn't look at him. Wouldn't.

The terror inside grew so thick it was choking her, flooding her. She couldn't keep doing that. Needed to see him. Had to. So she could tell Michael. Michael was there to help. He could tell Daisy. God...Daisy. Tears squeezed out of her eyes and Tanya had to bite back the scream that was building in her throat. They had been planning to go into town and watch a movie. Get a few drinks...just have a girl day.

They wouldn't do that now. There would never be another girl day. She'd never take her daughter shopping for that dress. Amy's first big dance was next month and Tanya wasn't ever going to see her, wouldn't be able to take pictures... She'd lost out on all of it.

Rage started to edge back the terror even though the blackness moved closer. *He* was moving closer. Turning, Tanya stared at the still body of the girl lying tied to the cot. *"I'm so sorry, sweetie,"* she whispered.

The girl just lay there.

Her body was still covered. She hadn't been battered...beaten...cut, or raped. Not yet. Tanya couldn't help but feel a little jealous. "You got off easy, baby. I wish I'd died before he touched me."

CR80

He felt the voice. At first, he was convinced it was his own imagination, but then, as it continued to echo inside his mind, he had to wonder.

And there was a stranger in town—one who had been seen talking to the sheriff. One who had been seen out where Tanya's body had been found. He was a big, mean looking bastard with sharp eyes.

He hadn't heard that voice, either, not until that man had shown up. Now it was like he wouldn't shut up. This was not good. Not at all. As the echo of the words ran through the man's mind, repeating themselves over and over, he started to worry.

Let her go... Let her go now, and maybe I won't kill you when I find you.

Shaken, he jogged out of the house and leaped into his truck, whipping it around and speeding for the cabin where the girl was kept. She lay there, sweet, innocuous...and dead.

He bellowed with rage, launching himself to the cot and grabbing one wrist. A pulse...there would be a pulse. She wasn't dead, she was playacting to try and get free. Stupid little bitch. She was going to pay for this. Damn it, nobody cheated him. Nobody.

But the skin was cool—she had a pasty, grayish blue cast to her skin and her eyes stared sightlessly up at the ceiling. There was a weird little curl to her lips, almost a smile. Mocking him.

She'd been dead a while.

He shot to his feet, pacing back and forth, dragging his hands through his hair and gnawing worriedly at his lower lip. What in the hell had happened? The ethyl chloride he'd used on her was harmless. And she'd woken up since then. What in the hell...

Spying her purse, he grabbed it and dumped it out. Hairspray, a comb, a cell phone with a dead battery, loose coins, two prescription bottles and a thick wad of cash. Something hit the floor with a musical clink and he knelt, eyeing the stainless steel bracelet with dread. The red caduceus winked up at him mockingly as he lifted it.

The medical terms didn't make much sense to him, the *V2* and the medical jargon was all but foreign to him. Except the words *cardiac murmur*—those words, he understood all too well.

Turning, he studied her face with disbelieving eyes.

She'd gone and had a fucking heart attack on him.

"You little bitch!" he screamed. "Bitch. Fucking bitch!"

He stood up and lashed out with his boot, kicking the cot.

In a fit of fury, he stormed across the cabin, cussing furiously, completely unaware that he was being watched.

Tanya hovered in the corner. Her own fear was slowly dissipating, washing away as the sense of irony settled in. She stared at the two bottles of pills and at the bracelet, moving closer. He cut her off and she shied away automatically, but he still came close. He stilled though and she watched as he shivered. Smiling, she moved over to the spilled pile of drugs by the girl's purse.

"Poor thing," she whispered. Died of a heart attack.

He came to an abrupt halt, staring around with wild eyes. "Who's there? Who the hell is that?"

Looking up, Tanya studied him. It was the first time she had consciously looked at him. His features came into focus... Recoiling in horror, she shied away, letting her mind blur his features again. *No...not ready...*part of her whispered. She wasn't ready to look at him. Wasn't ready to remember what he had done. How he had laughed when she screamed and cried.

But the other part of her thought logically. Realistically.

He heard her.

"You can hear me," she said flatly.

"Who in the fuck is here?" he demanded. His eyes kept wheeling around in his head as he searched the room for her.

Slowly, Tanya stood, a smile curving her lips as she moved closer. Reaching out, she touched his cheek. *"Take a guess."*

CRINGE

A cold touch drifted down his spine, bringing Michael out of his restless sleep. It wasn't the first time he had been wokened like this and he knew it wouldn't be the last. A restless spirit hovered around him and he swallowed back the furious shout that threatened to escape him. *Too late.* Bitter knowledge burned inside him but he clamped a tight lid on it.

The poor girl didn't need his anger.

"Hi," he said quietly, wondering if she would be stuck here, or if she was just a little lost.

There weren't any words from her. Just a sense of confusion.

"It's okay—takes a little time to move on sometimes," he

said softly.

She sighed. He felt it like a breeze moving through the air. She was afraid, worried. She knew what had happened—she was angry, and she wanted her mother. Finally, images of her mom made her hurt enough, made her angry enough that she was able to speak. *"Why did I leave...what's going to happen to my mom? She'll never know."*

"I'm sorry."

"What do I do? Am I stuck here?"

At least this much, he could help with. "No...no, you're not stuck. You can move on any time you're ready to let go."

"I can't go until I know Mom will be okay."

Michael promised, "I'll make sure your mom knows that you've moved on. That's what I do."

There was the beauty of youth, though. Sometimes, they did still accept what you told them. It took a while to coax her to move along, but eventually she did. She started to see the white light—one thing that the movies had gotten right. She moved toward it and there was one less ghost in his life.

But that meant somewhere out there, a young woman lay dead.

"You couldn't have just left."

"Neither could you."

Lucas stood by the window, materializing out of thin air, his form more ghostly than normal. *"You make me seem a lot more altruistic than I am. I cared about two things when I was alive, Mike. Me. You. That was it."*

Walking past the window, Michael didn't spare his brother a glance as he said, "Don't give me that line. If you knew innocent girls were being killed, would you just walk away? This last one was just a girl. Younger than you were." Mike was quiet for a minute and then he looked back at Lucas. "People knew what she was doing to us, man. They knew what she tried to do to me. How many times did you have to save me from it, Lucas? Were there times that I didn't even know about?"

Lucas' silence was answer enough. Mike had always suspected it but now he knew. His mother had been willing to sacrifice Mike for Lucas' sake, but now he knew the truth. She would have sacrificed him to score some coke. Mike wanted to be angry but he realized he just didn't care.

"People knew. They walked away. Time after time. If somebody had done something, we might have made it out of there."

"You did make it out of there. Hell, so did I. Just not quite the way I planned."

Nausea churned in Michael's gut. "That's not funny, Lucas."

Lucas laughed bitterly. *"I wasn't trying to be funny, pal. But I did get out. You think I wanted to hang around there waiting until it was the right time to get away from her? Every second we hung around, you were in danger. And that last night, I could have killed her. What if they'd found you? We did get out. I'm just sorry it was hell on you for as long as it was."*

Hell—Dear God, that didn't even cover it. How many nights had he lain awake wondering if dawn would ever come, and the monsters would fade with the light, if the voices that whispered to him were demonic dreams manifested by his own mind or if they were real?

It had taken him years to come to grips with the fact that they were real. Even longer to not wake up terrified when that ghostly touch came on him at night.

He saw ghosts. They touched him, spoke to him, whispered to him—and begged him for help in finding their killers. He never saw those who passed peacefully at the sunset of their lives. Only those whose lives were ended far too early.

With a weary sigh, he flicked on the switch in the bathroom, squinting at the overly bright light . Turning on the water, he bent over and splashed it on his face until the rest of the cobwebs faded. With his hands braced on the tiled edges of the sink, he stared at his reflection. He was starting to look old. It wasn't lines on his face, though, or gray in his hair. His hair was still a deep, dark brown and the only lines on his face were the little ones fanning out from his eyes.

It was the eyes that made him look old.

"You going to look for the girl? You never have that much luck finding them once they've passed on."

Drying his face on the towel, Michael said, "I'm going to find the sheriff. Then I'll go out to the field. The lady there will know the girl's passed. If she's not ready to help now, she will be soon."

⊂⊃

Sarah's bark woke her up. Sitting up, Daisy whistled and the retriever obediently left the window and came over to her, ears perked and waiting. "Who's out there, girl?" she asked softly, dragging a hand through her hair. Her curls tangled around her fingers and she sighed. She'd been so damned tired, she'd gone to bed before her hair had dried all the way.

Bad move for a woman whose hair curled the way hers did.

She stood and moved over to the window, peering through the blinds. The sleek little convertible moving up the road wasn't one she recognized. The full moon shining down was bright enough for her to see pretty well—buffed to a high shine, late model, and the top was down. She didn't know a person in town who owned that kind of car.

And since she didn't recognize it, Daisy had a good idea who it was.

FBI Agent Michael O'Rourke.

It was the middle of the night. She didn't have to be a cop to know it was a bad sign, an agent showing up on her front door this late. Turning away from the window, she moved to her dresser and pulled out a pair of jeans. Drawing them up over her hips, she grabbed the bra she'd draped over the foot of the bed and put it on. Just as the car pulled up in front of the house, she tugged a skinny strapped tank top on. Glancing in the mirror, she made a face at her reflection. Her hair was a mess.

Making a side trip to the bathroom, she splashed some cold water on her face and slicked her damp hands over her hair. The door bell rang. Turning away from the mirror, she padded away out of the bathroom and down the hall.

Sarah waited patiently at the door, her liquid eyes black in the darkness. Reaching out, Daisy turned on the light, giving her eyes a second to adjust before looking through the Judas hole. "Out kind of late, aren't you?" she asked as she unlocked the chain to let him in.

His eyes were grim. There was a chill to his features that made her gut go cold. And suddenly, Daisy wished she had stayed in bed. Wouldn't have mattered though. She felt cold all over. A cop knew what was wrong when a person was wokened in the middle of the night. It was because somebody had died.

"Why are you here?" she asked softly, backing away from him. She rested her hips against the hall table and folded her arms around her chest.

"She's gone."

"Tanya?" Daisy asked, clenching her jaw.

"No...Tanya hasn't passed on yet," he said quietly. He continued to watch her closely and she saw the answer in his eyes.

Daisy had never seen anybody who looked as haunted as he did. She prayed she'd never see it again. Swallowing the knot in throat, she said huskily, "Then you're going to have to explain who you are talking about. Tanya is the only one who has died recently."

"I told you that he had taken somebody else."

It seemed like the pit of her belly dropped out. Closing her eyes, she said, "No. You said he just took her." One hand closed into a tight fist and she fought against the useless burst of fury. *No.*

"He didn't kill her. She died."

Perplexed, Daisy opened her eyes and glared at him. She shoved off the table and planted her hands on her hips. "Damn it, O'Rourke, you're not making much sense. Now granted, it is the middle of the night and I'm in dire need of a caffeine rush. But if you're going to come here and tell me that a girl is dead—" She clamped her mouth shut and hissed out a breath. She took a deep breath. Tried to think, turned his words over in her head. Nope. Still didn't make sense. Looking back at him, she said in a tight voice, "You need to remember something. I'm a cop. I'm the town sheriff. I take a dead girl pretty damned seriously. Especially since we have a killer using my town as his hunting ground."

His lashes lowered, hiding the haunting blue of his eyes. "She was sick—bad heart. I told you that. I think her heart gave out."

With that, he turned on his heel and started for the door.

"Hey!"

He paused, looking over his shoulder.

"Where in the hell do you think you're going?"

"Out to the field. Tanya might be ready to talk to me."

Propping her hands on her hips, Daisy stared at him.

"Why? What changes things from this morning?"

"Because a girl is dead," Michael said, his tone patient, as though he was talking to a small child.

"Yeah and this morning, talking might have *saved* her."

Michael's lips curled in a sad smile. "I don't think so—you don't understand, Sheriff. The deceased, they are like kids. Like a young one, scared, confused and alone in the dark. She couldn't this morning—it just wasn't time, not for her."

"So because it *wasn't time* for her, some young girl was raped and tortured, probably scared to death—" her voice faded away at the look on his face.

"No. She wasn't hurt. I don't know what happened. But there—wasn't that tortured touch to her. I need to go. Are you coming?"

Damned jerk, Daisy thought a few minutes later as she drove over the rough roads. He sat next to her in silence. Hell, she couldn't even hear him breathing. *Spends so much time with his ghosts, he acts like one.*

It was unsettling. She couldn't hear him. He sat so still he could have been carved from marble—yet her senses were entirely too attuned to him.

He smelled good. Trapped in the close confines of the car, she was aware of just *how* good he smelled. Daisy had always been a sucker for the way a guy smelled. She didn't particularly care for cologne on a man, just the clean smell of soap and male.

And damn, this particular male was something else.

She was entirely too aware of him.

Being this close to him made her skin feel hot and itchy, made her aware of the way her clothes felt against her flesh, how her hair blew around her face in the breeze. Her heart started to slam against her ribcage and her breathing sped up. Against the steering wheel, she could feel her palms getting sweaty.

Up ahead, the gravel road ended and she had to turn off onto the dirt road. Eventually, that would end and there would be little more than two ruts in the dirt to follow and then they'd have to get out and walk the rest of the way to the field. She was looking forward to it, because she had to get out of this damned truck.

Then maybe she could think of something else beside him.

Alone, in the middle of the night, with a man she didn't really know and there were murders being committed in her county, and the only thing that Daisy could really think about was how damned good he smelled.

Twenty minutes later, she had her wish.

Following behind him, she slammed her flashlight against her thigh and tried to figure how *this* had happened. "You know, I am the sheriff. I think I should be the one walking in front."

He didn't say anything.

Daisy slid her gaze down the length of his back. And stared at his ass. Again.

Now she wasn't thinking about how good he smelled. For the past fifteen minutes, she had been trailing after him and in the bright patches of moonlight, she had been left to admire one very fine ass. "Any reason why you insist on being in front?" she asked irritably.

"Not sure where she is."

Tanya.

As they crossed into the clearing, she reached up to rub at her temple. "I'm still not entirely sure why we came out here. How can she help us? How can you even be sure you'll see…"

Something cold brushed against her. Daisy froze, jerking around, but she couldn't see anything.

Her eyes flew to Michael's face but he wasn't looking at her. He seemed to be staring at somebody just to Daisy's left, somebody roughly Daisy's height. His eyes were gentle, a soft smile on his face.

He didn't say a word.

"Why is Daisy here?"

Michael shrugged. He focused his thoughts, projecting them so that he didn't have to speak them aloud for them to be heard, *"She's the sheriff—if something's happened, shouldn't she know?"*

"Why?" Tanya's voice was flat and grim, her eyes angry. *"It's too late to do anything now."*

"She's trying, Tanya. She can't turn back time. He isn't leaving any clues. She can only do so much," Mike said, trying not to let her sense his frustration.

Tanya's eyes closed. *"I know. The girl's dead though. So am I. Can she stop him from doing it again?"* Her image wavered, a certain sign of rising emotion.

"I don't know...that might be up to you."

Tanya's eyes flew open. *"What can I do? Damn it, I'm stuck here. Here or at that damned cabin where he...where he..."* Her voice faded away and her eyes looked stricken as she stared at him, her image wavering in and out of sight.

"Tell me who he is. Can you see him yet?"

She spun away from him. *"No! I don't want to see him...he's just...just there! I can't—"*

Michael sighed. Running a hand through his hair, he glanced at Daisy. She was staring at him, her eyes wide and apprehensive. She'd sensed something from Tanya. Tanya had passed too close to her. The sheriff was a sensitive. She'd felt the cool touch of the deceased. He looked away from her pretty face and focused on Tanya. *"It's okay—don't force it then."*

Looking at Daisy, he said, quietly, "Come on. Lets go for a drive." Maybe he'd get lucky and just feel something lingering from the young girl's passing. Daisy stared at him.

"We just went for a drive. *Here.* Now we're going for another one?" she demanded sarcastically. "What's with all the silent stares?"

Michael shook his head. "Nothing. There's nothing here right now."

"Nothing my butt," Daisy snorted, propping her hands on her hips. Arching one elegant brow at him, she said, "What's going on?"

Michael repeated, "Nothing." He walked between the two women, one living, one caught between the world and what waited beyond. The cool icy touch of death grazed his flesh as Tanya's arm brushed his. On the other side, he felt the warmth of life and the sweet scent of Daisy's body flooded his head.

"Where are you going? I thought you came here to help."

"You're not ready to help me. I'll do it another way," he responded, trying unsuccessfully to block Daisy's scent from his head. She smelled too sweet.

"Where are you going?"

"We're leaving," he responded shortly. Too damned many voices in his head. "Nothing here right now."

"The hell there isn't. I felt something—damn it, you're the spookiest damned person I've ever met in my life. If you weren't talking to somebody then I'll eat my badge."

Michael stopped. Tanya circled around them, staring at him with shuttered eyes. *"You're supposed to help me—isn't that why you can see me? But you're just going to leave. Why aren't you helping?"*

"I will help you—when it's time." Turning away, he looked at Daisy. "Tanya's here. But she still can't help me. Can't help us. I'm sorry. There's nothing we can do until she's ready."

"Stop talking about me like I'm not here," Tanya said angrily. *"What in the hell do you want from me?"*

Daisy stared at him warily, watching as he looked off to the left. Her eyes narrowed as she studied him. Her mouth parted and she whispered, "The diner...damn it, you were talking to somebody at the diner. Damn it, was there somebody you were talking to at the diner?"

Arching a brow, he asked levelly, "Did you *see* me talking to anybody at the diner?"

She scowled at him, her rosebud mouth puckering up as she replied snottily, "I didn't see you talking to anybody just now either, but I'd bet my next paycheck you were talking to somebody." She stood there, glaring at him in the moonlight with her hands fisted on her hips, her eyes glinting with temper.

And Michael suddenly had only one thing on his mind.

Kissing that scowl off her face.

Forget about the dead crying out for justice. Forget about the voices that had crowded his brain for far too long. Forget about the malevolent evil that darkened this small town.

He wanted to kiss her. It was the weirdest thing too. Because Michael didn't forget about his responsibilities. He hadn't ever been able to silence the voices in his mind.

Her eyes flicked to his mouth and he heard her soft intake of breath. Taking a step, he heard a branch break under his foot. She spun away and he closed his eyes, muttering under his breath. *You've lost your mind.*

But another part of him said, *This is the closest to sane you've ever been.*

Turning away, he found himself staring at Tanya. Her gaze moved back and forth between him and Daisy, her pale, transparent features still full of fury. *"You're just going to leave? There has to be something else you can do. How can you just leave?"*

"Because until you are ready to help me, there's nothing I can do here," Michael told her as gently as he could. Then he walked away.

After a minute, he heard Daisy falling in step behind him.

You've lost your mind, Daisy told herself.

Had he almost kissed her?

Had she almost kissed *him*?

And damn it, she was really disappointed when that kiss hadn't happened.

Murder investigation, hell-*O*! she shouted at herself. She really needed to sit herself down and have a talk, explain the basic rules of common sense. The weird guy passing through town wasn't the best guy to have a fling with—well, some people might argue he was the perfect guy for a fling. But Daisy didn't do flings. And if she did...well she just didn't. She was also a little busy trying to catch a serial killer before he killed one more woman. Definitely not the ideal time for any kind of romantic interlude.

A couple hours of good, hard, mind-blowing sex might just clear your head and let you think better. Okay, that was her libido talking.

She needed some sleep, that was what she needed. Well, sleep or a self-induced orgasm. Any of that might help a little. But instead of going home and telling tall, dark and strange here to get lost and come back when it was light out, they were out driving.

Stuck in a car with a man who did the weirdest things to her system. He made her skin buzz and at the same time, there was something about him that really, *really* freaked her out. He didn't talk, either. He just sat there, his hands resting on his thighs as he stared outside.

What in the hell he was looking at, she didn't know. Where they were going? She didn't know that either. At least earlier there was a destination. He'd been talking to Tanya in the field. She knew he had been. Now though, she wasn't so sure what his game plan was. Driving down 402 when it wasn't even three in the morning wasn't how she had planned to spend her night.

"I should have made some coffee," she muttered. She pressed her fingers against her eyes and rubbed, but it didn't make it any easier to hold her eyes open.

"He picked her up here."

Daisy hit the brakes. "What?" she demanded. Turning on the overhead light, she looked at him, feeling a cold chill dance up her spine. His eyes were glowing again.

"He picked her up here," he said quietly, staring off into the darkness. "She was hitchhiking. Wanted to go to Indianapolis—she'd never been. There was a play she wanted to see. Mom was afraid she'd get sick."

Daisy had absolutely no idea what to say. Swallowing, she shifted her gaze forward and realized she was still in the middle of the road. Easing the car to the shoulder, she shifted to park and turned the overhead light off. "Who is she? I can't do anything until I know she is."

He didn't hear a word she said. "She was walking—it was late, almost dark. She'd thought she'd get to town before it got dark. He pulled up and he just looked so safe...so normal."

Her palms were sweating. That icy cold sweat. Fear and rage clamored for equal footing inside her. Rage at whoever in the hell was doing this in her town. Fear that it was happening...and with such apparent ease...

And she was also uneasy as hell.

Michael O'Rourke was entirely too spooky. He didn't seem quite human. "Can you tell me something that will help me stop them?" she asked, her voice rough with emotion.

"She saw his face." He continued to stare out the window, but his voice seemed a little more focused, a little more there.

"You...you aren't talking to her, are you?"

He blinked and the glow faded from his eyes. A sad, but relieved smile curled his lips and he glanced at her. "No...no, she's gone. It's just—kind of like an echo."

"What's this about his face?" Daisy asked, closing her hands tightly around the steering wheel.

The smile that lit his face now wasn't sad, or relieved. It was downright mean. "She saw his face...I can't see him yet. But I'll know him."

Closing her eyes, Daisy thunked her head down on the steering wheel. "Damn it, shouldn't it be easier than this? Can't you just tell me who he is so I can go grab him?"

Michael started to laugh. "If you just go and grab him, even if I could tell you a name, you'd never be able to keep him. You're a cop, Daisy. Think like one. There has to be proof. He'll give himself away—when he does that, there's going to be proof."

Growling, she turned her head and glared at him. "Don't you think I've been looking for proof all this time? And while I wait, he'll grab another girl. If she died before he had his fun like you think, then he is going to be pissed."

Through the shadows, she could just barely see his face. The dim glow coming from the dashboard didn't give off much light. She watched as he leaned his head back against the seat and sighed. "I don't think he's going to grab another right now. He's not pissed—he's scared. Something has him scared."

Chapter Four

Tanya hovered in the darkness, watching him. He had already methodically stripped the girl naked and right now, the clothes were burning away in the fireplace. Thanks to the gasoline he'd doused them in, there wouldn't be anything left of them but cinders and ashes.

Anger burned in the pit of her belly and frustration ate at her. Stuck here...stuck, trapped. Watching while he started to lift the still, pale body of the girl in his arms. Tanya didn't even know her name.

"They'll find you—why are you wasting your time?" When he jumped, it made her smile.

His hands were shaking as he pulled away from the girl and spun around. His eyes were wide and terrified as he searched the room. "Go *away!*" he rasped.

Tanya grinned evilly. *"I can't. You trapped me here. I can't leave until I do something."*

"Who in the fuck are you?" he screamed. His face was angry, florid and red.

She hadn't ever seen such emotion... Her heart stuttered in her chest as she found herself staring into his eyes. Nononono...not him. Not him.

Her fury exploded through her and she didn't realize she had moved until he started to scream when she flew through the air. Wind started to whistle through the room.

"Bastard!" Her voice echoed through the room like a banshee's wail. She reached for him unconsciously and as she did, she saw his eyes move toward her hand and she realized he could see her.

She could see herself. Her hand was visible, pale and misty, transparent. But she could see it. Looking up, she met his eyes and knew that he saw her. Focusing the fury inside her, Tanya said to the man she had known all her life, *"You son of a bitch—I'm going to haunt you for as long as you live."*

He ran. Hard and fast. He was almost to town when reality settled in and he made himself slow down and suck his breath.

No. He hadn't seen her. She was dead. She screamed out his name, over and over, and then begged him to kill her. They always begged...his mind started to drift and a happy, dazed smile curled his lips as he remembered. The sound of their screams was such a sweet, erotic thrill.

Then a cold wind seemed to whisper over him and his smile faded. *I'm going to haunt you for as long as you live.* That voice, it wasn't like anything he'd ever heard, echoing around him, within him. She had come back. They didn't do that. They couldn't—damn it, this was all *wrong*. It was her fault. That little bitch. Fury and terror welled inside him and he wanted to lash out, but he didn't know how. His newest little toy was dead. She'd died before he could even have any fun with her. And damn it! She was still at the cabin—needed to get her out.

He started to turn and go back to get her.

No.

Memories of that face, that pale ghostly face rose in his mind and he knew he wouldn't go back. Not yet.

That face. Her eyes had been dark, too dark, like black pools in the pale circle of her face and she had screamed at him—it had sounded like death's war cry. He drove home, parking in the garage, but instead of climbing out, he just sat there for long moments.

"None of this is going right," he muttered, licking his lips. First that weird guy showed up in town. He didn't want changes. Changes weren't good right now. It hurt the status quo. Changes made the sheriff nervous and she was already nervous as hell—plus she started looking at odd things the minute he showed up.

Then the girl died.

Then the voices coming from the dark.

Now *her.*

A ghost.

He laughed hysterically. Ghosts weren't real, right? How in the world could ghosts be real? He shoved a hand through his hair and finally climbed out of the car. He edged around the car and made his way through the tight confines of the garage to the house.

It was dark inside and quiet. He needed the silence. He wanted to sleep, needed the quiet. He almost headed for the bedroom. A short nap, maybe a quick shower, and it would clear his head. He could think again and decide what he was going to do.

One glance at the clock though told him he didn't have the time.

Almost time for his shift to start.

CRGO

Michael came awake at the knock on the door.

His neck was stiff, his mouth was dry as cotton and his back hurt like hell after falling asleep at the desk. Slowly, he stood and stretched, trying to ease the kinks in his muscles. It didn't do much good.

"Yeah?" He wasn't going to open that door until he knew it was the innkeeper. That woman made the Bureau look soft when it came to interrogation. Mike wasn't going through the inquisition again.

"It's Daisy."

The sound of her soft, husky voice started a low burn deep in his gut. His cock jerked a little and he pressed a hand against his fly. Just hearing her voice and he got hard. "Just a minute." He glanced at the computer. He'd bumped the mouse when he woke up and the images on the Bureau's website glared at him. He wasn't working this case in any official capacity, but he'd hoped there might be something in the Bureau's database that might help.

He'd been logged out due to inactivity but he didn't want the pretty sheriff seeing him there. If he had something to tell her, maybe. He didn't want her worrying that a lot more feds were going to show up, in an official capacity, and start poaching.

Mike had spent most of the night checking databases,

hoping to find something. But no luck.

He padded over to the door and muffled a yawn. Shoving a hand through his hair, he opened the door. She looked a lot more awake than he felt, he thought tiredly. She held up a piece of paper but instead of looking at it, he just stared into her furious eyes. "She was fifteen. *Fifteen.*"

Michael felt yet another crack etch itself into his heart as he looked at the flyer. Kerri Etheridge. Fifteen. Runaway from Denton, Indiana. The bright red font across the bottom alerted authorities to the fact that she had a heart murmur.

"Heart attack," he said, closing his eyes. A blessing in disguise.

"You already knew that," Daisy said, her voice trembling with rage.

Michael glanced at her as he reached out and gently tugged the flyer from her. "I suspected it," he said, stepping to the side. She frowned at him but came in, crossing her arms over her chest. Turning around, she watched him while he closed the door.

Kerri. Pretty name. "She's worried about her mom." Michael closed his eyes. "She wants her mom to know what happened. She just wanted to go to a play." He crumpled the flyer in his fist, clenching his jaw. Impotent fury ate at him. He wanted to hit something. Anything. But instead of pounding on something with his fists, he dropped down onto the bed and stared at the crumpled flyer. "All she wanted to do was see a play."

"I can't say anything to her mom until I find her," Daisy said quietly. "Nobody has even seen her. If I say something now, without proof—that would be cruel, Michael."

"I know. Daisy, you don't seem to understand—I've been doing this a long time." *Too long...*

"You've been doing this *too* long."

His eyes flew up to meet hers and an unwitting smile curled his lips. He watched as she moved forward and knelt down in front of him. "This hurts you," she whispered, staring up at him. "I'm sorry. I wish I didn't need you to help me."

Michael reached out and traced his fingers along the curve of her cheek. "This is what I do, ma'am," he drawled. "Nothing to apologize about." Dropping his gaze to her mouth, he finally gave into the urge that had been driving him nuts ever since he'd seen her. Threading his hand through her hair, he drew her a little closer, slowly, giving her the chance to pull away.

Her mouth felt soft and she tasted like warm honey. He traced the seam of her lips with his tongue and her lips opened under his. With a groan, he eased off the edge of the bed and wrapped his arms around her, pressing his hands against her back. Her breasts flattened against his chest as he eased her up against him. Michael skimmed his fingers up her back so he could fist a hand in her hair. Pulling back, he scraped his teeth over the curve of her neck. "You taste good," he muttered huskily.

He could feel her heart slamming against his. She felt so damned alive—need fogged his brain and he couldn't think beyond anything but feeling that life, tasting it, bathing himself in it.

Reaching up, he grabbed the neckline of her shirt and jerked. Buttons popped and went flying. Shoving the edges of the shirt open, he stared down at the pale flesh of her breasts rising over the red silk cups of her bra.

He tumbled her down onto her back and buried his face against her breasts. The soft scents of vanilla and lavender lingered there and the warm, sweet scent filled his head.

"Michael..." Her voice was a soft hungry little whimper that made his blood burn even hotter.

The leather of her gun harness got in the way. With quick, impatient jerks of his hands, he unbuckled it and shoved it away before reaching below her to unfasten her bra. He tossed that aside and sat back on his heels to stare down at her. Her nipples were rosy pink—hard as ice.

His mouth watered and he hunkered down over her. Michael slid his hands under her and lifted her torso up to meet his mouth so that he could catch one plump nipple in his mouth. The other one, he caught with his thumb and forefinger, rolling it back and forth, pinching it lightly. She cried out sharply, her hands coming up to cup his shoulders. Her nails dug into his shoulders and she arched against him.

The heat of her was driving him mad. Everything about her felt warm, alive... Pulling back, he sucked air into starving lungs while he stared into her eyes. The soft golden-green eyes looked as hungry as he felt. "I want you," he muttered hoarsely. "So much I hurt with it. If you can't do this, tell me now, while I can still stop."

His eyes looked so damned tortured, Daisy thought. How in the hell had this happened? She'd come here because of a lost child—one she knew was dead. All she had was his word. She barely knew the man, but his eyes didn't lie. She'd come here because she had a job to do. How had she ended up half naked on the floor?

Daisy wasn't quite sure. But her belly was a hot, molten mass of need and she wanted him so bad, she hurt from it. She'd been too damned lonely for too damned long, and looking in his eyes did something to soothe that ache. Something that she couldn't even begin to describe.

She didn't need to, either.

Daisy didn't need excuses, reasons, anything. What she needed was him. Sleep hadn't done anything to ease the ache and the self-induced orgasm hadn't done a damn thing. This would.

Feeling his heat and strength against her while he pumped in and out, that would ease the ache. "I don't want you to stop," she murmured as she slid her arms up and wrapped them around his neck. Daisy drew him down against her, whimpering softly as the warm weight of his body crushed her into the floor.

He swore roughly and pulled away from her, crouching on his knees as he tore at her jeans. His hands were clumsy with need and there was a desperate look in his eyes. Kicking her tennis shoes away, she tried to help him but he just batted her hands away. Arching a brow at him, she rose on her elbows and smiled at him. "Demanding."

"Not usually," he mumbled. He slid her a look under his lashes and her mouth went dry. "I can't remember ever wanting a woman the way I want you, though."

Michael continued to hold her gaze with his as he stripped her jeans away, keeping the flat of his hands pressed against her thighs and just using the downward stroke of his hands to take the sturdy cloth down. She felt a hot flush rise to her cheeks as his eyes moved down, locking on her naked body with focused intent. "You're not wearing any underwear."

She smiled, shrugging a little. "Habit—I never wear panties with jeans."

A wolfish smile lit his features and his eyes once more met hers. She felt the heat from that look and it damned near singed her. It also hit her in the heart like a sucker punch—for once, that damnable grim look was gone from his face. "You shouldn't have told me that. I'll never be able to think straight around you again," he said, shaking his head slightly.

Flashing him a wide grin, she winked. "Oh, goodie..." Reaching down, she traced her fingers over his thigh. "You're overdressed, you know."

His lips brushed over hers. "Maybe I am." She watched as he rose and when he stepped away, she rolled over onto her belly to watch him as he walked across the room. Light filtered in through the gap in the curtains from the bathroom, but that was all. She'd like more light, wanted a room full of bright sunshine so she could sit down and stare at him at her leisure.

That body of his was amazing. His shoulders were wide and powerful, his chest tapering down into a flat belly and narrow hips. As he reached into the closet, she rose onto her elbow and admired the play of muscles in his back and arms. Hell, she knew women who loved to take trips into town and throw money away at strip joints. They were wasted—not one of them had a damn thing on Michael O'Rourke.

He wasn't doing a thing except rooting through a duffle bag, and he was wearing a worn out pair of jeans. When he pulled out a cellophane wrapped condom, she arched a brow and drawled, "I have to say, I'm damned glad to see you carry it in there, and not your wallet. I've never been impressed with men who carry them in their wallet."

Michael just looked at her, that small smile of his on his mouth. He crossed back to her and held out his hand, waiting for her to rise and take it.

She did and then her heart melted as he pulled her against him and just held her for a minute. *You're in trouble, Dasynda!* her brain screamed. *Big major trouble! He'll leave when his job here is done.*

She knew that. She also knew nothing had ever felt quite as right as his arms around her. Snuggling against him, she murmured, "You're still over dressed."

Daisy shivered as one big warm hand slid up her back, cupping the back of her head and then tangling in her hair before arching her head back. His mouth covered hers and she opened her lips, groaning as he kissed her deeply. He backed her up against the bed—she felt the edge of it against her legs just a moment before he urged her backward, covering her body with his.

He shifted his weight to keep from crushing her and she worked her hand between them, tugging at the button of his jeans, then easing the zipper down. She felt his groan as she slid her fingers inside his shorts, closing her fingers around him. He felt hard and smooth under her fingers, silk and steel. An ache pulsed through her womb and she rocked against him. Daisy managed to get in one quick, caressing stroke before he tore away and shoved his jeans down.

"You're hell on my mental state," he muttered shortly, glaring at her as he kicked his jeans away.

Daisy pushed up on her elbow, staring at him with a smile. Cellophane ripped and she watched him as he rolled the rubber down his cock before she looked at him with a wide grin. "You know, I think I'm actually probably really good on your mental state," she murmured.

Her grin faded away as he crushed her into the mattress. She sucked her breath as he pushed one knee between her legs, then wedged his hips between her thighs. Dark midnight eyes stared into hers as he pressed against her. Her lashes fluttered closed and he murmured, "No. Don't close your eyes—I want to see you."

Daisy felt exposed under that look. Foolish—she was naked in his arms, and he was pushing inside of her, but it was that watchful gaze that made her feel vulnerable. Too vulnerable, too exposed and she didn't like it. But she did want to see him. Dragging her lids back up, she stared at him as he slowly started to sink inside her.

The stretching sensation was unbearable. Catching her lower lip between her teeth, she arched up against him as he pushed inside her. He lowered his head, pressing a soothing kiss against her mouth. Skimming one hand down her side, he slid it under her hip, lifting her up against him.

Michael held her gaze with his as he pulled out. She sucked air in raggedly, trying to make her tense body relax. A lazy smile curved his mouth as he stretched out atop her, taking her hands in his, gently bringing them up by her head. The head of his cock was still inside her sex, throbbing, teasing the sensitive tissues there. He rotated his hips a little with his next stroke and Daisy gasped. He did it again and again, teasing her clit. "Shhhh...that's it," he muttered against her lips. "Relax."

Relax—hell, no. "I can't relax," she muttered. She arched up against him, taking too much in, too fast. She hissed and instinctively clenched her thighs.

Shifting against her, he cradled her head in his hands, lowering his head and taking her mouth. He also started to rock against her. Slow, gentle rolling motions that did little more than stroke his body against her clit. "Relax," he murmured again. He bit her lower lip gently and then sucked on it. One big hand gripped her hips, holding her still as he started to rotate his hips against her once more.

Heat built inside her like a volcano, escalating with each slow, teasing stroke. The pain eased a little more. Daisy wrapped her arms around his torso, raking her nails down his sides, arching against him, trying to rock her hips up and take him deeper inside. Michael just laughed softly, continuing those slow, gentle thrusts.

Little mini shocks started to quake in her belly, rippling through her sex. Daisy hooked her heels around him, trying to ride the thick ridge of flesh harder. As he sank just a little deeper, she moaned in satisfaction. A deep rumbling laugh escaped Michael and then he rose up on his hands.

The glittering look in his eyes was all the warning she had.

He took her thighs in his hands, draping them over his arms, then he started shafting her, hard, deep strokes. The bed started to shake beneath them. Daisy felt her heart slam into her throat as he rode her. Dear heaven, he was so damned deep—each stroke rocked her to the very core.

Staring up at him, eyes wide, she felt icy hot chills skittering all through her. Her skin felt too hot, too tight, too itchy. She couldn't breathe, couldn't see—the iron-hard thickness of his cock burned inside her, throbbing, aching. The rest of the world faded away and all she knew was his body moving over hers, his cock shuttling back and forth inside her sex. So hot, so deep, so tight.

Too hot. Too deep—too much, too much... "Stop," she gasped out, curling her hands over his shoulders. She pressed the heels of her hands against him but she wasn't sure if she wanted to push him away or pull him closer.

"Stop?" he whispered, sliding his hand over one sweat slicked thigh, cupping the curve of her rump in his hand.

"Why?"

Staring blindly up at him, she said, "I can't...I can't..."

He just smiled. Lowering his head, he kissed her just below her ear and then he murmured, "You can." He reached between them and touched her clit. That one light touch did it. The orgasm ripped through her with an intensity that left her screaming breathlessly. And Michael continued to thrust inside her. Even as she came moaning back down to earth, he pumped inside, lowering his head to suckle on her nipples, first one and then the other.

"You still think you can't?" he whispered when she had her breath back.

"Huh?" she whimpered, staring up at him with blind eyes. Hunger and need left her uncomprehending. Her sex clutched greedily around his cock as he thrust against her. She clung to his arms, trying to make sense of his words.

He laughed, lowering his head to kiss her roughly.

Gathering her up against him, Michael buried his face against her neck. With short, deep thrusts, he rode her. Daisy rocked up to meet him, another climax building low in her belly even though she was still reeling from the first one. When he raked her neck with his teeth, she moaned raggedly. The brush of his fingers down her arm was like live electricity touching her skin.

The pounding of his hips against her grew more desperate—he shifted against her, slamming his hands down into the mattress by her head, rising up over her. With glittering eyes, Mike stared down at her, watching her so closely, staring at her so intently.

Daisy reached up, closing her hands over his biceps, digging her nails into the taut skin there as she lifted her hips up. The thick, steely flesh of his cock stroked over the sensitive, slick tissues of her sex—her heart slammed against her ribs while the heat built inside her, stretching her skin, threatening to spill out.

"Come for me," he whispered harshly, sliding his hand down her thigh and catching her knee, lifting it up over his hip. "Come for me, Daisy..."

As he pushed into her one more time, she did, clamping down around him and climaxing with a ragged scream. Her nails raked down his flesh, and she writhed under him, bucking in his arms.

He throbbed inside her—she felt the rhythmic jerking sensations of his cock. Moaning, her hands slid limply from his arms and he sank down against her, his head resting between her breasts.

Once she was able to breathe again, she whispered weakly, "How's your state of mind now?"

"I dunno," he murmured. "Maybe we should do that again and then see what happens."

"Again just might kill me," Daisy said, snickering.

"Ummm. Me, too. Hell of a way to go." Michael had to admit, he felt a hell of a lot better than he had been in a very long time. He could feel the furious pounding of her heart against his cheek, and the smell of hot woman filled his head.

The hot, snug silk of her sex still gloved his cock and he groaned as the tissues convulsed around him. "Gotta tell ya. I feel pretty damned good right now," he muttered. Sliding his hand up her side, he cupped her breast in his hand, rolling her nipple in his hand and watching it pucker.

She made a sound, that half moan, half laugh. "Don't do that—I'm practically dead already."

"I'm telling you—it wouldn't be a bad way to go." Her nipple was pink and tight and if he could just manage to move, he wanted to lick it again and taste her. Mike figured he could spend the next fifty years tasting her and he still wouldn't be satisfied. *Bad. This is bad.*

Daisy sighed. "I'd agree—but I've got a case to solve before I can think about dying."

"Yeah, you do. *We* do. She's mine—I have to help you finish this." He stared into her eyes and murmured, "I hope you understand."

A gentle smile curved her lips. "I do. And I have to tell you, I'm glad."

Working his arms around her, he rolled onto his back, bringing her with him. She sprawled on top of him and lifted up on her elbow, staring down at him. "This isn't the best way for you to spend your afternoon," he said. Her soft hazel eyes looked entirely too serious now.

She smiled a little. "Hey, I'm entitled to a lunch break." The smile faded. "I've got to find this girl, Michael. If we go around when I get off of work, do you think you might... Hell, how does it work?"

He reached up, pushing a silken lock of golden hair behind her ear. "Hard to explain that part. Kind of like a radio signal, sometimes. Best way to explain it. Sometimes I pick things up. Sometimes I don't. And yes. We can go whenever you're ready to."

She lifted a brow. "Ready? That will be exactly never. How can you be ready..." Daisy closed her eyes. "She was just a baby."

"I know. I wish I could make this easier. But nothing will." Michael held still as she lowered her head and pressed her lips to his.

"I *need* to do it now. But I'd have a hard time explaining it. I've got a meeting at one and five hundred other things I'm supposed to do before quitting time. Bureaucratic bullshit. I've got a killer to catch and I'm attending a committee meeting to discuss the need for a new stoplight."

"Hey, a town this small, isn't a new stoplight like a big step?" Mike teased.

It worked. A faint smile tipped up the corners of her mouth. "Yeah. A very big step." She sighed and cuddled against his chest. "You know, it's going to be a hell of a lot harder to concentrate on any of it now."

Ten minutes later, he watched as she climbed out of the shower, long streamers of dark brown hair dripping water down her sleek body. "Aren't you worried that people saw you come in here?" he asked, propping his shoulder against the door.

"I'm sure fifteen people saw me come in here. And I'm equally sure most of them have already called the majority of their friends and told them I'm here. So either you're my prime suspect, or we're having a torrid affair," Daisy said with a wry smile. "Either one is much more believable than the truth." Her voice broke off and she flashed him a wicked grin. "Well, I guess the torrid affair could be the truth now. But I can't exactly make it public knowledge that you're some sort of psychic bloodhound, can I?"

Michael ran his tongue along the surface of his teeth, watching as she started to dry off. "You aren't real big on beating around the bush, are you?"

She shrugged. "No. Wastes time." Slowly, she straightened, hooking the towel around her neck. "You know, I can't say I've had a lot of torrid affairs. Does one encounter count?"

Arching a brow at her, he said, "I'm not sure."

The blood drained out of his head, pooling in his groin as she moved up and pressed her nude body against him, wrapping her arms around him. "Well, I think maybe we might want to try for a repeat. If you're interested. That way, we can at least give truth to the torrid affair thing."

Chuckling, he trailed his fingers down her spine, he said, "Interested?" Nudging his cock against her belly, he asked, "What do you think? Am I interested?"

She hummed softly in her throat. "I think that's a yes."

Chapter Five

The darkness had been hanging over his head all afternoon, like a damned cloud.

Ever since Daisy had left.

When the phone rang, he answered it with a short, "Yeah?" He knew he sounded pissed, but he couldn't help it. Even the sound of Daisy's voice didn't help.

"Hey. You okay?"

Michael tried to force himself to sound a little less distant as he responded, "Sorry, Daisy. Just feeling—odd. Are we ready?"

"Yes. I'm out front." Her voice was neutral, not quite mad, but...*cautious.*

Hell, he couldn't blame her. A few hours ago they'd been in bed together and he answered the phone sounding like a bear with a hangover. He couldn't help it, though. Something was wrong. It hung in the air, a storm waiting to break.

Grabbing his jacket, Michael started to head out of the room, but then he turned back. His bag was in the closet. His gun was in it. Slowly, he crossed over to it, taking the bag down and withdrawing the Glock and the holster. He slid the holster on and buckled it into place, staring stonily into the distance.

"Things are getting ready to go down, brother."

"I know that."

Lucas came walking into view, appearing out of the corner of his eye, his face blank. *"You don't like guns."*

"No, I don't. But I carry one when I have to."

"The pretty sheriff the have-to this time?" Lucas asked, leaning against the table. *"I got some vibes earlier."* He wagged

his eyebrows and grinned.

Michael studied his brother with narrowed eyes. "You picking up eavesdropping?"

Lucas laughed. His image seemed to fade away for a minute and then he refocused, a little clearer, a little more solid. *"No, but damn, if I did, I wouldn't tell you. You'd just find a way to spoil my fun. It would be about the closest to living I've been in twenty years."* He shrugged, staring out the window as he added, *"I just know you, Mike. She's different—she means something to you."*

"Yes." That was all Mike would admit to. He didn't want to think about it, much less talk about it. The idea of caring about somebody was just too damn foreign to him. He'd given up on those kinds of emotions a long, long time ago.

"You know who you're looking for?"

Shaking his head, Michael methodically loaded his gun. That done, he slid the Glock into the holster and then pulled his jacket on. "No. If I did, you think I'd just be standing here?"

Michael lifted his eyes and stared at Lucas. "Do you know anything?"

Lucas smirked at Michael and said sardonically, *"If I did, do you think I'd just be standing here?"* The smile faded and his eyes closed.

Tension swelled in the room and Michael clenched one hand into a fist as Lucas wavered in and out of view for a moment. *"Things are changing around you, Michael. I don't understand what it is, not completely. But be careful—I made myself a promise and I can't move on until I see it done. Eternity is a long time to spend trapped here."*

Before Michael could form a single word, Lucas was gone. Snarling in frustration, he stalked out of the room. Ghosts—the most frustrating creatures on the damned planet.

They came, they went, they dropped ominous little comments like that and then before a person could ask so much as one damned question, they disappeared.

And Michael couldn't exactly stick a beeper on them, either.

Jogging down the steps, he slid silently out the door before Mrs. Maria Cambridge even saw him. No doubt she'd have fifty questions—she did every time she saw him. Michael would have loved to have stayed someplace else but Mitchell wasn't exactly a hotbed of tourism trade.

This small B&B was about all the town had to offer other than a hotel ten miles down the highway. And Michael's gut instinct had insisted he stay here. Crossing the sidewalk, he ducked into the car just as the door to the B&B opened behind him. He saw Daisy waving and he grinned.

"She's going to be so damned mad you slid past her again. She always manages to pin her guests down for interrogation...I mean friendly conversation, but you've evaded her entirely too well."

Michael shifted in the seat so that he could look at Daisy while he talked. "I doubt I have anything too interesting to tell her."

Daisy arched a brow, but remained silent.

"Okay, I don't have anything interesting I *would* tell her."

"Hmmm."

He didn't like the sound of that disinterested hum. Sighing, he ran a hand through his hair. Michael said softly, "I pissed you off, didn't I?"

She smiled brightly. "Why ever would you think that?"

Staring at her, he just waited. She pulled away from the curb, driving slowly down the busy street. People were leaving work, or coming into the small town for dinner at the diner. About as busy as this small place ever got.

She remained silent under his watchful gaze for long moments and then finally, hazel eyes slid his way. "I don't care to be brushed aside so quickly."

"You're talking about when I answered the phone just now," Michael said softly.

She didn't respond but the look in her eyes was answer enough.

"I wasn't brushing you off." Michael closed his eyes. "And I'm sorry if I made you think that." His gut started to churn and he didn't know if it was from the conversation's path, or something darker.

She slowed to a stop at the light and Michael could feel her watching him. He had to force the words out as he said, "There's just...something—"

Something cold brushed down his spine.

Turning his head, he found himself staring at a parked

squad car. It was painted the same beige and browns as hundreds of other sheriff's deputies' cars throughout the country.

Nothing at all ominous about it. It sat parked in front of the bank, and Michael watched, unable to breathe, as a slender girl with short, spiky red hair came walking out. She passed by the deputy's car and paused to wave.

Michael couldn't see the man inside, but it didn't matter.

"That's him," he rasped hoarsely.

Blood seemed to flood his vision. Thick oozing red streams of it that poured across his line of sight like some bizarre Hollywood effect. Voices started to whisper. Then scream.

The voices of the dead had risen to banshee wails and it was sheer will that kept him from clapping his hands over his ears in an effort to drown the voices out. None of them made sense. There were no words, just those pain-filled, tortured cries, the mourning cries of those silenced far too soon, crying out for justice, begging for peace.

Even those who weren't trapped could suffer when their killer kept killing.

A hand came up, touching his arm. "Michael!"

Darkness swarmed up and flooded his vision—there was a roaring in his ears.

"Damn it, Michael, what in the hell is wrong?" The hand squeezed his arm, shaking him lightly.

He focused on that voice. *That* voice was alive. It was real. She was real. Sucking air in, he breathed in the scent of her. Vanilla. Wildflowers. Life. *Daisy...* Opening his eyes, he stared at her.

She was staring at him with turbulent eyes. "Damn it, what is wrong?" she demanded.

Her voice was too loud, rasping, grating on his nerves, but he seized on it, focusing on her voice, on the sound of her breathing. He forced himself to relax, made his lungs work again, forcing air in and out of his lungs, as he stared at her.

"If you don't answer me..."

Hoarsely, he said, "I'm okay—will be."

She blinked. "Damn it, you practically have a seizure on me and you tell me that you're going to be okay?"

Michael ran a shaking hand through his hair. He was

sweating—covered all over with that nasty sweat that only came with fear. And rage churned in his gut. All the emotion pent up inside him made it damned hard to think, to focus on anything. "Sorry—hits like that sometimes."

Daisy stared at him. Shit. Her hand curled into a fist and she was tempted to just swing out and pop him on the end of that cleft chin. Instead, she took a deep breath and made herself pull to the side of the road, out of the flow of traffic as she muttered furiously to herself.

"Hits like that sometimes," she repeated, trying very hard not to growl. "You practically have a seizure. And all you have to say is *hits like that sometimes.*"

Michael slid a look her way. His eyes were glowing. That had started just when he had gone stiff as a damned poker in the seat next to her, one hand flying up to the window, pressed flat. The other hand had briefly locked around hers, although she wondered if he remembered that at all.

He had arched up off the seat, his eyes rolling back, teeth bared. Never made a sound.

If his eyes hadn't been glowing that surreal shade of blue... As it was, that was the one thing that had kept her from calling for an ambulance. If an EMT had shown up and Michael stared at him with those glowing blue eyes, Daisy would have *more* trouble on her hands.

"Maybe you could have *warned* me about that," she snapped. Damn it, she was still scared to death. Turning sideways in the seat, she glared at him. "Now why don't you tell me exactly what it was that hit you?"

Michael wasn't looking at her though. He was staring past her shoulder, looking at something just beyond her. Or someone.

She turned, glancing behind her, but didn't see anything out of the ordinary. Just Mitchell on a Thursday night. "What?" she asked warily.

"It's him." There was no emotion on his face. None in his voice. Yet she sensed a rage so deep, part of her wanted to hide.

She turned again, trying to find who he was talking about. "Who?" she asked huskily, looking at the men walking by. She knew these men. Some she'd known since she was a baby— some she'd gone to school with. Hell, Marc Tanner, he'd been

her first crush.
"The deputy."

Chapter Six

She turned back to him with turbulent eyes. Shaking her head, she said flatly, "No."

Michael whispered, "He's stained with blood. I can't see him beyond the blood—I don't even know what he looks like."

"Look again!" Daisy said shakily. She reached for the handle to get out, but Michael leaned over and caught her arm.

"You don't want to believe me."

"You're damned right I don't!" she half screamed, trying to jerk away. "Damn it, that's *Jake*. He's like a brother to me. What in the hell do you know?"

Michael looked away from her face. Looking back at the deputy's car, he watched as the door opened slowly. He couldn't see the man though. It was like he had just been blotted away, his image replaced with a blood smear. "Because I look at him and see blood. Nothing but blood. And I hear their screams. Tanya haunts him. She won't leave him alone."

Daisy turned back around, and Michael could see the tears rolling down her cheeks as she stared at the deputy. Michael watched as the blood stained figure followed the woman from the bank. "She's next—he's been watching her for some time. He won't take her for awhile, but he dreams about it."

"Shut up," Daisy whispered harshly. "Damn it, just shut up." Dear God, she was going to be sick. She knew it. Not Jake. Damn it, he had been there when they had found two of the victims. *Tanya.* He'd been there when they were looking for Tanya. Daisy moaned and pressed the back of her hand to her mouth, muffling the sound.

"I'm sorry."

Tears all but choked her. "If you are wrong about this..."

Michael sighed. "I'm not."

She looked at him. He felt his heart break as she stared at him with haunted eyes. "I know."

CR&O

Jake owned a cabin a good thirty miles outside of town. Daisy sat at the computer in the county clerk's office, pulling up the files she needed. She did it with a blank mind. She couldn't think about what she was doing, or why.

If she did—if she did, she'd break. So she didn't think about it. She focused on the menial task, blocking out all other thought.

"What are you doing?" Michael asked.

He'd been very quiet, his voice neutral, almost as if he wasn't sure how to handle her right now. Hell, Daisy wasn't sure how to handle herself right now. She felt like she was going to shatter.

Slowly, focusing on each word, she said, "Looking for an address. Or an area. Jake...Jake owns a cabin." She flicked him a glance. "You said there was one."

Looking back at the screen, she continued to search through the files. Finally, she found the program she needed. "Damned clerks. Always updating things," she muttered. "They've changed the program they used to use."

She typed in Jake's information and waited. A few seconds later, the data scrolled on the screen. She printed the sheet out and stood up. Even though she couldn't hear him, she knew he was behind her. His quiet presence didn't set her on edge quite the same way it had before. It was almost like her system had adjusted to him—started trusting him on some very deep, very basic level.

She believed him. He was right about Jake. She knew it. The knowledge hit her like a fist in the belly. Tears burned in her eyes.

She really believed him.

Oh, dear God. Closing her eyes, she pressed the back of her hand to her mouth, trying to silence the tears rising inside her.

His fingers brushed against the back of her neck and she tore away, whispering harshly, "Don't. Okay? Just don't."

Clutching the address in her hand, she slid out of the room before he could say anything. Hell, what in the world could he say? He could try saying he was sorry, but what would that do?

It wouldn't make this any easier. Nothing would. Nothing ever could.

One of my best friends is a killer.

CR80

You can't...not right now.

But he couldn't go back there alone. That bitch—her voice drove him crazy. And he *needed*...needed it. Hadn't had any fun with that last one—needed to feel that rush, needed to hear her scream again. Maybe, just maybe, it would ease the pain in his head, wash away the fog. Pain cleansed. Purified. Yes. It did.

He'd take her. Grab her. And when he made her scream, he would be able to think again.

Her...the faces all blended together. Their faces seemed to merge into one. The face shattered—reshifted. Formed.

Finally a face he could recognize. Somebody he could reach out, touch...take.

The voice of caution kept murmuring, *No, you can't, you can't...too soon, too soon.*

But he had to. He had to grab another one. Had to do something to shut up *that* voice. Had to shut her up. Or drown her out. The screams would drown out that voice. He knew it.

"Do it," he muttered. Swiping the back of his hand over the back of his mouth, he nodded. He watched as she pulled over, a satisfied smile on his face. Slow leak—imagine that.

Jake Morris turned on the flashers and parked behind Sandy Hampton. Casting a quick look around, he climbed out of the car and crossed over to her. "Hey, Sandy...what's the matter here?"

CR80

Michael climbed out of the car, staring off into the woods.

They were parked in front of a dark quiet cabin. "Fishing rental. I've had to come out here a few times. People lose their keys, set the grill on fire...one woman locked her husband out because he'd spent five hours out on the lake and left her here alone."

He didn't say anything, tucking his hands into his pockets, as he looked off into the distance.

"We'll have to hike it from here. I'm not exactly sure where we are going. The lake is through this stand of trees. Jake's cabin is north of us, set back a little from the lake's edge." Daisy unlocked the trunk, digging out two flashlights and tossing one his way. "I'm not sure where. We're going to have to hunt for it."

He caught it automatically without ever looking her way. Softly, Michael said, "I can find it."

"You can find it," she repeated slowly. Daisy closed the trunk and turned to look at him. "How can you do that?" she asked quietly.

"I feel it. Let's go."

Michael smiled a little as he heard her disgusted sigh. But then, he lost track of her, of the night, of the trees. Everything faded away as the voices of the dead rose in the night around him. Not all of them had passed on. Some weren't strong enough—it took a lot of strength for a dead person's soul to be able to cross the veil that separated life and death. The trauma alone weakened them. But being here, this close to where their lives ended, Michael felt them.

The maelstrom of emotion pulled at him. His jaw clenched as he waded through it—like wading through waist-high mud. And the closer he got to his goal, the more his own anger grew.

There were a hell of a lot more than four victims. Mike felt the brush of so many souls that he lost count of them all. But there were dozens. He'd been killing for years.

Tanya felt him.

"You found me..."

Focusing his thought required too much effort. Out loud, he said quietly, "I told you I would."

Behind him, Daisy said, "Huh?"

He shook his head and continued to talk to the ghost. She hadn't fully manifested yet, but she hadn't crossed over. Her own anger and pain had fueled it and soon, it would be too late. If he didn't help her move beyond this soon, she'd become one of the few things he did fear.

Poltergeists were the only ghosts that could cause harm. Their rage empowered them with a strength that was easily five times that of what they had in life. Guiding a poltergeist into the hereafter wasn't easy—Michael had done it before, but only twice. "I told you I would," he repeated, just as much to reassure himself as her. "We'll stop him."

"You'd better hurry. There's another woman here. I can't watch this again, Michael. I can't—something is happening inside me. I don't know what it is, but I can't control it. Every time I look at him, I feel so angry, I don't even know myself."

Behind him, Daisy asked quietly, "Michael...? Who are you talking to?"

"Tanya, don't you think you should be angry?" he asked as he jumped over a log. Turning, he held out a hand to Daisy only to find her staring at him with dark, troubled eyes.

"You're a spooky bastard, you know that, O'Rourke?" she said flatly even as she accepted his hand. She let him help her climb over the fallen tree that reached nearly to her waist. She dusted her hands off and muttered, "A very spooky bastard."

Slanting a grin at her, he turned back to the path and focused once more on Tanya. Nothing like trying to play a counselor to the deceased. She didn't need to try to suppress that rage—that didn't work. She had to let go of it if she wanted to move on. But they couldn't let it spiral out of control either.

"Angry...yes, I have a right to be angry. But not at her...and I scared her. He came in with her—and I lost it. Now she's just as scared of me as he is. And what did she do? Nothing. The only thing she did was be stupid. We were both stupid..." Tanya's voice and presence faded from his mind.

Michael stopped in the middle of the trail and tried to center his attention on what was around him, instead of what lay before him. Daisy stood behind him, her breathing soft and steady, but he could feel the tension rolling from her in waves. "We're close," he said quietly.

Daisy laughed—it was a high, wild sound. Her eyes were dark and terrified in the pale circle of her face, but he didn't once wonder if she would be able to handle this. "I figured that out while you were carrying on conversations with the dead. You couldn't have given me a warning about that, either?"

A bitter smile curled his lips and he looked at her. "My life is a little too weird for any warning label to cover it," he murmured. And that realization made him feel very, very bitter.

CRITER

Adrenaline pulsed through him. Fear ate away at him, but he shoved it aside. He had to hear it, had to feel it—the screams weren't the same unless he felt her flesh. Until she struggled.

And it wasn't *right* when he was afraid.

He wouldn't be afraid once he touched her. His hands were clumsy as he went to work on her clothes and he hated it. He wasn't supposed to be afraid. It wasn't right.

At least *she* had finally shut up. Jake still couldn't believe that bitch had caused him this kind of trouble—haunting him. How could she haunt him? They'd grown up together...

A wild laugh escaped him as he cut away the soft pants that clung to Sandy's body. The sight of the cloth falling away calmed him inside. He could focus again.

The shaking in his hands eased and the roaring in his ears faded away, letting him focus on her fear. As he ran one palm down her thigh, pleasure spiked inside him. This was better. So much better.

He liked how she looked in them. They clung to her ass and thighs, then loosened, draping around her lower legs. She had such a pretty ass. He wanted to untie her ankles and turn her over, stare at her soft white curves, but he couldn't get careless right now. No—not now. Can't cut her loose—she'd wake up soon. Sandy had passed out, scared to death after *she* had been here. Wouldn't do for her to wake up and be half free.

Still, he slid his hands under her and cupped her ass, molding the soft, firm curves. Sandy moaned and Jake felt the anticipation roll through him. Blood pulsed hot and heavy through him, pooling in his groin. His penis felt thick and hard. Pushing up on his knees once more, he used his knife to cut away her panties.

Her lashes started to flutter open just as he reached for the button of his khakis. Lowering the zipper, he smiled at her, knowing that would be the first thing she saw.

"Jake...?"

He smiled. They were always confused at first. "Hi, Sandy." Covering her body with his, he kissed her.

She struggled to turn her head. "Jake—what are you doing?"

Fear started to crawl into her voice and he could see it when she started to remember. Her body tensed as she struggled, but the ropes only had so much give. He tied them so that she could move just enough, so that he could spread her thighs wide if he wanted. He usually preferred to keep their legs together when he mounted them. It was tighter that way. And he could feel them struggle better.

He donned a rubber before he covered her body with his. Ducking his head, he whispered into her ear, "Scream for me, Sandy."

A sob escaped her. "Damn it, Jake, what in the hell are you doing?"

CR80

Daisy stared at the car with a heavy heart.

It was Jake's work truck. It was parked in front of the cabin and judging from the worn path, Jake came out here on a fairly regular basis. She didn't want to think about what he did out here.

The windows were covered with thick wooden shutters, but she could see light seeping under them. A perfect place for a crime—they were far away from the nearest neighbor. Sound would carry on the water, but his cabin was far enough back from the lake that it would dampen the sound. Far enough back that it wouldn't be seen. The shutters would silence even more sound.

"You bastard," she whispered, starting to move past Michael.

He caught her arm, trying to push her behind him. That was when she saw the gun. Narrowing her eyes, she whispered, "I really hope you have a license for that."

Michael just cocked a brow at her.

Of course he had a license. He was a fucking FBI agent. So what if he didn't exactly look like one. Daisy hissed out a breath. Still, this wasn't his job. It was hers. The women Jake had killed, they were hers. He started forward and she grabbed his arm, jerking on him. His eyes met hers and she shook her head furiously.

He glared at her.

Daisy just glared back and then she shoved in front of him, drawing her gun and holding it in a loose grip by her thigh. She heard him sigh behind her and she grinned. Nice to be the one frustrating somebody for a change.

She could hear voices now, muffled, too indistinct to really make out. The walls were soundproofed or something. Daisy ought to be able to hear him better than this. Done to keep anybody from hearing the screams. Damn it. They were on a slippery slope here and she knew it. Jake had a woman in there, one he was planning to kill and Daisy had absolutely no legal reason for being out there.

Somehow, she didn't think it would fly if she explained to a judge and jury that the reason she arrested Jake was because a psychic had told her that Jake was a killer. Going on the word of a psychic who worked for the FBI might sound cool, but it wouldn't hold up in court. Hell, it wasn't enough for a search warrant.

She'd had a vague plan, finding some kind of evidence to implicate him, plant it if she had to, something, anything, whatever it took to stop him.

Instead, she had a killer on her hands, no reason for being here, and hell, yes, she could arrest him, but other than assault—all those thoughts cluttered her mind as she drew closer to the front door.

Get her out of there now—details later...

Just barely she could hear a soft male laugh. A woman's terrified cry. "...what in the hell are you doing..."

She stepped back but before she could even look at him, Michael had guessed what she wanted. He busted the solid wooden door down with one swift kick and stepped inside. Daisy followed, her gun focused on Jake's head. "Yeah, Jake," she said flatly. "What in the hell are you doing?"

He lay sprawled atop Sandy's pinned body, his khakis shoved low, the rest of him clothed. He rolled away from her, jerking his pants up, and Daisy saw him grab the gun on the table by the cot.

"Put it down, Jake."

He laughed as he crouched on the floor behind the cot, keeping Sandy's pinned, terrified body between them. "Hello,

Daisy." Something black and ugly filled his eyes as he looked at Michael. "I don't think I will put it down. You need to put yours down, though. Otherwise..."

Nausea churned in her gut as Jake lowered his head and pressed his lips to Sandy's brow. Then he replaced his lips with the gun's muzzle. The cold, matte black metal pressed into soft white flesh and Daisy could see Sandy's flesh give way as Jake dug in. "*You* put your gun down, Daisy. Otherwise...she won't leave here alive."

Daisy shook her head. "You're talking to another cop here, Jake."

Jake barked out a laugh. "A cop? Hell, I'm a second rate deputy in a second rate town, playing Barney to your Andy. Stuck here in Mayberry, practically. I don't see myself as the next shoo-in for *Law & Order*."

He cocked his head, trailing the fingers of his other hand along Sandy's body. She whimpered, cringing away from his touch, turning her head and staring at Daisy with wide, terrified eyes. "Now, put the gun down—both of you."

A soft chuckle drifted through the room.

Daisy shivered at the sound. That wasn't Michael—and by the look on Jake's face, it wasn't him either. It was soft, feminine and scary as hell. When the voice came, it took everything she had in her to keep from dropping the gun and flinging herself at Michael in terror.

"*Guns...why are you so worried about guns? That's not what killed me.*"

Jake shoved away from the cot, staring around the cabin. His eyes were wide, almost black in his suddenly pale face. "Go *away.*"

"*I will. When I know you're burning in hell.*"

An unseen wind started to whip through the room, tearing at Daisy's clothes. She squinted her eyes against it, watching Jake. She ducked to the floor as he started to wave his gun around through the air. From the corner of her eye, she could see Michael doing the same.

"Tanya, don't scare him so bad that he starts shooting at thin air," Michael said.

With a desperate laugh, Daisy echoed, "Please, Tanya." *Now, I'm talking to a dead woman...* "I'd rather get her out of here in one piece, and me as well. And I'd like to make sure he can't do this to anybody else."

A soft sound echoed around them. Like a sigh. *"Don't worry. He won't. He won't hurt anybody. Ever."*

"Make her go away!" Jake screeched, turning his head to stare at them with wild eyes. He grabbed Sandy, fisting his hand in her hair.

He pressed the gun to her cheek, hard. "Make her go away or I'll kill this bitch and give her company."

Daisy stood slowly, shaking her head. "Don't do that, Jake. Come on—leave Sandy alone. This isn't her fault."

"No. It's *her* fault." He glanced up at the ceiling again. Unable to keep from looking, Daisy followed the path his eyes took. And there she saw her. A pale white figure just hovering there.

The wind blew faster and harder. It got colder. And the colder it got, the clearer that figure became. *"My fault. My fault—you bastard..."* Tanya started to laugh. She moved closer, a mean smile on her mouth. *"You're the one afraid now, aren't you?"*

Drifting down from the ceiling, she started to circle around Jake and he flinched, letting go of Sandy and scuttling away. He cowered in the corner as the misty white form moved closer.

"Nononononononono!" he screamed harshly, swinging out with one hand. It seemed like he had forgotten he was even holding the gun, just slapping out blindly in terror.

"I screamed that, didn't I? How often did I beg for help? Beg you to stop? You laughed. You wanted me to scream—now it's my turn." Tanya's voice rose and fell, getting louder and louder until it echoed off the walls.

Michael sat there, listening to that terrifying voice with dread. She continued to taunt her killer, her voice low and full of hate. The rage and anger spiraling inside her. It flooded the small confines of the cabin. All that emotion was going to explode and the results were going to be ugly and scary as hell.

She was pulling herself back into this world, too completely. Too entirely. Leaning over, he put his mouth to Daisy's ear. "Get the girl loose. Got a knife?"

Daisy gave a slight nod and started to inch away, moving backward until she could press her back to the wall. Once there, she circled around the room, watching Jake carefully.

Jake never once looked her way. He was too focused on Tanya. Nobody else in the world mattered to him.

Michael waited until he saw Daisy kneel by Sandy's side before he spoke to Tanya. "Is he worth it?"

Tanya barely seemed to realize he was talking to her. She was too busy whirling around Jake, her laughter high, a wicked edge to it that made his skin crawl. *"Scream for me!"* And her voice sounded just a little more solid. Long plumes of misty white trailed from her as she tormented him, making her seem larger than she really was.

Michael focused—it was harder now than ever before. All that wild manic energy that she drew in with her was scrambling his brain. *"Tanya!"*

The whirling white form seemed to settle a little and she turned, staring at Michael. *"Go away now,"* she said quietly.

Shaking his head, Michael said, "I can't. You said you could feel something odd, something inside you changing. Rage is taking a hold of you, Tanya. Ghosts and rage don't mix well. Ghosts and rage—you let rage settle inside you, Tanya, you'll never move on. Being stuck here, is that what you want?"

She stilled. *"I want him to pay."* Hatred filled her eyes and she stared at Jake malevolently. *"I want him scared and begging for his life."*

Tanya looked back at Jake and Michael cursed under his breath as she started to scream at Jake again. She reached out, her arms long, much longer than a human's, and grabbed him. Michael dove across the floor as she flung Jake across the room. "This makes him pay—but you pay as well. Don't punish yourself for his crimes. You don't want to be trapped, Tanya. Let it go. I'll take care of him."

"I...I don't think I can do that."

Michael closed his eyes as her anger began to pulse within him—getting too strong. Too out of control. "Are you ready to make us suffer with him?"

Daisy crouched in the corner with Sandy huddled against her. There had been an old, rough blanket laying on the floor and Daisy had given it to the younger woman, but Sandy was still trembling. Soft little mewls of fear kept rising in her throat and she stared sightlessly at the wall. Her entire body was shaking,

She was going into shock. Daisy had to get her out of there but she didn't know how. She sure as hell couldn't carry Sandy back to the car. It had been a good mile hike to get here and a rough one, at that.

It didn't help that the very air around them felt heavy, icy with terror. It was like the way the air felt thick and humid right before a summer storm broke open right over your head, but instead of thick, muggy air, when Daisy breathed in, it was chills and fear that clogged her lungs.

Closing her eyes helped a little. Forcing her breathing to level while she counted to ten. No—twenty. Twenty was a little better. She'd prefer a thousand, but she really needed to figure a way out of this mess.

Her mind raced. This sure as hell hadn't been covered in training years ago, and it wasn't anything she'd ever picked up through experience either. Part of her knew she needed to get Sandy someplace safe, someplace where she could get medical treatment.

The other part didn't want to do a damn thing that would draw Tanya's attention away from Michael. And yeah, she wanted to hear more about this *us suffering with him* part.

"I won't hurt anybody else—just him." Tanya's voice was low and angry and there was a sadistic look in her eyes that made Daisy's skin crawl.

Michael cocked his head, staring at the incorporeal form as though he was talking to somebody on the street about the damned weather. "But you already have—you scared her earlier, didn't you? You already told me that. You can keep it to where only he can hear you, but you're losing control. The anger is taking control."

Chills ran down Daisy's spine as she watched the emotions that flickered on Tanya's face. She seemed to getting more and more *solid* with every passing moment. That really *really* bothered Daisy—because she also sensed a wariness about Michael. Not in the way he held himself, or even the way he talked.

She doubted that Tanya sensed it at all.

But he was worried. Very worried.

"Listen to me, Tanya. If that anger takes over completely—if you let go, you'll lose yourself. And passing on, you will never be able to do it. You'll be trapped here, nothing more than a thing of anger and rage that nothing short of God's intervention will stop. I won't be able to help you."

Okay, now *that* sounded bad. Images of the movie *The Grudge* began to roll through Daisy's mind. Before she realized she was going to say anything, she heard herself speak, "He's not worth that, Tanya. Anger wasn't something you had use for in life. Remember how I always held grudges? You never did. Said you were too lazy, but it wasn't that. You just didn't have any use for anger. Not then. Don't let it take over now."

Seconds later, it was like the storm just rolled away. The terror was gone. Daisy was no longer trembling and Sandy finally stopped whimpering in mindless terror. Daisy squeezed Sandy's shoulder and then looked to Tanya.

Or tried to—Tanya wasn't so easy to see any more.

"You always had the most annoying habit of being right, Daisy," Tanya said. Her voice sounded distant, like it was coming from down a well. The wind whipping through the cabin stopped—there was a soft sighing sound and then just silence.

"Tanya?"

Michael glanced at her. "She's gone."

Daisy gaped at him. "That fast?"

That crooked grin appeared for the briefest second. "Sometimes, it just takes the right words. You had them. I didn't." Then he blinked. As he looked away, she had the briefest glimpse of his eyes. That look was going to stick with her a long, long time.

"I have to take him in, Michael. And we have to hurry. She's going into shock."

Michael looked away from Jake for a moment. Jake was still huddled on the floor, his arms over his head. Of the four of them, Jake still seemed to be suffering the after-effects of whatever Tanya had been doing. He was bawling like a baby. A disgusted sneer curled Michael's mouth and then he looked at Daisy. "Prison's too good for him."

As he moved toward Sandy, Daisy thought that danger had been averted.

Obviously not.

"She'll sleep now," Michael said less than a minute later as Daisy was slowly, carefully approaching Jake.

Daisy looked back at Sandy. "Damn it, shock victims aren't

supposed to sleep!"

His eyes met hers very briefly. "She's not in shock any more."

Daisy tried to block him from Jake, but he merely moved around her with that easy, effortless grace, crouching in front of the fallen man. He watched Jake for the longest time with that piercing, glowing gaze. "Tanya's gone."

Jake yelped at her name and looked up. Whatever he saw on Michael's face didn't set him at ease. He cringed away. Daisy suspected if he could have disappeared into the wall, that's exactly what he would have done. "Get away from me," he whimpered, sounding more like a child than a grown man.

Michael nodded. "I will. They want you more than I do anyway."

"They...?" Jake whispered timidly, his eyes wheeling around the room.

Daisy glanced around too. Holy hell. Please, not more. She couldn't handle anything else weird tonight. Maybe never. She might be ruined for ghost flicks for life. But there was nothing else in the room. Nobody else. Just the four of them.

She looked back to the two men in time to see Michael reaching out. He held nothing in his hand, yet Jake screeched in terror. "No! Don't fucking touch me!"

Michael did, though. Something odd happened when he touched his fingers to Jake's temple. There was a glow—a faint echo of the blue glow she saw in Michael's eyes. And for the briefest second, Jake's dark brown eyes glowed blue.

A keening wail escaped the deputy. He buried his face in his arms. "No—make them stop. Don't...take it away, please, please, please!"

Michael stood, turning his back on Jake without a word.

Daisy continued to stare at Jake with wide eyes, watching as he slowly started to rise, batting at thin air. His eyes were desperately searching the air for something, and he kept shouting out, screaming at something that Daisy couldn't see.

"What did you do?"

Michael's face was weary. "Giving the rest of them peace. They just want to know why." He stopped in his tracks, staring at her.

Daisy shook her head. "But there isn't a why. Men can't

always explain why they kill," she said softly, watching as Jake continued to spin around, staring into the air and swinging his arms as though he was trying to fend something, or someone, off. "Are...are they all trapped?"

"No. Just—at unrest. Most of them have moved on, but they can still see him, feel him. Each time he kills, it leaves a mark on them. When he's gone—"

Daisy shook her head. "Gone? No. No gone. He's going to prison."

Michael looked at her, a sad smile on his face.

"What?" she demanded. "What do you know?"

"They won't let him live that long."

Before she could puzzle that one out, Jake took off running. At some point, he'd dropped his gun and Daisy breathed out a sigh of relief as she went after him. Chasing somebody with a gun was something she'd planned on leaving behind her when she left Louisville Metro.

Jake ran east, heading for the lake. She hit the button on the flashlight and followed after him. Branches slapped at her face, tangled in her hair and she could feel leaves, twigs and mud sliding under her boots as she ran. "Just let me stay on my feet," she prayed silently.

The path curved and she struggled to close the distance between her and Jake before he got around the bend. She lost sight of him, though as the path continued to weave in and out of the trees. Blood pounded in her ears and her heart was racing so fast that she couldn't hear anything else.

"Damn it, where in the hell are you?" she muttered.

"Am I wasting my breath if I tell you that you don't need to chase him?"

Hell. She hadn't even heard Michael leave the cabin. Slowing to a stop, she stared ahead. "Go back and stay with Sandy. And yes, you'd be wasting your breath. Get Sandy to the car—I assume you know how to use a radio. Call for back up."

Michael sighed and she felt his hand brush down her hair. "You'll find him in the lake. I'll wait until I hear from you to call for back up."

Spinning around, she glared at his retreating back. "Damn it, I said..."

Distantly, she heard a splash. Sound carried on the water.

And the lake was close now. A few hundred feet away. That was a big splash too. Turning back to the trail, she started to jog, and then run. The trees broke open around her and she made her way to the dock, shining the flashlight around warily. Jake was nowhere to be seen. "Wait until you hear from me to call for back up," she muttered, shaking her head. Damn his stubborn hide.

An owl hooted and Daisy jumped.

"Oh screw this," she said furiously. She'd go back and call for back up.

But even as she turned, her flashlight flickered off the lake, reflecting light back at her. Michael's words echoed through her mind. *You'll find him in the lake.*

In the lake. Daisy swallowed. Not on the lake. Not by the lake. In the lake. Dragging her tongue over dry lips, she walked over the weathered boards of the dock. The heels of her boots echoed hollowly with every step. A fish jumped somewhere and the splash made her jump yet again. "I swear, I'm sleeping with the lights on every night for a month," she breathed softly as she edged closer, shining the flashlight's beam out over the surface of the water. Jake wouldn't try to swim to the other side at night, would he? Easier to get away just by making his way around the lake's shore. Hell of a lot safer too.

She reached the edge of the dock and scowled. "Damn it." She let the light fall to her side but as it did, it shone on a pale face. Eyes wide. A hideous death mask.

Daisy screamed. Clapping a hand over her mouth, she stared down into the water at Jake's still face. "Oh, dear God," she whispered quietly.

It hadn't even been ten minutes since he had taken off running from the cabin. Maybe four minutes since she had heard the splash.

And now—

They won't let him live that long.

Chapter Seven

It was late the following night when she finished the official report.

Officially, Jake Morris' death was an accident. He'd tried to run when Daisy attempted to arrest him. Why was she out there? A wonderful standby—an anonymous tip. And since Jake wasn't around to lawyer up and have her worry too much about him getting out of prison on technicalities, she felt safe using it.

Officially, the report looked very cut and dry. Probably one of the neatest little wrap up jobs on a major case in history. No question of his guilt, not with everything they'd found in the cabin and no need to worry about him getting off on some technicality at the trial. All nice and tidy with no loose ends.

Unofficially—it was the most bizarre night of her life. The most terrifying. One that was going to be the source of nightmares for some time, she had no doubt. It was definitely one that she hoped never to repeat again.

Yet as she finished printing the report out, she couldn't help feel a little bitter.

Michael was going to leave.

He had stayed here only because there was a ghost who couldn't move on. And now that Tanya had moved on, he would too.

A few days. A handful of days, she'd known that man. She didn't know much of anything about him, other than the fact that he had the saddest blue eyes, a smile that melted her knees—and he was too damn spooky to describe. But she desperately wanted him to stay. There were men in this town she'd known off and on all her life and she wouldn't miss any of them if she up and decided to move back to Louisville. Not that it would happen, but Michael, she was going to miss him. She already did.

How had he come to mean so much in such a short amount of time?

Sighing, she propped her elbows on the desk, rubbing at her eyes with her fingers. Chances are, he was already gone. They'd spoken briefly at the hospital. Michael had told her that Sandy wouldn't remember a lot of what had happened. Vague memories of Jake grabbing her, and nothing else.

She was rather curious about that, but he'd just given her that small, mysterious smile of his. And that was all the answer she would get. Daisy could fill in the blanks though. If he could make Sandy sleep, do something to keep her from going into shock—wiping a few memories away was probably just another talent.

A part of her cringed at the thought. Memories were personal—should Sandy's have been touched? But every time Daisy closed her eyes, she remembered what happened at the cabin. Sandy would have enough bad memories just from Jake grabbing her, just thinking about what *might* have happened. She didn't need memories of ghosts on top of it.

"You should be at home. You're exhausted."

Daisy jumped. Looking up at Michael, she slammed her hand down on the table and snapped, "Don't do that!"

His eyes softened. "I'm sorry." He closed the door behind him and leaned back against it, studying her. "Were you able to sleep any today?"

Daisy shook her head. "No. I'll sleep tonight. Maybe. Then again, it may be a few days before I can sleep." She paused, looking down at the report in front of her. It was done. All she had to do was sign it. "Almost done here." A knot formed in her throat as she saw the bag over his shoulder. "You're leaving."

The thick fringe of his lashes drooped, shielding his eyes. "My job here is done," he said quietly, lifting his shoulder restlessly.

He looked back at her, his gaze resting on her mouth for a brief second. Then he met her gaze and forced a smile. "So it's time to go."

It wasn't the first time Daisy had thought about it, but now, she looked at him and wondered, really wondered, just how deep the loneliness inside him ran. "You ever get tired of just the job, Michael?" she asked softly.

"It's all there is for me."

Slowly, Daisy rose from her desk, moving around it. She held his gaze as she drew nearer and hoped the knot in her throat wasn't going to choke her before she could finish saying goodbye. "Is it that way because you want it to be? Or because you don't think you can have anything else?"

He had no answer. Daisy forced a smile. "Maybe you don't know. Think about it." Rising on her toes, she pressed her lips to his mouth gently. "When you know—I'd be interested in hearing the answer. Because if you think it's the second one, I'd like the chance to prove you wrong."

She started to pull away and his hands came up, cupping the back of her neck and pulling her closer. His tongue traced the outline of her lips and then pushed inside. Desperate goodbye sex was so...desperate, but Daisy couldn't pull away.

She slid her hands under his shirt, feeling the smooth play of hard muscle under his skin. He felt so warm, strong—so alive. It was weird. Daisy hadn't realized it until just that moment, but she hadn't felt this alive for a long, long time. When he left, it was going to leave a hole inside her and that life would drain away, leaving her empty.

But she wasn't going to ask him to stay. If that was what he wanted, he'd do it. If he was going to leave, Daisy wanted one more memory with him. She rose up against him and he wrapped his arms around her, lifting her off the floor. "You taste so good," he muttered.

"Mmmm. So do you." She could feel tears burning her eyes but she wasn't going to cry.

She left then, walking away from him before he could see the tears gleaming in her eyes.

CRΣΘ

"Don't do this, Mike."

The long endless stretch of highway unfurled beneath him as Michael headed out of Mitchell.

And riding shotgun with him was his brother. Sighing, he glanced at Lucas. "Don't do what?"

"Don't just walk away from her."

His gut knotted even thinking about it. He didn't want to walk away. He wanted to turn the car around and go back to her, wrap his arms around her and hold her until she got some rest. Then he wanted to kiss her awake and make love to her, long and slow.

But it wasn't going to happen. Right now, he was functioning on sheer instinct. Case solved, job done, drive away, find some quiet place, and rest. That was what he needed— what he tried to do any time he did a job.

"This wasn't a damned job! You aren't on the payroll for this."

Michael snorted. "The agency doesn't just pick and choose where I'm going to go, Lucas. I go, and just end up in places like this. That's how my life works." Bitterly, he muttered, "This is all there is."

"Just because it always has, does that mean it has to stay that way? You have a choice—a chance at a real life. Reach for it." Lucas shook his head. *"Don't do this, Mikey. She's your chance."*

"I can't."

"Why?" Lucas demanded. Anger surged through him and his form went from damn near invisible to almost solid as he glared at Michael. *"After all this time, don't you deserve it?"*

That, Michael didn't know. "I don't know." Then he shook his head. Yeah, he did. He knew all right. He *didn't* deserve any kind of normal life. Even if he did, he couldn't have it. "I don't have a normal life—I wouldn't know what it was like if it bit me on the ass. But I don't deserve it, Lucas."

"Why not? Over me? Let it go, Mikey. You were twelve years old, damn it. You can't keep punishing yourself for not protecting me. I was the big brother—it was my job to protect you, not the other way around." Lucas shook his head and said, *"Let it go, Michael. Give up your ghosts."*

Now Michael laughed. "That's impossible. The door's been opened—I can't close it."

Lucas smiled sadly. *"You don't have to. Just...stop hunting for us. If somebody needs you, they'll find you. Tanya did. You may never have a completely normal life. I get that. But you can have a happy one. If you'll reach for it."*

Daisy's image bloomed in his mind's eye. Groaning, he slowed down and edged his car to the side of the road.

A happy life—not something he'd ever really thought much about. He didn't know if he was in love with her. Michael wasn't certain he really even understood love. But she was the first woman he'd ever met that made him wonder about it. Sex was easy. Love, though—he wasn't so certain about that. Yeah, she made him wonder, made him yearn and wish. Made him want.

I'd like the chance to prove you wrong...

A smile appeared on his face. She could do it. If anybody could, it was her. There had been a few brief moments with her when he hadn't thought about the ghosts, when he hadn't thought about Lucas, when he hadn't thought about anything but her. "I barely know her," Michael said softly.

"Then get to know her. Isn't that what dating is for?"

Leaning his head back, Michael chuckled. "Dating." He spent his life talking to ghosts and hunting down their killers. Dating seemed just a little too—tame.

"It's called real life, Mike. Reach for it."

CRSO

The lady was so damned tired, not even Sarah's warning bark woke her up. She hadn't even fed Sarah when she came home. She'd stripped off her clothes as she walked to the bed and fell face down. It had been daylight then and now it was black and still the lady slept.

The retriever watched the door with wide, liquid eyes as the doorknob jiggled. Tumblers rolled. It unlocked and moments later, the deadbolt followed suit. It swung open to reveal a man. He paused by the dog, tucking something inside his jacket, before crouching down in front of her.

Sarah could smell her lady on him.

"I'm no threat," he murmured.

Deep voice...nice voice...Sarah leaned into his hand as he scratched behind her ears. Ooooohhhh...nice hands.

He chuckled. "I think you know that."

When he headed down the hallway, Sarah followed behind curiously. She'd hoped maybe he would get her some food, but he couldn't look away from the lady. He stood in the doorway for a minute, just staring at her. Sarah finally went and curled up below the window.

People never made any sense to her. She could tell what he wanted just by the way he smelled. And all he did was stand there.

She was sound asleep. Michael hadn't sensed anybody awake inside the house as he climbed from his truck. Well, other than the dog. He'd have to talk with Daisy about that dog too. He knew he had a way with animals, but that dog was entirely too friendly, too trusting.

Leaning his shoulder against the doorjamb, he just stared at her. Moonlight shone in through the window, painting her skin with a soft, silvery glow, turning her hair to a pale blonde. In sleep, she looked so soft and delicate. She was an Amazon, though. She had the heart of a warrior. What had happened at the cabin would have had most people running for the hills, but instead of running, instead of breaking down and crying, she had stood up and faced down a poltergeist. Tanya's rage had been increasing with every breath. Mike's blood had long since gone cold with fear.

But Daisy had stood up and faced Tanya. Brought her back from the very brink.

He didn't think he'd ever met anyone with that kind of strength.

He wanted to climb in bed and cuddle up behind her, just wrap his arms around her while she slept. For a few minutes, he stood there, waiting to see if she'd wake up. Michael almost left. Almost... He slowly slid out of his jacket, draping it over the foot of the bed. Then his boots. He left the rest of his clothes on. She wasn't wearing much of anything, he could tell. If he climbed in bed with her naked—well, he was already going to have some explaining to do.

Stretching out on top of the cover, he pressed up against her back, sliding his arm around her waist. Daisy sighed, snuggling back against him. Michael smothered a groan as the soft curves of her ass pressed against his hips. The blood in his veins re-routed and all headed south, leaving him questioning his sanity.

His cock ached. Unable to help himself, he arched his hips and pressed just a little tighter against her.

Daisy sighed in her sleep. "Michael..." Then she shifted a little, wrapping her arm so that she could lay her hand atop his.

A satisfied little hum escaped her and then she was still.

Behind her, Michael lay staring into the darkness. The sound of his name on her lips as she slept was a memory he was going to carry with him for a very long time. It was hours before he slept. But he didn't give a damn. Even though he ached with weariness, he was content to just lie there, holding her.

CR&O

Heat.

Daisy groaned, trying to struggle out from under the covers. Although why in the hell...

Her hand pressed against warm male flesh. Covered with soft cotton, but still, warm male flesh. A familiar scent flooded her head. A hungry wet heat began to pulse in her womb even before she opened her eyes. *Michael*—

He lay on his side, facing her. Early morning sunlight streamed in through the windows, falling across his face. He had little golden flecks in his blue eyes, Daisy mused. She hadn't noticed that before. His lashes were ridiculously long, especially for a man. He was probably one of the most beautiful men she'd ever seen.

And he was lying in her bed. Daisy swallowed, confused, the cobwebs in her brain keeping her from talking for a minute. Lust and exhaustion did not make it easy to form coherent thoughts. She'd be damned if she'd just babble. Finally, she licked her lips. "I thought you'd left."

"I did." He reached up with his hand, tracing his fingers over her cheek, along her nose and her lips. She shivered under that light touch, but never stopped looking into his eyes.

Damn, he had such beautiful eyes. That dark blue, so warm. Just one look from him was enough to make her get weak in the knees.

He was so big, so full of brutal strength, yet so amazingly gentle. He had cradled Sandy like she was made of glass as he carried her to the car. Sandy had curled up against him, like she knew he would keep her safe. She had good instincts.

"If you left—why are you in my bed?"

A faint smile curled his lips. "Decided to take you up on

that offer," he murmured. He moved then, rolling so that she was under him. He settled himself in the cradle of her thighs and she whimpered as hot little jolts of pleasure rocketed through her system.

Daisy would have been really pleased with their positions, except he was still fully clothed. Licking her lips, she focused on his words and not on how amazing he felt pressed against her. "Offer..."

"Hmmm," he murmured, his voice a low, rough purr as he bent low and pressed his lips against her neck. "The changing my mind thing. You said you wouldn't mind trying to change my mind. I'm here to let you do that. That is, if you can."

For one second, her mind went blank. And then Daisy started to laugh. Wrapping her arms around his neck, she smiled at him, "Oh, yeah. I think I can manage that." Lowering her lashes, she murmured, "And the first order of business is getting you out of those clothes—you have this bad habit of being overdressed..."

He grinned back at her and then all thought fled as he covered her mouth with his.

Vicious Vixen

Chapter One

If there was a better way to wake up, Graeme wasn't so sure he wanted to know. Her mouth was already cruising down over his chest as he pushed through the foggy place between slumber and waking. When he opened his eyes, she already had her hand wrapped around his cock, holding him steady as she took him in her mouth.

It was slow and sleepy, sweet and easy. One of the miracles of this woman he loved. Sometimes it was like this, like some sweet dream that couldn't possibly be real. Then other times it was heat and fire and raw power, something that had to be real, because the intensity of it could never exist within dreams.

Sweat bloomed on their bodies as she moved up and straddled his hips, taking him deep inside. She was hot, hot as fire, wet and silky soft around him, her pussy wrapping around his aching flesh in a slick, snug grasp. Her pale hair fell around her shoulders, down her back. Graeme reached up and fisted his hands in the long strands, pulling her down and covering her smiling mouth with his.

"I love you," he muttered. But he ached inside. She'd never say it back. She never did.

But she sighed against his mouth and whispered, "I love you..."

Love.

What a joke.

Had he been dreaming? He didn't really know if he slept in this place, but whatever that was, it had been a dream. So he had to have been asleep. At least he assumed he was sleeping. Nothing really made sense here.

A dead man dreaming made about as much sense as Vixen admitting she loved him.

Graeme's bitter laugh echoed in his head but it made no sound. In this weird place between life and death, all too often there were no sounds. When he could hear much of anything, it was muffled. It was kind of like that twilight sleep, all fogged and hazy, but instead of everything taking on that surreal quality, sound and scent were more defined. Everything—sight, sound, memory, thought—was more pronounced, yet in an odd sort of fashion—hazed.

Only his thoughts and memories seemed real.

Well, usually.

There was something of a pattern to life here. Periods of activity that mostly mimicked day, when light was pronounced and all the travelers in the way station left their "homes" and milled around with each other. There were no jobs here, no place to go, nothing to do. There really wasn't much interaction between the travelers, beyond seeing each other. Graeme hadn't thought death could be this boring. When he left his home—if it could be called such—all he did was wander around and think about things he'd rather not remember. Like Vixen…

It was frustrating as hell, but he couldn't *not* do it. Any kind of interaction happened outside his place. Within it, he hardly seemed to exist. Within his home, it was too hard to think, too hard to focus and thankfully, too hard to remember.

Yet another reason why that dream was so out of place.

He had thought of her. Too often, in fact, and sometimes he would retreat to his home because there, he lost enough of himself that he didn't have to think of her. Considering that being in his home was a respite from memories of her, Graeme couldn't figure out why in the hell he went out there with the others so often.

Unless he was just into self-torture.

Or maybe it's because you miss her…

Missed her. Why in the hell would he miss her?

If it wasn't for Vixen, he wouldn't be here.

Hell, everybody had been right about her. Graeme was the one who'd been wrong. When the time came, she'd stuck a knife inside him like he was just another street thug she was getting off the street.

He hadn't even mattered.

Quit thinking about her.

But it was too late. The tidal wave of memories had started and Graeme was just going to have to ride it out.

They called her vicious.

They called her vindictive.

They called her violent, volatile...

But Graeme Lawson, arrogant bastard he was, he had simply called her his.

She was a mercenary little bitch, and she had been the entire time he'd known her. Going on eight years now...or at least it had been just before he died. How much time had passed since then, he didn't know. He didn't know if she missed him, if she thought of him, if she ever regretted what she'd done.

Unlikely.

Graeme hadn't ever known Vixen to regret anything, ever feel guilt, ever look back and think about the *what-ifs* in life. It wasn't that she was cruel or evil—she was a woman borne of pain, a woman who hadn't ever known anything remotely easy in life. She was, simply put, a survivor and she did whatever in the hell she had to do to survive.

Her childhood had been one long, endless struggle, as had much of her teenaged years. That was when he'd entered her life, tried to make things a bit easier on her, but even then, she hadn't wanted help.

She'd been a wild, sly little thief. Seventeen and out to pick as many pockets as she could before moving on, finding a new hunting ground. When she'd slipped her nimble fingers into his pocket, he'd grabbed that skinny wrist, prepared to find one of the loud-mouthed hoods who had been eying him ever since he'd come to Blanton.

The mid-sized town was just south of Chicago and Graeme hadn't been overly happy about the assignment that had brought him there. But his boss wanted a meeting with a low-level thug living in Blanton.

Normally, guys who made their money selling stolen property weren't the sort of thing Graeme's boss would worry about. The problem was this particular thug was selling his goods in a section of town that really didn't need the attention of the police.

Graeme had been sent down with a warning and a

115

message. The message hadn't been acknowledged. The warning had been brushed off. When Graeme went to lean a little harder, guns had been drawn. Graeme had spent the rest of the afternoon making sure nothing could be tracked back to him or his boss.

He'd been on his way back to his car when he crossed paths with a thief.

A quick thief, but not quick enough. He grabbed a thin, almost bony wrist, squeezed and moved. He moved them out of the street, ducking into a shallow alcove. A mostly unnecessary precaution because in this part of Blanton, few people paid any attention to anything unless they absolutely had to.

He'd expected to find a hood and he'd been prepared to pound him into the pavement. Nobody stole from him. Ever.

What he'd found was a skinny girl. A girl with eyes too big for her narrow face. When he slammed her into the wall, the cap on her head fell off and long, silvery-blonde hair went tumbling to her shoulders.

One look...and he'd fallen in love.

She'd driven a knee in his balls. He was a wanted man and had killed more men than he could remember. Hell, he had just walked out of a building where five different men had guns aimed at him and now all of them were dead. But a skinny girl with big, dark eyes managed to send him to his knees, holding his aching balls while she disappeared like a ghost.

Their first meeting hadn't exactly left an impact on her. When she made her way to Chicago two years later, she hadn't known who he was, but he'd known her. She had been nineteen, but already her eyes showed a wisdom and weariness beyond her years. Graeme was twenty-five at the time. If any other nineteen-year-old female placed before him, he knew he wouldn't have looked twice. They were either still too innocent or too convinced they were completely grown up and neither appealed to him.

He saw none of that in Vixen.

Again, he'd been out on assignment. Graeme wasn't under any delusion about his importance to his boss. He was an effective tool, he obeyed orders and he didn't ask questions.

At least not until he broke into the small apartment of a thief that had pissed off the boss. This time, it wasn't a low-level thug drawing too much police attention—that would have been too easy, too simple.

No, this time the thief had actually been stealing the product.

Graeme knew his job. He'd give a message. Give a warning—*and* get the goods back that the thief had stolen from the boss. If the goods were gone, then he'd take the money instead.

Most people had enough sense to fear Graeme, and if they weren't afraid of Graeme, they were definitely afraid of the boss. Usually only took one request and he had money in his hand.

Along with that message, he'd give a warning. But this time, he never delivered the first message.

It had been her.

He'd been waiting inside her apartment and when she'd come through the door, his heart had stopped.

She wasn't who he had expected to see walk through that door and as he stared at her, an icy-cold rage unlike anything he'd ever known had encompassed him.

One of the boss's men, a rather unpleasant bastard by the name of Carlos, had been the one to track down this address. He'd beaten it out of a vagrant who hadn't been wise enough to move out of the area after seeing a deal go straight to hell a few days earlier.

Nothing had been said about the thief being a woman.

Which meant Carlos hadn't known. The vagrant must not have shared that bit of information.

Graeme had recognized her easily, watching from the shadows as she came through the door, pulling a cap off her hair and sighing as she ran her fingers through the tangled mess. Slender fingers had undone the buttons marching down the front of her plain peacoat and she'd shrugged out of it to reveal a slender, rather waifish figure.

She'd been halfway across the floor when she noticed him, but she hadn't screamed. Hadn't tried to run. He saw in the lines of her body that she was prepared to fight, saw the resignation in her eyes and he knew she had done this before, squared off with a man, forced to protect herself.

He'd fallen just a little more in love as he faced her and she'd yet to say even two words to him.

Vixen didn't know it, but before he had so much as kissed

her, he'd changed everything he was, placed his neck on the line—risked everything for her. He'd made himself change who he was—over her. Not because he had ever really cared that he was walking a wide road that led straight to hell, but because the road he took was a dangerous one and he didn't want that danger spilling onto her.

Because she'd be with him.

Or so he had always thought.

CRED

The walk down memory lane was just the beginning.

A shadowy figure, hooded, covered from head to toe in a concealing robe, appeared before Graeme. The being's presence suddenly made everything more substantial. Graeme could hear again, feel again, speak. When he shoved a hand through his hair, he felt the wiry curls cropped close to his scalp. Automatically, he touched his face, ran a hand across his chest, cracked his knuckles.

Just *feeling* something again was beyond description. Too bad he didn't realize there would be a cost.

"It is time."

"Time for what?" Graeme asked, wary. But somewhere inside, he already knew.

Judgment. What else? Why else would he be here?

"No. The time for judgment is not yet upon you. I speak of something else—but it will affect your day of judgment, Graeme."

"What are you talking about?" Graeme couldn't see his—her—its—face and he hated that. He wanted to see the eyes. A ghost from the past whispered in his ear, *"The eyes are the gateway to the soul."*

"It's time to make amends. To save one such as you. To redeem yourself."

Although Graeme didn't remember leaving his home, he was no longer within that obscure cocoon. He was in what appeared to be the afterlife's version of a movie theater.

The star of the show was Vixen herself.

He couldn't exactly see any kind of screen, any kind of projector, but he could see her, life-size, lovely and sleek, walking by. The image of her was so real, at first he tried to reach out and touch her. That was when he realized it was some sort of illusion, maybe a hologram. Something.

Except he could smell her. Almost even feel the silken glide of her hair as it blew across his face.

"What is this?"

"Salvation. Redemption."

This afterlife business was a pathetic joke and this had better be another humorless little torture, a way for the beings around him to amuse themselves. Time had no meaning in this place, and for all he knew he could have been there for centuries. He was guessing a couple of years, though, going by how Vixen looked. Her hair had grown out—the last time he'd seen her, right before she stabbed a knife into his heart, her pale, silvery blonde hair had been cropped to chin length and now it was well past her shoulders. It had always grown fast, but not that fast, so he figured it had to have been at least a few years.

He looked away from her and faced the being that had brought him to this place. Being—because there was something completely androgynous about the cloaked and shadowed figure. A sexless voice, a sexless affect. A seriously annoying manner of refusing to answer anything Graeme asked—but that didn't keep him from asking another question.

"You have got to be kidding me."

Under the cloak, its shoulders rose, fell. From under the hood, its voice rang out, clear, pure and bell-like. Gentle, but firm. "We do not kid in matters of salvation and redemption, Graeme."

Graeme snorted.

The being, as though puzzled by Graeme's derision, cocked its head. Graeme didn't need to see the being's face to know he was being scrutinized. Shit, he could *feel* the weight of that stare. Feeling somebody's stare was the closest he'd come to physical sensation in far too long. "So which is this? Redemption? Salvation? Or just plain torture?"

The cowled head swung back and forth. "We do not torture. Your own guilt is torture enough, is it not?"

"Guilt?" he asked. "Guilt isn't something I waste time on."

"No? I feel a great deal of guilt coming from within you."

Simple statement.

119

True enough.

But it infuriated him.

The ability to physically feel again wasn't a blessing just then. He was too damned pissed off and it would have been easier if the fury had that softening haze to it. Hands closed into fists, he glared at the cloaked being in front of him and demanded, "What did I ever do to Vixen to feel guilty about? I loved her."

"Oh, Vixen isn't the one you feel guilt over. Indeed, if you hadn't met her, you wouldn't be here."

Graeme grunted and glanced back over his shoulder at Vixen's image. It was like whatever had captured her image had changed, moving in for a close-up as she walked down a street. All he could see was her face, her eyes, so dark in her pale face. "You got that right. If I hadn't ever met her, she couldn't have stuck a knife in me and I'd still be alive."

It laughed. There was nothing mocking in the sound, though. It was more sad than anything. "No, Graeme. You would have died long before now...but nothing you had done in your life before meeting Vixen would have awarded you one last chance. She changed you. She made you better. Make no mistake, Graeme, her presence in your life and the changes you made for her are why you are here. Instead of..."

These beings didn't spend a lot of time on special effects or anything, which made it all that more effective when something freaky did happen. As the silvery white light surrounded Graeme went orange-red, the air blistered fire-hot. The heat threatened to melt the skin from his bones. It seared his lungs and stole his voice.

Then it was gone.

"You really don't want to live eternity like that, do you?"

Instinctively, he reached up and rubbed his burning eyes. That was when he noticed his hands. That was when he *saw* his hands. They were red from the heat, blistering, but already the blisters were fading away into nothingness. "And some wonder why in the hell a lot of people don't choose to believe in God, in heaven or in hell. If *He* is such a decent, loving-type God, He wouldn't threaten to send people *there*."

The air in the room grew weighted, heavy with sadness and the being sighed. There was censure in that unseen gaze, Graeme could feel it. "Graeme, He sends nobody anywhere. He gives them the choice. Gives all of us the choice." A long, slender arm lifted, the belled sleeves obscuring everything but the fingertips from view as it passed over Graeme's hands.

Even the faint, lingering itch of heat faded. Just like that. "She changed you, Graeme. Meeting her unlocked a door inside of you that nothing else could do—but even with that door opened, it couldn't erase the darkness within you."

He hissed in surprise when the being touched him—and he actually felt it. He was still reeling over being able to feel, but being touched—it was almost painful. The being touched him on the back, in the exact spot where Vixen had plunged a six-inch stiletto—one that Graeme had given her. In response to the being's touch, Graeme felt an icy-cold pain tear through him, brutal in its intensity—hell. It hadn't hurt that much when Vixen had killed him.

"This is salvation. This is redemption."

The voice was changing, deepening. A hand came up, closed over Graeme's shoulder and squeezed—and Graeme felt it. Its hand was warm, too warm, painful in contrast to the ice rushing through his system. "I'm a little past salvation," Graeme said, trying to pull away.

But he couldn't move.

"It isn't your salvation, Graeme. It's hers."

Then the being let go and glided away. The shadowed face glanced in Graeme's direction and then away, nodding to the panoramic view of Vixen on the hunt. "Her salvation." Then its gaze cut to Graeme and it added, "Your redemption."

"What in the hell are you talking about?"

Chapter Two

What an absolute bitch-slap from fate.

From heaven. Or God. Or whatever divine mess had landed him here.

Here. Back on earth, alive and trapped inside a body that felt nothing like his own.

Three days had passed since he'd been dropped back onto Earth from wherever in hell—or heaven—he'd been. Three days—now that was really weird, being aware of the passage of time, seeing the sunlight shining down on the concrete canyons of Chicago, watching as the sun sank behind the horizon and trying to see the stars past all the city lights.

He could see again, could hear, could feel.

Graeme felt real again. Felt alive.

But he wasn't so sure he liked it. Actually, the more he thought about it, the *less* he liked it. He was cold. Bitterly cold, but it had nothing to do with the cold air of an early spring day in Chicago.

Her salvation. And your redemption.

Graeme wasn't the kind of guy that put much thought into what existed beyond death. He'd always figured he'd get there sooner rather than later, but until it happened, he didn't want to deal with it. If pressed, he would have admitted his doubts about the existence in some divine power. Doubts—shit, they hadn't been doubts.

He hadn't believed *at all.*

If such things as God, heaven, hell, angels and the devil actually existed, then Graeme was heading straight to hell. But he hadn't ever worried about it, because he had never been given any reason to believe in a "higher power". No miracles for him. The closest he'd ever come to a miracle was Vixen and look where that had landed him.

The being hadn't come out right and said it, but Graeme got the impression if he succeeded on this whacked-out Biblical version of *Mission Impossible*, then he'd get that pass through the pearly gates. If he failed, he might as well resign himself to an eternity of fiery torment. Not what he wanted, but he was already preparing himself for that eventuality.

He couldn't save Vixen. Even if he thought he might have a chance, she wouldn't let him.

She had made her choices.

Just as he had.

Just as everybody he'd seen while he was lost in the void. The void where he had existed since his death was sort of a waiting room to wherever the deceased's true destination lay. Most only stayed for a little while and Graeme had lost track of how many he'd watched fade away before his eyes—sometimes with a serene, peaceful smile, eyes warm with acceptance and joy.

Others had gone screaming and struggling and pleading. When the being had come for Graeme, he'd figured whatever furlough he had in the way station was over and he was going to burn.

It was what he'd been expecting ever since his body started to die around him and he realized that he'd been wrong.

There was something after death.

It was funny, as he lay dying, he'd realized just how wrong he'd been. Some innate knowledge had filled him and he'd known death wasn't the end, just as he'd known it was too late for him—too late for her, too, because he couldn't hold onto his fading life long enough to tell Vixen what he knew.

Sometimes the beings appeared as the damned were taken away, almost some kind of support group as the deceased fought to remain—they never came for the believers, Graeme had discovered. Those who smiled that peaceful smile and often gazed around with pity before fading away to heaven.

For the anxious, sometimes the beings came, although it didn't make much sense to Graeme. That kind, considerate pity was worthless if an eternity of torment awaited.

The beings very often came for the arrogant and the terrified. They fought the hardest and that fighting disrupted the peaceful non-existence in the way station. Apparently, the beings didn't like having the peace disturbed.

So when this lone being had appeared before Graeme, he'd told himself he wasn't going to fight. Wasn't going to struggle. He'd accept what lay before him just like he'd accepted the rather crappy hand he'd been dealt in life.

Even if terror wrapped around him like it did for so many others before him, he was determined to go to whatever hell awaited with some measure of dignity. But no terror came.

He didn't get a one-way ticket to hell, either. Or at least he hadn't received it yet.

No, what he'd been given, as far as he could tell, was one last chance.

To save her, and somehow himself.

He had a choice—save Vixen from the road she was walking, and get that chance to go someplace other than an endless pit of fire. Or he could just choose the endless pit of fire.

It wasn't a choice he understood, but they hadn't been too inclined to enlighten him when he'd tried asking.

Why? Why me? Why am I getting a second chance and why should I try to save the woman who killed me?

You love her, do you not? The being hadn't needed an answer.

Yes. Graeme still loved her. Even though she'd betrayed him. Even though she'd lied to him. Even though she'd killed him. He still loved her.

She hadn't loved him in return but he did know she'd cared about him. Vixen didn't care for many people, and Graeme was too honest to delude himself into believing she'd cared for him just for the sake of his own pride or a need for her. She'd cared. In life, he'd let that be enough.

Now he had to hope it would be. Even though he doubted he had any chance at all of saving her, he had to hope he was wrong. That there was a chance.

Otherwise his love hadn't done her a damn bit of good.

"Stop stalling already," he muttered.

Stalling. That was exactly what he'd been doing for the past thirty minutes—stalling. He needed to just get over it, because he really didn't know how much time he had. He squinted as he stepped outside, automatically lowering a pair of mirrored sunglasses to shield eyes that had become sensitive to the sun.

It had been three years since he'd seen sunlight. Three years since he'd breathed oxygen, needed food, rest or even something as mundane as taking a leak.

He didn't know exactly how he knew this—he'd been unaware of the passage of time since he'd opened his eyes and found himself in the way station between heaven and hell. But he now knew exactly how much time had passed since Vixen had effectively, and fairly painlessly, ended his life.

Just as he knew he was no longer in his body.

Even before he'd moved around and realized everything felt off, he knew he was physically different. He knew that his close-cropped black hair was now shoulder-length, shaggy and gold-streaked, like he'd spent the past three years in the sun, instead of dead. His voice was rougher, gruffer and raspy, almost like a smoker's voice, although Graeme hadn't once smoked a day in his life. Well, not in his previous life and he really had no intention of smoking in this life, no matter how short it might be.

He knew that his body had changed as well—he'd been built like a defensive linebacker, standing six foot four, weighing close to 250, with big hands and big feet. Vixen had always felt so delicate in his arms, under him or straddling his hips and moving in that slow, teasing way of hers as she took him closer to heaven than he ever expected he'd go.

Now, his body felt—strange. He pegged himself a good six inches shorter, a good seventy pounds lighter. Shorter, with a much leaner build, he felt almost weightless as he took a few slow steps. A car horn sounded off in the street and it rang in his ears like somebody had just blared a siren right next to him. Somebody crashed into him and an innate sense of irritation rose, only to fade away as he turned his head and saw a heavily pregnant woman struggling to juggle a box filled to overflowing. She listed to the side, the box overbalancing her.

Without thinking twice, he reached out, steadied her and as she gave him a grateful smile, he took the box from her. The smile on his face shouldn't have come as easily as it did. Graeme wasn't a smiling sort by nature.

Nor was he the helpful sort. Even though he'd spent the five years since meeting Vixen trying to move away from his hard, ugly life, kindness wasn't one of his better virtues.

Neither was friendly, easy chatter—but that didn't keep him from asking the woman if he could help her with the box. Some deep, hidden voice advised him, *Women don't trust my kind to help with anything. No smart woman is going to trust a strange guy anyway.*

Judging by the look on her face, that was exactly her mindset. However, before Graeme could decide what to do, the suspicion in her eyes faded and her smile warmed. "I just need to get it into my car, if you don't mind," she said, gesturing to the pay-per-hour parking lot a half-block down the road.

Ten minutes later, he was once more out on the sidewalk, walking down Lake Shore Drive. His mind was a jumble of questions and curiosity—what was he doing here? Where did he start? *How* did he start?

But then his skin went hot and tight. A shiver raced down his spine. Blood drained south and for the first time in three years, he wasn't just missing the idea of sex—he was so damned turned on he could hardly breathe for it.

Vixen...

And he hadn't even seen her yet.

But she was here.

Vixen was here.

Chapter Three

Nobody would be able to tell by looking at her, that Vixen Markham was so damned pissed off she could barely see straight.

Nobody knew her well enough to realize the blank, empty mask she wore had been designed to keep people out, to keep them from guessing her thoughts, to keep them from trying to reach out and connect—designed just to keep them *away*.

It worked.

Not even Hawthorne, the sick bastard, realized just how much she hid inside. So much for his belief that the eyes revealed all. It was something he liked to say often—*the eyes are the gateway to the soul.*

But if that were true, he'd have her dead before she even had time to blink. One glimpse inside her head where she made no attempts to hide her hatred of him from herself. If he looked in her eyes and saw her soul, he'd see her disgust of him. Then he'd see her dead.

But Vixen was skilled at keeping people at a distance. It was one of her talents.

Not always, a silken voice whispered in her head.

There had been one man she hadn't been able to keep away from. One man who had seen beyond the mask to the woman underneath. One man who had connected with her—in every sense of the word.

A man who'd lied to her. Betrayed her. Made a fool of her. Used her.

After three years, it seemed she should have been able to *not* think about Graeme Mackenzie Lawson. Been able to remember that night without cringing, without wanting to cry or scream. She'd done the right thing. She'd done what she'd always done—she'd taken care of herself.

This was the first time that she had ever felt guilt over doing what was necessary.

So Graeme was responsible for introducing her to yet another wonderful thing.

Self-doubt. Worse—*guilt.*

Neither were emotions she had time for. Patience for. Tolerance for. She didn't want or need them. However, she couldn't move past them. Fortunately, thinking about Graeme right now wasn't capable of laying her low. She was too damned mad.

Vixen would take anger over guilt any day. Anger was so much better and right now, she was so damned angry she could barely think.

Angry—and a little scared.

Carlos had stood by the boss's side, watching her with a smirk on his ugly, scarred mouth, as though he knew how she'd react to the recent assignment. As though he wanted one specific reaction out of her—refusal.

Nobody refused Gerard Hawthorne. It simply wasn't done.

But he'd never requested anything like this from her before.

Should have seen it coming, she thought bitterly. Over the past three years, he'd been nudging her closer and closer to the lines she had drawn for herself, lines she'd vowed she'd never cross.

Vixen had no problem getting her hands dirty.

She had no problem killing if it was necessary, if the mark was somebody who needed killing. Or rather, if the mark fit *her* idea of somebody who needed killing. Death didn't bother her.

Innocent death did bother her, though. That was her line. It was one she fought long and hard not to cross. It was her line— as long as she didn't cross it, then she could face herself in the mirror and know she was seeing a person, not just a monster.

Hawthorne wouldn't give a damn about Vixen's personal lines. For all his lip service about how he admired her, respected her, it was just that. Nothing but talk, and empty talk at that. What Hawthorne wanted was to get in her pants. He'd wanted it for years but Hawthorne knew better than to try and force her into it. She'd killed over less. She'd follow his orders when it came to business, and he knew it. Likewise, he also knew that forcing Vixen into his bed wasn't going to work. He either didn't want her enough to try and force it, or he was arrogant enough to want her to happily agree to be his little whore.

So he continued his silver-tongue routine and she continued to ignore him about anything that wasn't related to business. That was the status quo and that was how she liked it.

But if she refused a business order from Hawthorne, Vixen knew how it would end for her. Badly.

The idea of her own death concerned her quite a bit, but she still couldn't wrap her mind around what she was expected to do. And why.

Kill the daughter of the mayor of Chicago.

Vixen knew why. The fucking mayor was in bed with Hawthorne—or at least in Hawthorne's pocket. But the election was coming up and the past few years hadn't been easy on the incumbent. If he didn't at least *look* like he was cracking down, making changes, pushing for lowered taxes and all the tap-dancing that politicians did, he was going to be voted out in the blink of an eye. He had a hard road ahead of him anyway thanks to the screwed-up economy, and it was going to be an uphill fight.

That spelled problems for people like Hawthorne. Hawthorne dealt with problems the same way he dealt with everything. Ruthlessly. Coldly.

Vixen wasn't surprised he'd decided to send a message to the mayor, but she hadn't expected this, and she hadn't expected that he would ask her to do it. The daughter was a twenty-something debutante who looked a lot like the mayor's dead wife. A wife he'd lost to cancer, and from everything Vix could tell, a wife he'd truly loved.

Vixen envied love and at the same time, she hated it. Hated how it made a person weak. Hated how it made a person doubt. Hated how it could make a person lie awake at night, crying, aching.

Until she'd known love, Vixen hadn't cried in longer than she could remember.

Not when she'd been nine and came home to find her always-stoned mother dead from an overdose.

129

Not when she'd ended up sleeping in an alley because there was no way in hell she was going to risk somebody at a shelter calling social services on her.

Not when some lowlife had broken two fingers on her right hand because she had moved in on "his" territory.

And not when she'd had evidence placed in front of her, depicting Graeme's betrayal.

But as she had sat on the floor next to Graeme's lifeless body, stroking his too-short black hair, she'd started to cry. That night, she'd cried for hours. She'd gone to the graveyard and watched as the plain, simple box was lowered into the ground—not a soul had come to tell him good-bye. There had been no flowers, no service. Nothing. As the dirt was shoveled over him, she'd cried.

When she'd returned a few hours later, her arms overflowing with flowers, she'd cried.

And every night for a week after.

Even three years later, she cried.

That was what love did.

It made a person weak.

Killing the mayor's pretty daughter would certainly make the man weak. Certainly make him afraid.

But Vixen couldn't picture herself doing it.

She *wouldn't* do it.

Heaving out a breath, she fought the urge to fidget, shove her hair back from her face, bite her nails, anything to work off some of the nervous, worried tension mounting inside. But such displays were a sign of weakness and she knew she was being watched. Vixen was always being watched, sometimes in subtle ways, sometimes not. Right now, the skin on the back of her neck crawled and she knew that Hawthorne was probably standing at the window of the spacious penthouse, staring down at her with that fucking telescope of his.

The bastard was a voyeur.

A favored way of killing time was for him to point that telescope towards any of the surrounding buildings and see what he could see, particularly any manner of sexual acts.

A few years ago, she hadn't known as much about him as she did now. The past three years had been very eye-opening, and none of what she'd learned was pleasant.

He'd bought the building next to Vixen's apartment shortly after Graeme's funeral. If Graeme hadn't once mentioned Hawthorne's love of peeping, it may not have dawned on her just why he'd bought it.

She'd gotten used to the spying and normally, she couldn't have cared less. He had bugs planted in her place and after the initial jolt of surprise, Vixen had shrugged it off and not once had she confronted him. If the sick fuck wanted to see her tits when she got out of the shower, so what? If he wanted to watch her as she went through her strenuous hour-long workout, big deal.

The one bug he had planted in her bedroom she'd dealt with and as long as she had privacy while she slept, that was all she cared about. Let him watch her sweat or shower or eat— hell, even if he had to watch her pee, she didn't care. It was the closest he would ever get to her and there were even times when she could laugh about it. Privately, of course.

But not today. Today, she didn't want him watching her, didn't want him near her, or even able to see her.

Hawthorne was a man who took what he wanted, but taking Vixen would require force. He was too aware of what she did when men tried to use force on her. He'd seen the results. Maybe that had been enough to make him just a bit squeamish. Or maybe it was a pride thing, because he seemed determined to seduce her, even going so far as to attempt romance.

It was a waste of time.

Vixen wasn't interested in Hawthorne—or any man, really. Nobody but Graeme. Whether that was a curse or a blessing, she didn't know. It was simply the way it was. Even when she lay in bed, burning with need, eaten up with lust, the man she wanted was cold and dead, and he was cold and dead by *her* hand.

Except for Graeme, none of the lives she'd taken over the past five years bothered her. It was cold, callous—and Vixen didn't give a damn. The men and women she'd killed were cohorts, competitors or other people who had crossed paths with Hawthorne and Hawthorne wasn't the kind of man to cross paths with the innocent type.

He was a reclusive bastard and only allowed certain people near him, cutting down on the possibility of innocent bystanders.

It was cold out, the air heavy with the promise of rain as she came to a halt at the intersection of Adam and Franklin. The Sears Tower jutted up in the sky, blocking out the sun. The wind started to kick up. It blew her hair into her face and she shoved it back.

Somebody bumped into her, blocked her path. She moved to go around without even looking at the man, but then a hand came up, closed over her elbow.

"Excuse me, ma'am."

It wasn't a familiar voice. Vixen was the type who never forgot a face, a voice, a name. The man standing before her was a man she'd never met before.

So the eerie sense of *déjà vu* washing over her was strange. But even stranger than that was the sudden impulse to take a step closer, although even half a step would put her far too close to him. Close enough to touch. Close enough to kiss.

Stranger still was the sudden urge to cry and laugh at the same time.

She followed none of the urges, just looked at him, his eyes hidden by a pair of sunglasses, with a long-practiced icy stare. Then she lowered her gaze to the hand grasping her arm, lingering for just a moment, before she looked back at him. The hint was far from subtle, yet he didn't let go.

"Excuse me."

Vixen lifted a brow and said, "You already said that. You're excused. Now, if you don't mind...?" She tugged against his hold.

A slow smile curled his lips. For some reason, the sight of it warmed something inside her. A place that had been far too cold, for far too long. It made her heart skip a beat and then start banging against her ribs hard and fast. Unbidden, she felt herself softening, her body trying to betray her.

Vixen steeled herself against it, just as she steeled herself as his fingers passed down her arm in a slow, lingering caress before he let go and stepped back.

Not very far.

He was still close enough that she could feel the heat of his body, and smell him. Vixen hadn't ever been too conscious of a man's scent, with the exception of Graeme. Graeme had been the exception to everything, a unique, singular exception.

But Vixen realized she wanted to lean against this total

stranger and bury her face against his chest or in the crook of his neck. Stiffening her shoulders, she jerked away and started back down the sidewalk.

She could feel his eyes burning into her neck with every step she took.

CREO

He watched until she turned the corner and then he closed his eyes and dropped his head. He wasn't cold anymore. That much was certain. Facing Vixen hadn't hit him the way he'd expected. He loved her, but he would have expected to feel anger when he faced her. Expected to bite back a hundred questions that he knew he couldn't ask.

All he'd felt when he looked at her was grief.

Vixen never showed her emotions, but he knew how to read her. Her eyes got dark when she was sad, and she held herself stiff and rigid when she was afraid or angry. They were minute tells, but nobody knew Vixen the way he did.

She was both angry and afraid right now, and there was an air of grief lingering around her.

And hunger. When she'd met his gaze, something moved through her eyes, just the quickest flash and then it was gone, but he knew that look. Just as he knew what it meant when her breath hitched in her chest, what it meant when she licked her lips, what it meant when she curled her hands into fists as though to keep from reaching out to touch. She'd wanted him in his first life, and she wanted him now. Now, just as then, she wasn't happy about it.

Wanting, needing, they were weaknesses as far as Vixen was concerned.

She didn't care for weaknesses.

Once she'd wanted him enough, cared for him enough, to allow herself that weakness.

He wondered what she'd do now.

Then he sighed, pushed a hand through his hair, scowling at the unfamiliar feel and weight of it. His hair was still thick, but it had a finer, softer quality to it. Didn't feel like his hair at all.

Briefly, a thought moved through his mind, but as he

muttered aloud, "Now what?" he realized he knew the answer.

Or at least part of him did.

He started to walk, following the path Vixen had taken.

He wasn't looking for her, though.

He was looking for something or someone else. He wasn't entirely sure which one, though.

ᑫᔆᓂ

Privacy was a precious commodity in her world. Even though she rarely let herself worry about Hawthorne's prying eyes or those of his men, Vixen needed a place to crash where she could have some privacy when she needed it.

Finding such a place wasn't hard. At least not for a woman of her talents. Talents, that was something she had plenty of, but they weren't the sort of things most people would want to boast about.

Breaking into a place without leaving a sign, robbing a man blind as she stood next to him on the subway, killing a person without leaving a mark.

She was a regular Girl Scout.

Finding a place where Hawthorne didn't have bugs planted or a bird's-eye view of her bedroom wasn't hard, but it was tedious. Not trusting him to leave her to her privacy, she moved her safe place every few months.

She'd been in the small, mid-scale apartment for just over a week. On one side lived a detective. On the other side lived a nurse. She hadn't seen much of them and preferred to keep it that way. She kept a low profile, low enough that there hadn't ever been mention of her in any of the investigations surrounding Hawthorne.

Which was a damn good thing with a detective living on one side of her. A lot of people in her position wouldn't want to sleep with a cop just on the other side of the wall. But Vixen didn't have any reason to worry being this close to a cop. She actually preferred having one close by her safe place—just another safeguard against Hawthorne prying into her life. He was far less likely to have his men go in and set up bugs when there was a chance a cop would notice.

So she didn't mind the cop. Vixen was glad she rarely saw

her neighbors. She wasn't the friendly type, and liked it that way.

The apartment across from her had been vacant for a few weeks, but judging by the sounds coming from behind the door, that had changed. She pushed her key into the deadbolt and turned it, but just before she could slip inside and shut herself off, the door behind her opened.

She didn't even have to see him.

Her body knew.

Her heartbeat sped up, her hands went damp and her knees got weak.

Shit, she thought silently.

"Hello again."

His voice was just as perfect now as it had been when he crashed into her less than an hour earlier. Slowly, she turned her head and met his gaze over her shoulder. "You."

He smiled. "Do you believe in coincidences?"

"No." She unlocked the second lock and opened the door. As she slipped inside, she glanced back at him.

"Are you always this friendly?" he asked, still giving her that inviting, open grin.

"Yes. Are you?"

He laughed. The sound of it was like velvet rubbing over her skin and she suppressed a shiver. "Actually, no."

Go inside, her head said firmly. *Shut the door. Get your head on straight.* But instead, she lingered in the doorway and studied his face. It was a nice face, she decided. The whole package was nice—broad shoulders, narrow waist, lean hips. Oh yes, very nice. With a body like that, he could be outright ugly from the shoulders up and he'd still have women checking him out.

But the face was every bit as nice as the body. Narrow, with elegant, clean lines, a wide mouth that she imagined knew how to kiss very well. Earlier, he'd worn a pair of mirrored shades that had kept her from seeing his eyes and he hadn't gotten around to taking them off yet.

"Why am I getting the special treatment?"

One of those wide shoulders moved in a negligent shrug. He reached up to push his sunglasses onto his head as he replied, but whatever he said fell on completely deaf ears.

Vixen's heartbeat faltered. Her hands were all slippery with sweat and blood roared in her ears.

His eyes.

Everything else faded away as she stared into eyes the color of blue neon. Eyes that color couldn't possibly be real, although she'd once known a man who had eyes that same impossible shade. She stumbled backward, fumbled the door open and all but fell inside. Shoving it closed behind her, she fumbled with the locks, a sob catching in her throat. Finally, she managed to secure them but her fingers shook too much to put the chain on. Blinded by tears, she pressed her forehead against the door and tried to breathe.

Tried to breathe, but couldn't.

His eyes.

Damn it, looking into his eyes, for just a second, it had been like she was looking into Graeme's eyes once more. Guilt churned in her gut, but the guilt wasn't what had her shaking like a leaf. It was grief.

She half-fell, half-leaned against the wall, slowly sliding down until she was crouched in the corner. Drawing her knees up to her chest, she hid her face against her legs and tried to block off the torrent of memories storming through her...

Then...

"What's your name?" He wore a suit. Even her naïve, young eyes could tell it was a pretty damn fancy suit.

He wasn't exactly good-looking, although he had beautiful eyes. An amazing shade of blue that couldn't possibly be real, but somehow she knew they were. He wouldn't be the type to wear contacts. So that neon blue had to be his. His dark hair was cut close and he had a broad face that matched his broad shoulders, his deep chest, big, muscled legs and big hands.

Vixen hated big men.

She was too damn short and big men always made her feel threatened, even though she was far from helpless. More than a few guys had learned that lesson the hard way. But for some reason, she didn't feel overwhelmed by the sheer size of him and the way he was looking at her didn't send fear scurrying through her.

"Vixen," she said, lifting her chin, refusing to let him see how nervous she was. "Don't know why in the hell you're asking. You prob'ly already know my name, what size panties I wear, what size shoes I wear and whether anybody will notice if I disappeared."

He lifted a brow, a faint smile on his face. "I didn't go through your underwear drawer or your closet." Then his gaze dropped to her feet and he added, "But I'd guess you wear a size five shoe."

His gaze moved up and lingered on her hips slowly and his lids drooped low over his eyes. "And size two."

She swallowed. Her belly went all hot, crazy considering that this man had broken into her apartment and she hadn't even realized he was in there until she walked into the living room and saw him sitting on the chair by the window.

Vixen should be terrified.

But she wasn't.

"Have we met?" The question slipped out of her before she realized she even wanted to ask. She'd remember if she'd met him, right? Those eyes. How in the hell could a woman forget those eyes?

He shrugged, big shoulders moving under that very nice suit. "I can't say I'd call it that. You tried to steal my wallet in Blanton, and then you tried to relocate my balls into my throat."

Vixen blinked, tried to remember. She couldn't place him, not going off just that—she'd racked plenty of guys and she'd stolen plenty of wallets. Her mother had taught her how to pick pockets before she could even tie her shoes and even though she'd mostly moved on to bigger things, she could rob a person blind in the blink of an eye. She rarely got caught. A cop in New York once and that one had landed her in juvie and then a foster home, where she'd stayed for exactly three days before she ran. After that, she'd left New York and was a lot more careful.

Blanton...shit.

Yeah, she remembered now.

Not his face really, and certainly not his eyes, but she remembered a hand closing over her wrist, squeezing. Squeezing. Then abruptly gone as the man stared down at her. Instinct had her racking him, and then running, before she caught more than a glimpse of his face.

"It looks as though you remember."

She shrugged, trying to keep the action casual and failing. "I dunno. I've swiped a lot of wallets."

"Vixen…" he murmured the name softly, almost as though testing out the sound of it. "Is that your real name?"

She curled her lip at him. "Yeah. My mom was fucking nuts."

He smiled. "It suits you." Then he sighed and shoved up out of the chair. "Vixen, you should have kept to lifting wallets."

Something about the way he said that made a chill race along her spine. "What the hell does it matter to you?"

He slipped his hands into his pockets. Studied her face. "Tuesday night."

That was all he said.

But she knew.

Falling back, she shifted and reached for the switchblade she had tucked inside her waistband. "What about Tuesday night?"

He sighed and rubbed a hand over his head. "You don't strike me as a fool, Vixen. And I assure you that I'm no fool, either. You know what I'm talking about. He wants it back."

"Yeah, I bet he does. Too fucking bad." She curled her lip in a sneer.

Briefly, lashes lowered over those blue eyes. "If you sold it, then perhaps you can get me the money. I might be able to convince him…" His voice trailed off as he looked at her face. "You haven't sold it."

"No."

"Hmmm. But I get the feeling if I tell you to get it for me, and I'll convince my boss to leave you alone, you're going to tell me that you can't."

Vixen shrugged. "Nope. I can't."

"Where is it?"

She grinned. "An evidence locker. I mailed it to the cops."

He blinked. Cocked his head and squinted at her, as though he couldn't quite understand what she'd said. "You stole it and sent it to the cops."

"Yeah. I figured it was the best place for it." She shrugged, tried to remember exactly what she'd been thinking when she stole the boxes from the storage shed. Vixen usually didn't give a damn about drugs, if somebody was buying them, selling them or taking them, as long they kept it away from her.

But those drugs bothered her. If somebody wanted to snort some coke, shoot heroin, she didn't give a damn. They'd fry their brains, maybe end up overdosing like her mother had when Vixen had been eleven years old. But those bottles and bottles of little white pills weren't the kind most people took willingly, or even knowingly.

She'd stolen one case of the smuggled Rohypnol and she'd mailed it to the cops with the address where they could find the rest, even though she knew it probably would get moved before they got there. That one case was going to have to be enough but now she wished that maybe she had risked making a so-called "anonymous" phone call to the cops.

"You had something you could have sold for thousands and you mailed it to the police," he said, speaking slowly, shaking his head.

She gave him a brazen, bold grin that hopefully hid how afraid she was and shrugged. "Yeah."

"Why?"

She glared at him. "Hell, maybe because I hate to think about a bunch of perverted rich boys buying it up and slipping it into a girl's drink so they can rape her."

"Somehow I didn't see you as the altruistic type."

"Altru... Huh?"

"Doing a selfless act. Just to do it."

Blood rushed to her face and she knew she was probably blushing a bright shade of pink. Shifting on her feet, she looked away from him. "That drug is fucked up. Somebody wants to fry their brain, hey, fine by me. But they shouldn't force it on somebody else." She rubbed her thumb along the blade she still held hidden behind her back, reassured by the smooth surface, the familiar weight of it in her hand. "How did you all find out I took it?"

"Security tapes taken from the storage facility. One of the boss's men recognized you, said he'd seen you in the area." He lifted a brow and murmured, "You should have been more careful, Vixen."

"Yeah, well, I'll remember that next time."

Not that she expected there would be a next time. He hadn't said his boss's name and she hadn't exactly seen a name written on the box of drugs she'd stolen, but she knew who this guy worked for.

Around here, there was pretty much one boss. Hawthorne was both revered and hated. Revered because he didn't concern himself with the petty thieves and small-time dealers as long as they stayed out of his way. Hated because when they didn't stay out of his way, there usually wasn't enough left to bury.

Vixen hadn't known the keys she had stolen had belonged to a man who worked for Hawthorne. She'd tried them in three other storage depots before she hit the jackpot and all she'd hoped to find was maybe some electronics or something, hopefully stuff that was easy to steal, easy to sell.

Not drugs.

And certainly not Roofies.

But when she'd seen them, she knew she'd stumbled into something of Hawthorne's. Instinct had told her to backtrack, real quick. She hadn't. Now she'd pay for it.

"You cost him twenty thousand dollars."

She sneered. Even though her belly went all cold and slippery with fear. "Hell, that man won't miss twenty K."

"Miss it, perhaps not. But he doesn't like people taking things from him."

"Got that much, thanks."

"Twenty thousand." He muttered it to himself this time and shook his head. He shot her a narrow look, those killer blue eyes going glacial.

"I don't give a shit how much money it was. Anybody who sells that kind of crap knows what it's going to be used for— they ought have somebody shove it down their throat and then, if they want to keep selling it, fine. Let them."

Now the look on his face changed, softening. She didn't like the concern she saw in his eyes, and she didn't trust it. "Vixen, has it happened to you?"

She laughed. "Hell, no. I don't do the party scene."

"Drugs don't get used just at parties."

Rolling her eyes, she said, "Yeah, I've heard that before. No, man. Nobody's ever slipped me anything. Nobody ever will. I'd kill them." She shrugged restlessly, remembering a night when she'd come to her apartment and heard moaning coming from next door. It had been weird enough, out of place enough, that she'd climbed out on the fire escape and investigated.

What she'd seen looked like something off a porn flick, her quiet, rather shy neighbor caught up in a three-way. It wouldn't have bothered Vixen at all, except she'd seen the woman's eyes. Glassy. Unfocused. Without a doubt, drugged. It had pissed her off enough that she called the cops and then beat tail, taking only what she had to have from her own apartment and getting out of dodge before the police showed up.

She'd watched from down the street as the police led the men away, watched as an ambulance drove the drugged victim away. It was the last time Vixen had seen her, and it was an image that stayed with her.

More than anything, it had been that memory that drove her to steal the Rohypnol. And she didn't regret it. Even considering hell was about to rain down on her, she didn't regret it.

He still watched her with measuring eyes and she had to fight the urge to turn away from that insightful gaze. Vixen knew better than to ever give somebody her back, but she really hated the way he looked at her. Like he could see clear through her.

"You know, this would have been easier if you'd just stolen the product to sell it for yourself."

"Easier for what? For you to beat the shit out of me? Kill me?" She lifted her chin and curled her fingers, beckoning him. "Give it a shot, slick. But you won't walk away without a mark. I guarantee it."

He laughed. "I'm not here to kill you. And I have no desire to beat you up, either."

"Why not? Ain't that what you do?"

"Isn't."

She paused, a little caught off-guard. "You mean you're not one of his thugs?"

He smiled. It wasn't a nice smile. It was the kind of smile a shark would have, if sharks smiled. "Oh, I'm one of his thugs, Vixen. Believe that. I was referring to your phrase... 'Ain't that what you do.' It should be 'Isn't that what you do.' And yes. That is exactly what I do. I'm supposed to come here and get the product or the money if it had already been sold, and deliver a warning."

"A warning. Yeah. I know what kind of warnings he gives. But if you think it's going to be easy, you're dead wrong."

"I have no intention of leaving a mark on you." He lowered himself back into the chair and brought up a leg, hooked his ankle over his knee. "I'll deal with my boss. I've done it before. As long as he gets his money, he'll be satisfied."

"I don't have any money."

He shrugged. "I do. I'll handle it."

Vixen narrowed her eyes, automatically falling back a step. She couldn't stop the sneer that curled her lips as she stared at him. "You'll take care of it. Man, aren't you a nice guy? And exactly what do you want for it?"

He lifted a brow and asked, "Did I say I wanted anything?"

"People don't shell out twenty grand just to be nice."

That made him laugh. It was a deep, rolling sound and even though it made absolutely no sense, she liked hearing it. It warmed something inside her. "Vixen, sweet, I'm not doing this to be nice. Quite frankly, nice is something that eludes me. So, no. I'm not doing it to be nice."

She glanced at his lap. "That means you want something. I bet I can guess what it is. Fuck that. I ain't a whore."

"If I thought you were, we wouldn't be having this conversation," he murmured. "I can't quite decide what you are, Vixen. Petty thief. Police informant—"

She stiffened. "Like hell!"

He shrugged. "You mailed the product to the police, and I imagine you told them where to find the rest of the product. That counts as informing, I believe. But I've decided that doesn't suit you either. Neither does a whore. So relax. When we have sex, it will be because we both want it, not for any other reason."

Vixen blinked. Then she reached up and stuck a finger in her ear, wiggled it like she had something caught in there. "Excuse me? *When* we have sex? What in the hell you mean by that?"

A strange little smile curled his lips. Something hot and liquid pulsed through her. It was an unfamiliar sensation. Vixen had spent half her life watching from the shadows as her mother fucked any guy who would help feed her habit. She didn't even remember how young she'd been when she first saw her mother having sex, but it had been young. Way too young. It left a mark on her and she found the idea of sex in general just distasteful. Men? Even more so.

So the rush of heat caught her by surprise.

"Yes, Vixen. When." He shoved up off the chair and advanced on her.

She started to circle away but stopped herself, held her ground as he moved in on her personal space, remained still as he reached up and cupped her face in his hand, cradling her chin.

His touch was gentle.

For a moment, she was so caught off-guard by that, she couldn't think of anything else. He stroked his thumb across her lip and an involuntary sigh escaped her.

"When, Vixen. It isn't a question of *if*, but of when. It will happen." His eyes narrowed on her face and the fingers on her chin tightened ever so slightly. "It's going to happen. I know it, and soon you'll know it too."

Chapter Four

Now...

She could look back to that night with crystalline clarity, and she hated it. Eight years had passed, but the memory hadn't dimmed at all. She hated it.

Hated that his features hadn't gotten even the slightest bit hazy.

Hated that she could still remember trying to find some bravado to face down that arrogance, but all she'd been able to do was lick her lips and wonder why she couldn't seem to breathe.

Graeme had been right.

It had happened.

But then again, Graeme was one of those annoying types who had been right about a lot of things. Bracing her back against the wall, she used it as a support as she shoved to her feet. Her legs wobbled underneath her and she ended up walking close to the wall and letting it support her as she made her way into the living room.

It wasn't much.

The only time she ever came here was when she needed a quiet, private place to crash from time to time. It had a futon that doubled as a bed, a TV she hadn't turned on even once, a bathroom the size of a closet and a kitchen that just might be the size of two closets. She kept water, diet soft drinks and canned stuff on hand but she didn't want anything to eat, anything to drink.

She just wanted to fall down on a soft, warm bed and huddle under the blankets as she waited for the misery to pass. The futon wasn't soft or even warm, but she managed to dig up a couple of blankets. Carting them back with her, she dumped them on the futon and sat, reaching under the leg of her tailored pants for the zipper to her boots.

They were custom-made, expensive, and the leather was soft as butter. Curling up on the futon, she lay down and stared at the boots as she drew the blankets over her body.

Years ago, she never would have imagined that she'd own something as soft and lovely as those boots, or that she'd have a closet full of designer clothes. That she could walk into the finest restaurant in town and be shown to the finest table, instead of kicked to the door. She wouldn't have believed that she could learn a second language, or that she would ever be good at much else besides stealing.

Graeme had told her otherwise.

She hadn't believed him. She'd resisted at first, resisted him when he tried to talk her into leaving behind her life of picking pockets or fencing stolen electronics, resisted when he bought her nice things, took her to nice places.

She'd had three years of being spoiled, being pampered— then a blight moved in, but by the time she'd realized it, it had been too late. The blight had been Hawthorne. He'd come to her three years after she'd met Graeme and spoke to her about working for him.

Graeme had politely suggested to her, in private, that she stay clear of Hawthorne. He could handle her "refusal", he would deliver the message to Hawthorne. She hadn't agreed.

With every job she took from Hawthorne, Graeme had told her she needed to back away before it was too late. At the time, she'd thought it was some weird, male possessiveness thing. It was the only thing that had made sense to her—at the time.

Later, though, once she realized that Graeme was playing a dangerous game, it had made plenty of sense. He'd been playing a dangerous game with Hawthorne for years. He never let anybody close enough to see, at least not until her. Vixen, he'd allowed to get close.

Close—close enough to get caught up in his life, close enough that he had tried to protect her. Right up until the very end when he had to make a choice—and he'd made the choice to get away from Hawthorne, even if it meant sacrificing her.

She thought maybe she could have loved him.

During their five years together, he had told her, more than once, that he loved her. She even believed him. Or at least she believed that Graeme believed he loved her. He was a stubborn man and once he got an idea in his head, nothing would sway it.

But it hadn't stopped him from betraying her.

Hadn't stopped him from selling her out with the rest of Hawthorne's men. If she hadn't killed him, she would have ended up in jail.

She knew that. She'd told herself that a hundred times. A thousand.

But still, even three years after she'd seen the evidence, she didn't believe it.

Not in her heart.

She closed her eyes as the tears started to fall and wished that she'd turned and run the other way when she saw Graeme sitting in her apartment all those years ago.

Run and not looked back.

Then...

"What am I doing here?"

Three weeks after he'd broken into her house, three weeks after she'd expected to either get her throat slit or take a beating that would put her in the hospital, she still didn't know what to make of Graeme Lawson.

She had no idea why he'd brought her to this posh, pretty condo. She had no idea why he would show up at her door at the oddest times, or at any time, really. Why he'd call her. Why he hunted her down for a meal and then walked her home as though he didn't want her out alone on the streets.

Vixen had lived alone on the streets for nearly half her life now, and even before her mother had died. It wasn't like the woman had ever been much of a parent. Other than teaching her how to steal, her mother hadn't done much for her.

In the past three weeks, Graeme had shown more care and consideration for her than her mother had shown in her entire life. He had paid his boss for the money she'd cost their "organization" when she stole the drugs. When she was out late at night, he often followed her, watching over her. Some of the hassling she dealt with on a regular basis abruptly stopped and she had no trouble figuring out why.

Exactly three days after he'd first broken into her apartment with the intention of delivering her "warning", she realized he'd gotten inside her place again. She'd come home, her belly an empty knot and an eviction notice burning a hole in her pocket, to discover that Graeme had been there. He'd picked her locks, again, and left her miniscule little refrigerator stocked, and not with the cheap staples she usually had to make do with. No hot dogs, eggs or bologna. There had been steaks, chicken, stuff for fresh salads, milk—and chocolate. Lots of chocolate.

He'd also paid the rent that she was two weeks late on, plus an additional month.

Turning in a slow circle, she studied the large, airy room. It was so clean, everything all new and shiny looking. Automatically, she tucked her hands into her pockets, afraid to touch anything for fear of getting it dirty. The plush white couch—looked like leather—wasn't the kind of thing that a street rat should sit on. The windows were crystal-clear and the sun shone through in a warm, golden fall of light, splashing on a vivid red carpet.

She felt him watching her and she jerked her chin up, met his gaze. "What am I doing here?"

He crossed towards her, reached up and tucked her hair behind her ear. His hand, hard, warm, but so tender, cupped her cheek and he stroked his thumb across her lip. The guy had a thing for touching her. Not those oily, sneaky touches that she'd been fighting off for most of her life. But things like touching her hair, stroking a hand down her back. Holding her hand. Or simply touching her face, his thumb rubbing across her lip in a slow, gentle stroke.

Soft touches. The kind she'd see every once in a while when she was working a busy street, the gentle sort of touches a man gave a woman and not just because he wanted to screw her.

"This place is empty. The previous tenant moved out a few weeks ago."

She glanced around. Man, if she lived in a place this pretty and clean, she'd never leave. "I don't get what that has to do with me."

Graeme had that small, secretive smile on his face. "Perhaps you'd like to move in."

She blanched. "I can't afford nothing like this. I ain't got a job. Even on my best day, I couldn't lift enough wallets to pay for something like this."

Graeme laughed. "I'd planned on something a little more lucrative."

Something hot and ugly formed in her belly and automatically, she stepped back. No fucking way. She'd done a lot of shit, but she wasn't about—

His eyes narrowed and he caught her chin in his hand. "I don't like the look on your face, Vixen." He squeezed gently. Not hard, but firm, forcing her to meet his gaze when she would have jerked away. "That face of yours, it's as transparent as glass. You really do need to work on that. I know exactly what you're thinking—and if I wasn't a suspicious bastard myself, I'd probably feel a bit insulted by now."

He lowered his face, brushed his lips across hers.

She tried to turn away, but he wouldn't let her. His other hand came up, hooking over the back of her neck and angling her face up to his. His lips brushed across her cheek. His teeth caught her lower lip and bit, soft and gentle. "You think I want to whore you out, Vixen?"

She stiffened, blood rushing to her face. But she didn't see any point in lying about it. At least not until he lifted his head and she glimpsed the thinly veiled fury in his gaze. Instead of lying, though, she just sneered. "You wouldn't be the first to think that. But it didn't happen then, ain't going to happen now."

He didn't respond to that directly. What he did was catch her hand in his, guiding it down between them. He forced her hand against the hot, steely length of his cock. Her eyes went wide and she jerked against his hold, but he didn't let go. What he did was rub himself against her hand as he whispered in her ear, "I've been living in this condition for the past three weeks. I see you and I want you. I think of you and I want you. I smell you and I want you." He raked his teeth down her neck and then straightened, slowly letting go of her hand. Convulsively, her fingers tightened around him before she let go.

He fisted a hand in her hair and kissed her, hard, deep, his touch rougher, greedier than it had been any other time. "I want you—and I think I'd kill if I saw another man touching you," He growled against her lips and then he took her mouth once more.

Shaken, a little bit scared, she stood in his embrace almost passively. He pulled away, bit by bit, first separating their bodies, then untangling his hand from her hair. Finally, he lifted his mouth from hers and took one step back.

Harsh flags of color ruddied his cheeks and his eyes burned into hers as he backed away until three feet separated them. "I knew the first time I saw you that I wanted you. The second time I saw you, I knew that I'd make you mine. I don't share, my pretty little Vixen."

"Ahhh..." She didn't have a damn thing to say. She couldn't think of a damn thing to say. Hell, she just couldn't think period.

A rueful laugh escaped him. "Struck speechless, Vixen? That has to be a first."

She licked her lips and sighed when she realized she could still taste him. Her body ached, her nipples throbbed and deep down low in her belly, she felt empty. Almost painfully so. Sex was a messy chore in her mind, but since meeting Graeme, she began to understand the appeal of it. Or at least the idea.

The idea still terrified her.

"I don't get what in the hell you want from me."

A smile tugged at the corners of his lips and he sighed, a weary, sort of sad sound. "I only want what you're willing to give me."

She gestured to the condo, confused. "And what in the hell is that? I can't afford a place like this, but you act like you expect me to just move in and you'll handle it. But why? If you don't want me whoring around..." Abruptly, she shut up.

Maybe...maybe he didn't want her whoring around for money. Maybe he just wanted her to be his whore. She blinked, taken aback by the fact that she didn't find the idea all that repulsive. His eyes narrowed on her face, and she realized, once more, he'd read her like an open book. "I want you in my bed, Vixen, I won't lie about that, but I don't expect you to sell yourself over it."

Shaking her head, she demanded, "Then why this?"

"Because I'm tired of worrying my head off over you living in that hellhole. I know what kind of shit happens there and I don't want you near it." He didn't yell. But the fury she heard in his voice was only that much more effective, silencing any argument that might have formed. He crossed back to her, reaching out and fisting his hand in the front of her shirt, jerking her against him. "Bad things happen, Vixen, all the time. I don't want them happening to you."

"I can take care of myself. I've been doing it for a long time."

His eyes closed and he lowered his head, pressing his brow to hers. Laying his hand across her face, he stroked her lip. Something in her heart warmed and for some reason, tears stung her eyes when he whispered, "I know that. But I want to take care of you."

His lips brushed against hers, a whisper of a caress and then he let her go, stepped back. Dipping his hand into his pocket, he pulled out a key ring. "It's your choice, Vixen. You can move in here, or not. But before you make that choice, I want you to know that the offer comes with no strings. I don't expect you to sleep with me over this place." He laughed, but it wasn't a happy sound. "All this place costs is money and I have more than I need."

He lay the key on the window sill and then walked past her.

She stood frozen with indecision for the longest time, but when she heard him open the door, she blurted out his name.

She turned, found him standing there, facing away from her with his hand wrapped around the doorknob, his big body tense. Her tongue didn't want to work anymore and her mouth was dry. So instead of trying to figure out something to say, she went with her instincts. That was what she was best at anyway.

She shrugged out of her beat-up canvas coat. It hit the floor with a soft, muffled thump as she reached for the hem of her shirt. She pulled it off and dropped it to the floor just as Graeme glanced behind him.

His eyes went wide. And dark. That unforgettable neon blue darkened to twilight as he turned, shutting the door as he leaned back against it, staring at her with a dumbfounded look. She toed her tennis shoes off without looking at him and then unbuttoned her jeans. Under them, she wore nothing but a pair of worn cotton panties and she wished she had something pretty to wear for him.

Wished she knew what she was doing.

She didn't, but she didn't let that stop her.

"What are you doing, Vixen?"

"Taking you at your word." Her voice shook. "You say you want me. I'm pretty sure I want you too."

He pushed off the door, his eyes locked on her face. Good.

That was good. If he looked at her skinny, short, too-pale body, she might just freak out.

"Pretty sure?" he parroted back.

"Yeah." Licking her lips, she shrugged restlessly and then lowered her head, staring at the floor. Would he believe her if she told him she hadn't done this before? She'd always hated the idea of sex. Watching her mom fuck one man after another before Vixen could even read had more or less left her disgusted with sex.

The grunting, the grabbing, the sweating. It didn't help that none of the men her mom had slept with were any sort of decent. Most of them had ignored her, but as she got older, a few of them had started giving her looks that had made her gut go cold with fear. Every now and then, Mom would see one of those looks and that was the one thing that would bring out any sort of protective instinct.

None of it had left Vixen with a positive outlook on sex, or men. Graeme was the one man she could actually considering doing it with—the only man she really wanted to think about doing it with. The thought of getting nekkid, hot and sweaty with him did the exact opposite of what happened any other time she thought about it.

The smooth gleam of his leather shoes appeared in her field of vision and she lifted her head to meet his stare.

Blood rushed to her cheeks and she figured she was probably about as red as she could get. "You're pretty sure you want me?" he murmured again.

"I..." The words locked in her throat. Hell, Vixen was pretty sure her knees were shaking by this point. *Get it over with!* a voice inside her head shrieked. In a rush, she blurted out, "I ain't ever done this before, Graeme."

He blinked. A muscle in his jaw jerked. Slowly, he rasped, "Never?"

Mute, she shook her head.

"Why now?"

Edgy, she shrugged. "Because you want me. And when you touch me, you make me wonder what it would be like. You make me want you, make me want this. I ain't ever wanted it before."

His lids drooped low, shielding his eyes, but he continued to stare at her. She could feel the hot, intense weight of his stare. He shrugged out of his long black coat and she gave him a shaky smile, stepped a little closer. But he didn't reach for her. He placed his coat on her shoulders, tucking her inside it. It fell to her ankles. He cupped her chin in his hand and angled her face up to his. "Not here," he whispered.

"Why not?"

A smile curled his lips and he kissed her, tracing the outline of her mouth with his tongue, before murmuring, "Your first time isn't going to be on the hard floor in an empty apartment, Vixen." He nuzzled her neck, his warm breath drifting over her bared skin in a teasing caress. "If I had any sort of decency in me, I'd wait. Make this something special for you. But I'm not waiting."

He lifted her and Vixen squealed, startled. Blood rushed to her cheeks and she buried her face against his shoulder as he cradled her to his chest. *Some hot guy sweeps her off her feet and she squeals like some sort of rich little princess.* But this wasn't just some guy.

This was Graeme. If he looked at some pretty prom queen the way he looked at Vixen, the girl would run so fast, her tiara or whatever in the hell it was would go flying. Graeme, with those intense, amazing eyes, the way he could look at a person with eyes so icy, their heart stopped—and the way he looked at her with eyes so damned hot, it was amazing he didn't leave scorch marks.

People looked at him with a mix of fear and respect and when they saw her with him, that odd fear/respect began to bleed over onto her.

She saw the way women looked at him and for once, she could understand the greedy desire written on their faces, because she felt the same thing when she looked at him. He never seemed to notice them, women who were a good eight inches taller than she was, with tits out to there, long legs, a butt that didn't look like it belonged to a pre-teen boy.

He noticed her.

He wanted her.

And that was enough to have nerves hit in the stomach with the force of a sledgehammer.

Curling her fingers into his coat, she breathed in his scent and tried to focus on something, anything but the fact that he was carrying her out of the apartment, down the hallway and into another apartment. He kicked the door shut and turned around, stooping just enough to flip the lock, all without putting her down. The lock slid home and there was a finality to the sound that had her swallowing in nervousness.

"You sure?" he whispered, brushing his lips against hers. "If you're not, better say something now, baby."

Lifting his head, he stared down at her with glittering eyes. "I'm not a gentleman who'll let you go if you change your mind, Vixen. If you think it could happen, tell me now before this goes any farther."

Vixen reached up and traced the outline of his mouth with her finger. "I don't spend a lot of time changing my mind."

"Good." His voice was gruff, rough, guttural and so damned sexy it sent shivers up and down her spine. He carried her out of the narrow entryway into a larger room with a high ceiling, huge windows that faced out over Lake Michigan and a thick, plush carpet the color of the midnight sky. She didn't see much beyond that because Graeme didn't slow down, walking through the room without once looking away from her.

He carried her into a bedroom—a bedroom that was probably bigger than her entire place, with a bed big enough for four, a fireplace that took up half the wall and more windows. By that lake-sized bed, he lowered her to her feet, his hands coming up to cradle her face as he lowered his mouth back to hers.

"You taste too good," he muttered. "Like cinnamon."

His lips brushed along her cheek, down her neck. "Like honey."

He sank to his knees in front of her and Vixen felt her knees go a little weak at the sight of him kneeling before her. His big hands came up, parted the jacket he had wrapped around her. Self-conscious, she tried to tug the jacket closed but all Graeme did was catch her wrists in his hands and force them back to her sides. He leaned forward and kissed her belly, circled his tongue around her navel. "Sweet. Soft."

He went lower, lower, smoothing her panties down until they fell to the floor. When he nuzzled the pale curls between her thighs, Vixen jolted and tried to back away. But the bed was right behind her and she ended up pinned between Graeme's body and the mattress. And then she wasn't pinned—he released her wrists and he banded an arm around her waist,

Shiloh Walker

lifting her until her feet left the floor and her breasts were on level with his mouth.

Leaning in, he took one swollen, pink nipple in his mouth. He licked her and that big, powerful body of his shuddered. "Sweet."

She arched against him, whimpering. The coat he'd wrapped around her shoulders fell down, caught in the bend of her elbows as she reached up, cupping his head in her hands. He bit down, lightly, letting go just as she felt the edge of pain. Graeme shifted his attention to her other breast and he kept at it until Vixen was sweating and panting out his name.

Between her thighs, she ached and deep in her belly, she felt empty. But as he lowered her to the bed, apprehension hit her. The smug bastard read her way too easy. He came down beside her, his hand cradling her cheek. "Too late now, my pretty little Vixen," he murmured, stroking a thumb across her lower lip. "You had your chance to back out."

She wished he couldn't read her so well and it was damn hard to fake bravery when she was wearing nothing more than her hair and his coat tangled around her elbows. She tried, though, giving him a wobbly sneer as she said, "I don't back out."

Graeme laughed and dipped his head long enough for him to catch her lower lip between his teeth and bite her softly. "Good." Watching her face, he slid a hand down her torso, over the flat of her belly, She hissed as the tips of his fingers brushed up against slick, wet flesh. Blood stained her cheeks red and she closed her eyes, turned her face away.

"You're wet for me," he rasped, circling one finger around her entrance. "Your pussy is already slick and hot... Fuck, feel how tight you are..."

His words ended on a groan as he pushed one thick, long finger inside her. He did it again, and again, but then he stopped. "Look at me."

Reluctantly, she turned her face back to his and stared at him. He started that teasing caress back up, pumping his finger in and out. "You like how that feels?" he asked.

Damn it, Vixen didn't know how she could blush any hotter, but that blunt, honest question, coupled with the expectant look in his eyes, had her flaming up again. "Yeah, I like it."

154

"Then don't look away." He added a second finger, then circled his thumb over her clit.

Vixen moaned and arched up, her lashes fluttering down over her eyes—but as soon as she broke eye contact, he stopped. Her lids flew open and she automatically rocked herself against him. "Don't stop."

"Then don't look away."

It went like that, Graeme screwing his fingers in and out of her pussy until she was moaning, this close to exploding under his touch, but as soon as she closed her eyes or looked away from his face, he stopped. She was sweating, panting his name, staring at his face as though nothing else existed. He twisted his wrist, reaching deep, deeper. Crying out his name, she felt something inside her give...explode...

Dark, vibrant colors ricocheted before her and she fell, moaning, into a dark abyss, moving against his hand and seeking more...

But he'd stopped touching her.

Growling, she shoved up on one elbow and reached down, locking her fingers around his wrist and holding him as she pumped her hips, riding his fingers until the storm inside her eased. When it did, she slumped back on the bed, unaware that she was smiling, unaware that Graeme was staring at her with desperate greed.

He moved, pulling his fingers from the tight grasp of her pussy and reaching up, cupping her chin in his hand and angling her mouth to his. "Fuck, you're a hot thing, aren't you?" he rasped, slanting his mouth over hers and kissing her as though he'd die if he didn't.

Keeping his mouth on hers, he rolled his weight between her thighs and then he shoved up, kneeling between her spread legs and staring at her with the look of a starving man. "Fuck, I could eat you up." He placed his hands on her thighs, just above her knees, and stroked upward until his thumbs met in the middle.

Vixen caught her breath, afraid to move, afraid to breathe, as hot anticipation washed through her. He shrugged out of his suit jacket, tossing it off to the side. His tie, his shirt, soon followed and then he straightened from his crouching position, reaching for his belt.

When she saw his cock, her breath lodged in her chest and

she blinked, looking from that thick column of flesh up to his face. *Oh, hell, no—*

He reached for her hand, brought it up to his sex. Vixen jerked back, but he wouldn't let go. "I'm no gentleman," he reminded her gruffly. "You're not leaving this bed any time soon, Vixen."

Mouth dry, she wrapped her fingers around his flesh, following the guidance of his hand and stroked him. "This is going to hurt," she said, her voice flat.

"Probably." He dipped his head and licked her mouth. "But I'll make it good. I swear." He reached down and caught her wrist, tugging it away and urging it down by her side.

Vixen braced herself, but he didn't cover her. He lay between her thighs, cupping her ass in his hands. Her eyes went wide as he dipped his head and pressed his mouth to her sex.

Vixen might be a virgin, but she wasn't naïve. She knew the ins and outs of sex and had seen pretty close to damn near everything, thanks to her mother. But she hadn't ever seen the appeal of oral sex. Giving it. Receiving it.

Not until Graeme placed his mouth on her. Not until he licked her entrance and then pushed his tongue inside her pussy, licking her, lapping at her flesh like she was a piece of candy. When she moaned and reached down, cupping his head between her hands and rising to meet him, he growled against her sensitive folds, his hands tightening on her butt and lifting her higher.

Too damn good. It felt too damn good. Nothing could feel as hot, intense, as sweetly sinful, as his tongue stroking in and out of her pussy...but then he shifted his focus to her clit and suckled it. At the same time, he lowered her butt back to the bed and slid a hand between her thighs, pushing two fingers inside her.

She screamed out his name. He worked her harder, twisting his wrist. His mouth became more urgent, more demanding. She started to come, everything inside her threatening to splinter into a million pieces. That was when he added a third finger and she was caught, spellbound, in the grip of an orgasm, barely even aware of the pain.

He brought her to climax again and again. When he finally pulled away and crawled back up her body, she was drained, dazed and too limp to move.

"Look at me," he whispered. His mouth was swollen and red. When he went to kiss her, she tried to duck her head, but he wouldn't let her. "Look at me," he ordered, covering her mouth with his.

Caught in the vivid blue of his eyes, she lay there as he kissed her, the taste of her on his mouth, but under that, she could taste him, dark and erotic. He lifted up, braced his weight on his elbows, hooking his forearms under hers, his hands at her shoulders and holding her still. Terror and heat swarmed inside her as he nudged the head of his thick cock against her sex.

"Don't look away," he whispered. "You gave me this...and I want all of it."

The pain was just a whisper at first, but as he pressed deep, deeper, it grew, hot and vicious, spreading through her. She cried out and closed her eyes.

His voice cut through the hot wash of pain. "Look at me!"

She did...and she found herself lost in his gaze.

"I want it all," he repeated. "I want the tears. I want to feel it as your body tries to accept me, accept this...and I want to watch you as it happens. You gave me this—you can't hold anything back. Not from me."

"It hurts." She hated the whimpering, pleading tone of her voice, but she couldn't stop it. Nor could she look away from him as he forged deeper and deeper, claiming her one slow inch at a time.

"I know it hurts." He dipped his head and nuzzled her neck. "And bastard that I am, I can't even say I'm sorry. I'm glad it hurts, glad this is the first time for you...glad I'm the man having this, having you...and damn it, Vixen, I'm keeping you."

He pulled back. Their gazes locked—and then he surged deep, this time not stopping until he had completely buried the thick, throbbing length of his cock inside her. Blinded by the pain, for a few minutes, she couldn't think beyond it. She tried to clutch her thighs together, but he lay with his hips snug against hers and she couldn't move, couldn't pull away so she had to just take it. Just when it started to ease, though, he began to move.

"Graeme, please...don't..." she pleaded.

He kissed her. Softly. Gently. But he didn't stop.

Shiloh Walker

The pain sliced through her and she arched up, helpless against it, against him. Balling her hands into fists, she shoved against him, half a mind to pull away, if she could manage. But then he reached between them, cupped one hip in a big hand and angled her hips higher. She moaned, closing her eyes as tears slid free. He pulled out and she braced herself for the pain when he pushed back inside.

It was there—

But this time, so was the pleasure. She gasped, her eyes going wide as she stared up at him. He rotated his hips against hers and she shivered as twin spirals of pain and pleasure streaked through her. She said his name again, but this time it was on a shivery sigh and she arched up to meet him.

He kissed her and she wrapped her arms around his neck and opened for him. His tongue moved against hers, traced her lips, pulled away to lick away her tears. "Say my name again," he muttered, nipping her earlobe.

"Graeme…" The soft, breathy little sound was nothing like her voice, but she couldn't manage anything more.

Then he moved higher on her body, let go of her hip and reached between her thighs, touching her clit—and Vixen couldn't even breathe, much less manage to speak his name. She lay there, her nails digging into his shoulders, full of his taste, his scent, his body moving over hers, his fingers stroking and teasing her clit. He took her from the farthest edge of pain into a pleasure so profound, she didn't know if she'd survive it.

As he rode her, Graeme whispered, muttered and teased her, his rough, sexy voice as erotic as the way his body moved over hers, within her. "Hot, sweet little pussy…that's it, pretty little Vixen, come…aw, fuck, you're so damn perfect…"

He shafted her, alternating from slow and lazy to quick, shallow thrusts. Sweat beaded, gleamed on their bodies and it wasn't too much longer before his breathing was as ragged, as erratic as hers. He aligned their bodies, skin to skin, and against her chest she could feel the driving, heavy rhythm of his heart. Catching her hands, he twined their fingers together and stretched her arms over her head. "You're mine, baby," he whispered against her lips. "Say it. Tell me you're mine."

Vixen couldn't breathe, couldn't breathe… "Yours, Graeme."

He growled. The sound of it was oddly triumphant. A hard-edged smile curled his lips and the rhythm of his strokes sped up, his hands tightened on hers. Inside her sex, his cock throbbed, swelled. "Come for me, Vixen. Come."

It hit hard, hot, fast. She gasped for air, but it was lodged, locked inside her lungs. Everything went dark as she spun off the edge of the world, falling...falling...only his arms, only his hands, only Graeme kept her from dissolving away entirely.

The orgasm held her in its grasp, her skin felt too hot, too tight and too small to contain it. Distantly, she felt him stiffen above, heard him swear as his body bucked. His cock jerked inside her pussy and when he came, she felt the hot, heated splash of semen jetting deep.

The moment stretched out forever, but even when Graeme moved, shifting to lay with his head on her belly, the sweet perfection of it didn't end. Their hands were still linked and he lifted one, pressed a kiss to the back of her palm.

Eventually, he shifted, moving up to lay beside her and drawing her into the curve of his body. Her last conscious thought was that he was once more touching her face, his hand on her face, cradling her head against his chest.

And his thumb. Stroking back and forth across her lower lip.

Now...

She wouldn't cry.

Vixen lay on the futon, shaken through and through, aching deep inside, both physically and emotionally. But she'd be damned if she'd cry. She'd done what she had to. More, she'd done exactly what Graeme had trained her to.

He was the one who took her rough-and-tumble, scrappy, street-fighter skills to the next level. He was the one who first put a bladed weapon in her hand and showed her how to use it. It had been for self-protection, he'd told her. Not too long after she'd moved into the apartment next to his, somebody had grabbed her on the street.

One of Graeme's rivals, somebody else working for the illusive Gerard Hawthorne, and somebody who wanted to be where Graeme was. She'd managed to surprise the guy, driving a knee into his balls and then swinging at his face with her key poking out from between her knuckles. She got away, but it was luck alone that made it possible. The man hadn't been prepared for a girl who had some inkling of how to fight. If there had been more than one, she never would have gotten away without more than a scare and a few bruises.

Both she and Graeme knew it and that was when he began teaching her not just how to fight, but how to kill. And he taught her a little too well.

Or she learned a little easily.

Learning anything actually came easily. Under Graeme's encouragement, she'd gotten her GED and discovered that she didn't just have street smarts, she had actual brains. She just never had much of a chance to discover that until she was burying herself in books and making the grade her first year of college.

By the second year, Vixen realized she hadn't ever understood hard work until she was juggling advanced algebra, Spanish, Classic Lit and the fine art of protecting her ass.

Not one of her college professors had a thing on Graeme when it came to slave-driving. What he taught her wasn't anything she could have learned in any formal setting. After the first year, he would have been happy to stop working with her, but when he'd suggested it, Vixen hadn't wanted to stop.

She didn't know what drove her.

She didn't understand why she craved to learn more, why one knife wasn't enough, and why perfecting her aim with a gun seemed as vital as taking another breath in the morning.

She didn't understand then.

Later she did. After Hawthorne pointed it out. *You're a natural-born killer, Vixen...don't look so insulted. You're a predator. Predators are as natural as prey.*

The first time she'd killed, she'd done it on her own. There had been a sweet, little old lady who liked to hand out paper flowers and feed pigeons at Grant Park. Her name was Alice, no last name, and she always had a flower made of pink paper for Vixen. Up until Graeme came into her life, Alice was the first and only person who had ever given her any sort of flower.

A couple of punks beat her to death for the hell of it, but escaped jail time because of a technicality.

Vixen wasn't much for caring about people, but she'd liked Alice. When she'd heard about the old woman's death, she had cried. It was the first time she could remember crying over a person. She hadn't even cried when her mom died. But she'd cried over that old woman.

When the grief passed, the fury welled and she'd waited with baited breath, actually putting her faith in the justice system for the first time in her life. Vixen wasn't the naïve type, and she wasn't the type to let somebody else do something she felt she should do.

But for some messed-up reason, when she heard those punks had been arrested, that there was a witness more than willing to testify, she'd wanted to think that maybe the system could get justice for a woman they'd failed.

It was the first and the last time she'd put faith in the police and the so-called justice system. When the three bastards were released from jail, she'd waited exactly one week before she killed the first one. A week later, she killed the second one.

By the time another week had passed, the third man was more than a little jumpy. Using the skills Graeme had refined, she'd broken into the man's house. It was a dump, falling apart both inside and out, although he had an entertainment system that would probably sell for as much as the house. Most of it, if not all, was probably stolen goods.

She couldn't have cared less about that.

If Vixen hadn't stolen, she never would have survived those first few years on the street. Going to a shelter, risking getting sucked into the system hadn't once occurred to her. It was steal to eat, steal to be warm, do it, or die. Dying just didn't hold much appeal to her.

It didn't seem too appealing to her third victim either. His name was Marco Ruiz. She'd waited in the shadows as Marco came in, his eyes sliding left, sliding right. In his right hand, he'd held a Glock, but the way his hand had shook, he probably couldn't have hit a target if he tried.

Graeme had come in while they were fighting. Vixen hadn't wanted to outright kill this one. He was the one who came up with the idea to attack Alice, and he was the one who'd beat on her the worst. He was the one who took her precious paper flowers and burned them in front of her while the old woman lay crying in pain and fear. Vixen wanted him to cry.

When he first saw her, he'd laughed. The fear went out of him and the hand holding the gun steadied—right up until she kicked it out of his grasp and launched herself at him. After she'd blacked his eye, broken his nose and smashed his balls with her knee, he wasn't laughing any more, but he hadn't been scared either.

It had infuriated her and if Graeme hadn't come in when he did, her fury might have made her slip.

Graeme had been pissed off at her, but he seemed to understand she had to do this. So he had stood by in silence and watched as she killed a killer.

It was two days later that Hawthorne stepped into her life.

Looking back now, a huge part of her wished she'd listened when Graeme told her it was a bad idea to get involved with Hawthorne. She'd thought it was out of some fucked-up notion of "protecting" her because she was a woman, because he saw her as his woman and he didn't want his woman involved in the kind of life he lived. She hadn't realized she'd been both right and wrong.

He had wanted to protect her. Because she was his woman. And he didn't want her involved in the kind of life he lived, but he also hadn't explained that he wanted out of that life, hadn't explained that he was doing everything possible to make it happen—for both of them.

Those explanations didn't come until later. By then, he wanted it desperately enough that he'd been willing to sacrifice her to get it.

Love was a lie.

He'd always told her he loved her, and she'd believed him. Even though she hadn't ever said it back, she'd believed him, she'd trusted him. He was the one man she'd thought would never hurt her, the one man she'd thought she could trust. She never would have betrayed him the way he'd betrayed her.

That was why she didn't believe in love.

And that was why she'd be damned if she'd cry over it.

Laying there on the futon, staring up at the stark white ceiling overhead, she kept telling herself that. Even as tears leaked out of her eyes to soak her hair and her pillow.

Then...

"I love you."

He murmured the words against her neck, his voice rough,

drowsy with sleep.

She started to tense, but made every muscle in her body relaxed. Made herself smile as she covered his hand with hers and squeezed. Part of her wanted to say it back. Vixen didn't understand love, but she knew with Graeme she felt safe. She felt protected. She felt needed. And she needed him as much as she thought he needed her. That was love, right?

If it wasn't...

He sighed and she felt the movement of it in his chest, pressed snug against her back. The arm around her waist tightened and then he moved, easing up off the bed to stare down at her. "Any time I tell you that, you tense up," he said, studying her with dark, unreadable eyes.

Vixen licked her lips and wondered what he wanted her to say.

He'd been telling her that he loved her for nearly two years, almost every time they fuc...made love. Sex equaled fucking, but neither sex nor fucking seemed to describe what happened with her and Graeme.

Sex, it was nothing but two bodies.

When Gracmc touched her, he was touching more than her body, touching her in a place that went deeper than her soul.

"I'm sorry. I just..." Her voice trailed off and she shrugged weakly, wished she could make herself say it back to him. He deserved to hear it, but not unless she meant it. Whatever sweet fairy tale love was, Graeme deserved it.

But she couldn't even think about saying I love you.

Graeme laid a hand on her cheek, his thumb rubbing across her lower lip. It was a familiar touch, so sweet and tender, so at odds with the man the rest of the world saw when they looked at him.

"You don't need to tense up. You don't need to worry. I'm not asking anything from you." He trailed the roughened tips of his fingers down over her neck, down between her breasts, along the line of her torso, lower...lower, until he could cup his hand over the mound of her sex.

She was still wet from him, still sensitive, still swollen, and when he circled the tip of his finger around the entrance of her pussy, she stiffened and bucked against him.

"I say it because I feel it," he whispered. His gaze caught and held hers as he pushed one thick, long finger inside her. "I touch you because I need it." He pressed the heel of his hand against her clit, staring at her face as he caressed her. With certain, deft touches, he brought her whimpering and moaning and hovering on the brink of orgasm before he pulled away and then rolled to lay between her thighs. "I make love to you because I want to listen to you moan my name, and have you fall asleep while I hold you."

He pushed inside, the thick, hot length of his cock throbbing within the clasp of her pussy. "I fuck you because I need to hear you scream my name," he rasped, lowering his head to kiss her.

Vixen moaned into his mouth, lifting her hands and looping them around his neck. When he would have pulled away, she followed his mouth with her own. Graeme chuckled against her lips and reached up, caught her hands and forced them to the bed beside her head. Holding her pinioned, he angled up, stared down at her face as he moved higher on her body.

Her nipples dragged against his chest, pulling a whimper from her. "I love you because I do," he whispered against her mouth. "It's not a trade, Vixen. You don't need to say anything or worry that I expect something back...just accept it."

He levered up onto his knees, kneeling between her thighs. She lay sprawled on her back, staring at him with dazed, hungry eyes as he slid his hands up along the outer curve of her calves, along her thighs, up to her hips. He gripped her waist and held her steady as he started to shaft her, pumping in and out of her body with slow, unhurried strokes. Even when she started to rock against him, tried to take his achingly hard cock deeper, faster, he held back. Groaning, she wrapped her legs around his waist and sat up, straddling his lap. Her weight drove her completely down on his length and she cried out, shuddering at the sensation.

The silky, hot pillar of flesh seemed to stretch and scald her, but it was the sweetest pain imaginable. Big hands cupped her ass as she started to ride him. Staring at each other, lost to the entire world, lost in the slick, silken glide of flesh against flesh, the hot, powerful punch of pleasure and the primal music created by harsh breathing and hungry moans.

His electric blue eyes burned as hot as flame. Tunneling the fingers of one hand through her hair, he fisted the silken stands and tugged, exposing the line of her neck. Scraping his teeth over the exposed curve, he rasped her name against skin gone slick with sweat.

That rough, sexy growl was almost as erotic as the feel of his free hand on her ass, guiding her rhythm. Almost as sweet as the slip-side caress of his chest against her breasts. Almost as sinful as the way his cock jerked and swelled inside her pussy as she clenched down around him and moaned out his name.

Almost.

"I love you," he growled against her ear. Untangling his hand from her hair, he cupped her face and forced her to meet his gaze. "Tell me that you believe it, that you believe me."

"I believe you."

He took her back down to the bed, his greater weight crushing her into the soft, plush mattress and tangle of silken sheets. He caught her hands, bore them down beside her head, his mouth coming down on her and kissing her as though he couldn't take anything separating them. His cock swelled. He pulled out, slowly, withdrawing until he had only the barest inch inside her.

Vixen caught her breath and then he drove his length inside her, shafting her deep and hard until she was screaming into his mouth and shuddering under him.

Her orgasm hit hard and fast, and still he kept moving, dragging a second and third climax from her before reaching his own. Above her, he stiffened and growled her name and she shuddered as he came deep inside her. Sinking down, he pillowed his head between her breasts and wrapped his arms around her waist. "I love you," he whispered.

She smoothed a hand up over his damp shoulder, cupped it over the back of his neck. She didn't say it back.

But she was closer.

Now...

Closer. Yeah. She'd been closer.

That had been less than two weeks before she saw the disc and the memory of that night burned into her mind, rising out of the recesses to haunt her when she least expected. Now it surged to the fore, drowning everything in its wake as she relived it.

She thought about how close she'd come to saying it back.

To believing him...believing in love. To believing in the promise she'd always felt in his touch, the way he'd cup her face in his palm and stroke his thumb along her lip. The promise she'd sensed when he lay awake at night holding her when sleep eluded him—holding her, like she was all he really needed.

But in the end, she'd learned what she'd suspected was the case all along. Love was a fairy tale. She sniffed, wiped the back of her hand across her cheeks and when she realized she was crying over all of this again, it only added to her depression.

Chapter Five

She was in there crying.

Graeme didn't know how he knew, but he did. She was crying. He could feel each hot tear as it slid down her cheek, and his chest ached in sympathy for the sobs she tried to suppress.

Yeah, I'm doing a hell of a job here, he thought bitterly, shoving off the couch to pace the room yet again. He figured he'd paced about five miles around the room since he'd retreated back inside four hours ago.

She'd been crying then too. It had stopped and his weird awareness of her faded away, only to return again a good thirty minutes ago. The tears weren't slowing, the pain wasn't easing and if Graeme had to feel this echo of her grief for too much longer, he was going to go mad.

"Fuck this," he muttered. He sent a dirty look upward and snarled, "How am I supposed to do a damn thing to help her? What am I supposed to—"

The phone rang.

It wasn't his phone. He didn't have a damn phone.

It was hers.

He could hear the ring though, as clearly as if the phone was two feet away. And her voice. Never mind that several walls and doors and a decent amount of drywall separated them. He might as well have been listening in on another line—her voice was that clear. It sounded weary when she answered and for a minute, the novelty of that was so unexpected, he didn't recognize the other voice on the line.

A seething rage erupted inside his gut as Hawthorne said, "We have business to discuss, Vixen."

"Is there some sort of deadline here?" The weariness was gone from her voice now, and it was the cool, emotionless voice of the ball-busting bitch that had slid a blade into Graeme's heart.

"No deadline, but I would like to finalize the deal. You've never walked away without discussing the final details."

"You've never asked me to take care of some innocent kid who just happened to be the child of a man you're pissed off at."

"Innocent." Hawthorne laughed. "Vixen, love, you don't really care about some woman you don't know."

"No. I don't. But not caring about her doesn't mean I'm okay with this. She's never done a damn thing to you, to me. She's no threat. There's no reason—"

"No reason?" Hawthorne cut her off and if her voice had been cool, his was arctic. "But there is a reason. I want it done. That's all the reason you need."

"How many years have I been doing this for you, Hawthorne?"

It would be five years. He'd been gone for three years and Hawthorne had drawn Vixen into his web two years before Graeme's death. Rage boiled inside Graeme as he continued to play an unknown, silent third party to their conversation. He'd known that Hawthorne was bad news for Vixen. He hadn't been concerned for himself, but then Vixen entered the picture. As long as she didn't place herself in Hawthorne's business matters, Graeme had known he could protect her.

He hadn't gone blindly into his life and he'd prepared for any eventuality—or so he had thought. Any preparation he'd made hadn't included Vixen placing herself in Hawthorne's organization. She'd hated the bastard and Graeme had counted on that keeping her safe.

But Hawthorne knew people.

He hadn't had more than a few brief conversations with Vixen, but he didn't need any direct contact with her to figure out her hot button. A woman who'd risk life and limb just to trash a shipment of Rohypnol was a woman who'd been willing to take a similar risk again. And Vixen, being the scrapping survivor she was, would definitely be interested if some money was added in.

Hawthorne had some competition edging in his territory but the newcomer had been a bit more ambitious than the small-timers who usually went ignored by Hawthorne. Graeme had been expecting to hear from Hawthorne about leaning harder—or just eliminating the man.

But the elimination order was offered to Vixen.

Hawthorne had dangled bait that Vixen wouldn't refuse— the date-rape drugs. She'd deny it, but she had a core of honor buried inside her closely guarded heart. For a while, each successive hit had been along those lines.

But then he started pushing the lines, blurring them. In the months before Graeme's death, there had been several things that Vixen had done that Graeme wouldn't have expected. Within a few years, Vixen was crossing lines that would be hard, or impossible to come back from. Before his death, Graeme had spent a great deal of time worrying about that, wondering when—*if*—she'd hit a line she wouldn't cross.

It had finally happened. That line she wouldn't cross. Graeme didn't know whether to feel relief that she had finally come to that line, or fear for her.

She knew how Hawthorne handled refusal.

Dragging his thoughts away from that, Graeme made himself focus on the conversation again.

"Vixen, perhaps we should talk." There was something in Hawthorne's voice that bothered Graeme, stilled something inside him.

The man wasn't surprised.

He wasn't surprised—and Graeme had a bad, bad feeling that Hawthorne had been hoping for just that response from Vixen. The question was why?

"No reason to talk right now," Vixen said.

Thanks to his newly acquired, not always reliable awareness of Vixen, Graeme realized that she was buying time. Buying time to figure a way out of this that wouldn't cost her life, or this unknown woman's life—and she also had just realized that Hawthorne had an agenda. "I'm still trying to decide how I want to handle this."

"So you aren't refusing me."

The disappointment in Hawthorne's voice was subtle, but it was there. Subtle. But Graeme suspected that Vixen had heard it as clearly as he did.

He was playing her, playing his fucked-up version of truth

or dare, and Graeme didn't need any sort of insight to know what Hawthorne's final dare would be. The knot of fury inside him expanded and Graeme wanted to kill. That was even the idea forming in his mind as he headed towards the door.

He'd thought about killing Hawthorne before. Often. Seemed to be the most expedient way to get away from the man, but something had kept him from it.

And something was going to stop him again, except this something was an outside force and not something of his own doing. Halfway to the door, his legs stopped cooperating. Hell, his entire damn body froze. He couldn't even angle his head to send a glare up at the sky. His vocal cords seemed to be working though and he managed to growl out, "What in the hell is this?"

The response came in words, that familiar, sexless voice whispering inside his mind, *"You're not here for vengeance. You're not here to kill. You're here for her."*

"Exactly. So let me take care of that fuc—"

"Please spare me the obscenities, Graeme. This isn't the way to save her. She still walks a dark road."

"Why do I get the feeling you'll keep my ass frozen here until I change my mind about killing him?"

"Because you're a clever man."

The unseen force freezing him in place faded slowly. First, he could move his hands, then his arms and torso. Finally, his legs. He shot a glare upwards and muttered, "A clever man wouldn't have landed in this mess."

CℜŁƆ

"How did I get into this mess?" Vixen hit the disconnect button and resisted the urge to hurl the sleek iPhone against the far wall.

She knew the answer to that, though. She'd gotten into this mess because she hadn't listened to Graeme. No matter why he'd told her she was better off not getting mixed up with Hawthorne, it had been good advice. Whether it was because he didn't want his woman involved with the drug dealer, whether it had been some weird caveman, chauvinistic urge, some altruistic need to keep her from getting tangled in his rather shady lifestyle, it had been good advice and now Vixen wished she'd steered far and clear of Gerard Hawthorne.

The people she'd killed over the past five years didn't bother her. Save for Graeme. Having his blood on her hands kept her awake at night. Missing him kept her awake. Needing him kept her awake.

For different reasons, killing the mayor's daughter would do the same thing. If she agreed to the hit, Vixen knew she'd see the girl's death play out in her dreams for the rest of her life. Vixen really didn't need anything else disturbing her sleep and she definitely didn't want some innocent kid's blood added to the marks against her.

Even when Hawthorne was giving her the assignment, Vixen had suspected something was up. There was more to it than what he was saying and the short, terse conversation with Hawthorne just now added to that suspicion.

He'd expected her to refuse the job.

He'd wanted her to.

Definitely something weird going on and Vixen was going to find out what. If Hawthorne was using her to further his own agenda, it was nothing new. He'd done it before, he'd do it in the future.

Unless you get away.

Her lip curled as she stalked into the bathroom. She splashed cold water on her face and studied the damage. Her eyes were a little puffy, but not too bad. She was pale, but she was always pale.

"Get away," she muttered, shaking her head. She freed the knot of hair, pulling the sticks that held her bun in place and tossing them on the bathroom counter. She picked up her brush, dragging it through her mass of hair.

"Graeme wanted to get away. Look what he'd been willing to do..." she muttered.

Then froze, her arm falling limp to her side.

Willing to do.

She didn't understand why it came to her, then. She'd thought through this so many times in the past, muttered about it, swore about it, beat her head against the wall and called herself ten different kinds of fool for believing in him.

But instead of thinking about what Graeme had been

willing to do, she found herself wondering just what Hawthorne was willing to do. Thinking about that, thinking about just how far Hawthorne would go, she had to admit, that with Hawthorne, there were no lines he wouldn't cross. Nothing he wouldn't do to get what he wanted. She'd always believed Graeme had lines. She herself had them.

Hawthorne had none. He'd do whatever it took, use whoever he had to use. And lie.

He'd lie without blinking twice and she knew that.

He could have lied about Graeme, and that wasn't news. "The disc. I saw the damn disc," she muttered.

Hawthorne had approached her, told her that he believed Graeme was playing both sides. Hawthorne claimed that Graeme was collecting evidence for the police, planning to sell out the people in Hawthorne's organization so he could eliminate the threat they posed to him, and so he could walk away from this life with a clean name.

She hadn't believed him. But then he showed her the disc.

She'd seen the evidence, heard the evidence. Graeme had mentioned her. There had been two cops and a district attorney at the meeting with him and the disc ran for more than an hour. If she hadn't heard it, she never would have believed Hawthorne.

But she had heard it.

She'd heard it and she'd known that if Graeme was willing to do anything to free himself from Hawthorne, then she needed to be willing to do whatever it took to stay out of jail.

She'd watched it, just that once. Watching it more than that wouldn't have been possible and there really wasn't any point, right? There was no way she could have mistaken Graeme or his voice. No way she could have missed seeing her own face when the cop pulled out a black and white and laid it in front of Graeme, tapped it with his finger and asked, "Who is she?"

Then...

"Who is she?"

"Why do you need to know about her? You're looking at Hawthorne."

"We're looking at everybody. You want the deal, then we get

her name."

"Vixen."

A lengthy pause and Vixen stood there staring at the screen, at the images, searching for something that would prove it to be a fake, or that Graeme had some sort of plan—some reason to explain why he was betraying her. But there was nothing.

"Vixen." There was a smirk on the female cop's face, one she wiped away the second Graeme's eyes flashed her way. "So what's Vixen got to do with Hawthorne? She work for him?"

"In a manner of speaking."

"So what does that mean? Does she fuck him or does she do something else?"

"I really don't see why it matters. She's not your concern."

The cops shared a long look and then glanced at the lawyer. The lawyer leaned forward and caught Graeme's gaze. "I'm afraid she is our concern, Graeme. We don't need somebody stepping into Hawthorne's shoes once we take him down. His whole organization has to go. Now is she part of it?"

Graeme looked away and all the camera revealed was the way the cops and the lawyer watched him, and the back of his averted head. But his voice, that came through loud and clear. "Yes."

There was more. Other pictures placed in front of Graeme and he gave a rundown on the person's name, his place in Hawthorne's organization, but Vixen was blind and deaf to everything else.

Graeme was going to sell her out. How in the hell could he... Shit, less than a month earlier, he'd been talking to her about trying to get out. Get away. She'd laughed. She knew he'd wanted out for a good long time, but Hawthorne wasn't the letting-go kind.

"He isn't going to have a choice," Graeme had told her.

All of a sudden, the confident, certain way he'd said that made a lot more sense to her.

Hawthorne didn't have a choice because he was going to be rotting away in some jail cell while Graeme disappeared and lost himself among the masses. He was a smart man—chances were that his terms for selling Hawthorne out had to do with destroying whatever record he had and some sort of deal for immunity.

If she hadn't watched as he merrily added her name to the list, she could have been amused. Maybe even a little proud and envious. But he'd sold her out.

The abrupt, sudden silence of the room hit her and she jerked out of her daze and found herself staring at the TV's blank screen. The disc was over.

It sort of felt like her life was too. But she wasn't going to think about that, and she wasn't going to watch that hateful thing again, with some stupid, weak hope in her heart that maybe she'd misunderstood, or missed something.

She'd misunderstood, all right.

When Graeme had told her that he loved her all those times, she'd believed him. Part of her even wanted to say it back to him—Vixen thought she probably did love him, but love was a foreign emotion for her and she didn't trust it. Didn't want to trust it.

She'd been wise not to.

She'd thought love meant not doing something that would hurt the one you loved worse than anything. She'd thought love meant protecting the one you loved. She'd believed Graeme would do whatever it took to take care of her.

She'd been horribly, awfully wrong.

Instead of watching the disc again, instead of fighting the urge to puke, scream and cry all at once, she took the disc out and secured it in her bag. It would go into her private safe-deposit box. It was one she'd gotten using a false identification that nobody, not even Graeme, knew about. It would go inside that box and when she looked back later and wondered if she'd made the right choice, she could watch it.

And remind herself she hadn't made the right choice, she'd made the only one.

Chapter Six

Now...

The ID Vixen needed wasn't kept at her penthouse, but inside another safe-deposit box. Getting from one bank to other ended up taking up the entire morning. A good hour of that was because she'd circled aimlessly, making sure Hawthorne's goons hadn't located her.

By the time she knew she wasn't being followed, morning had come and gone. Even the rush of lunch hour quieted. When she walked into the bank, it wasn't busy, but there were enough bodies milling around that she knew she wouldn't stand out as she took care of her business.

She disappeared into the vault and when she emerged less than ten minutes later, in her left pocket, she had the false driver's license declaring her to be one Elizabeth Bary. Elizabeth was married to a nameless, faceless accountant, she shopped at all the right stores and she rarely overindulged.

Elizabeth was also friendly, polite and had a smile for everybody she met.

It was hard now to keep that false smile on her face as she left the bank, and even harder to keep it on her face as she took the L-train back uptown. But she wasn't heading for Hawthorne's place. No, her destination was a few miles away. If she knew Slicer, he was holed up in front of his computers and his gaming console. He'd probably be wearing clothes that were two or three days past clean, he'd have a glazed, dazed look in his eyes and when he saw her, that fogginess would disappear in a rush of terror.

If she was right...he was screwed.

It took another forty-five minutes to get to Slicer's place

and every damn second seemed to last an hour. Part of her wondered why she was bothering. She had her suspicions and even if Slicer confirmed those, what would it change? In the end, nothing. In the end, it wouldn't matter all that much.

Oh, she'd kill Slicer over this.

And Hawthorne.

Along with anybody else who was involved. But it wasn't going to undo what she'd done. She couldn't take it back, and she had a bad feeling she was going to realize she just couldn't live with herself any more.

It would be easier if she just didn't know the truth, but Vixen couldn't take the easy way.

She had to know.

Slicer lived in one of the many derelict housing projects in Chicago's west side. This one had seen better days, but she knew worse hellholes existed. As she climbed the steps, the grimy floor made a sucking sound at her boots and she grimaced. Although it was cool outside, the air in the narrow, confined stairwell was hot and stale, smelling of things she didn't want to classify.

It sent her back. Sent her back to the time in her life when she'd lived in places far worse than this one. Places she didn't want to go back to.

Pushing all of that out of her mind, she continued to climb the steps. Slicer lived on the fourth floor in a corner unit. Thankfully, the inside was far better than the outside. It was no suite at the Ritz, but Slicer was a fanatic about his equipment and part of taking care of it, in Slicer's mind, was making sure the place stayed somewhat clean. She knocked and spoke through the door. Keeping her voice pitched low, she said pleasantly, "If you don't open the door, I'm going to open it for you, Slicer. And I'm already in a bitch of a mood. Don't make it worse."

In less than twenty seconds, she heard the series of locks being undone and when the door opened just an inch, she kept a sweet smile on her face even as she stepped back and lashed out, kicking the door. The kick served as an outlet for all the rage, fury and guilt trapped inside her and when it flew back and smacked into Slicer's scrawny body, she had to grin.

He stumbled back from the door, his beady eyes wide and glassy. "Vixen. What...what are you doing here? Nobody called me, told me you was coming over."

She stalked towards him, her smile fading. "Nobody knows I'm here." She slid a hand into her pocket and plucked out the disc. "I'm here because you and me are going to watch a movie, Slicer."

He gave her a wobbly smile, revealing badly yellowed, crooked teeth. "I ain't got no time for watching movies, Vixen. Busy, busy."

"Oh, you'll make time for this, Slicer."

He had a good six inches on her. Even as scrawny as he was, he had a good forty pounds on her too. Yet he looked at her with the same fear a rabbit would give a hawk. He'd always been nervy around her, but this was extreme. His gaze locked on the disc in her hand and he reached up, swiped the back of his hand over his mouth.

"What kind of movie we watching, Vixen?"

"You'll see." She brushed past him, walking past the very nice entertainment center he had set up in his narrow living room and into the room that served as bedroom and workroom. His bed was a Murphy, tucked up out of the way. The consoles, monitor and other techy gadgets she couldn't name took up more room than the bed. She had no idea where he kept his clothes because the door of the miniscule closet had been taken off and more of his equipment was neatly shelved within.

She took the one chair in front of the main computer and slid the disc out of the envelope. When she went to slide it into the disc drive, he made as if to grab her. Fear for his precious tools gave him a moment of bravery, but when she looked his way, he pulled back.

"I don't like people messing with my stuff," he mumbled.

"Don't worry, Slicer. I won't hurt the equipment." She settled back in the seat as the disc started to play. From the corner of her eye, she glanced at him and added, "Yet."

He stared at the monitor, a look of sick fascination on his face and she suspected he hadn't heard a word she said. "You know what this movie is about, Slicer? Have you seen it before?"

His muddy brown eyes glanced at her, then away. He licked his lips, rubbed the palms of his hands up and down his pants. "Why we watching this, Vixen?"

Gently, she reminded him, "You didn't answer my question.

Have you seen this?"

He swallowed. Gave a jerky nod.

"When?"

He shrugged. "Few years ago."

Vixen nodded. Closed her eyes and took a deep breath. When she opened them, she focused on the monitor instead of Slicer. Her heart ripped a little as she watched Graeme slide into the booth across from the cops and the lawyer. "Are they really cops? He really a lawyer?"

Slicer didn't answer immediately. She looked at him and he looked like he just might start sobbing at any moment. "Yeah. They are. Graeme was feeding them shit about Hawthorne, helping them build a case against him. Hawthorne found out and he was pissed. Knew he had to get rid of Graeme but—" His words ended abruptly.

Vixen stroked a hand down her leg and Slicer's gaze focused on her hand, watched as she slid her fingers inside her boot and drew the thin stiletto from the custom-made sheath. "But what?"

He spoke so fast, his words seemed to trip over each other. "He knew he had to be careful about how he did Graeme. Cuz of you. If he sent one of his boys after Graeme, you'd know it was his work."

"Why not just kill me?"

He blushed. Beet red. Looked down at his feet, shook his head back and forth. "Well, he...uh, Vixen, I think..."

Rolling her eyes, Vixen said, "He wants to get in my pants for some weird reason. That's not news. I'm not that good a piece of ass, Slicer."

"It's because you aren't scared of him," Slicer whispered. "Because you won't do him even though you know he wants it. People do whatever he wants. But you don't."

Vixen nodded. "Okay." She looked back at the disc, watched as the cop laid her picture flat on the table. "What am I looking at, Slicer? Did Graeme sell me out?"

It was a low, almost soundless whisper. But to her, it rang through the room like a crack of thunder.

"No. He wouldn't have sold you out, Vixen. Not ever."

She closed her eyes and fought the scream inside. She couldn't let it out. Not now. Later. When she could scream and not worry if she choked on it. She couldn't choke on it, though, not until she killed Hawthorne.

Slowly, she rose from the chair. She didn't bother reaching for the disc. She didn't need it. "Is it your work?"

For some reason, Slicer no longer looked so terrified as he stood in front of her. He looked sort of resigned.

"Yeah. It's mine." He blew out a ragged breath and shoved a hand through his coarse, overlong black hair. "I'm sorry, Vixen."

She gave him a humorless smile. "You're sorry." Lowering her head, she studied the toes of her boots. She twirled the stiletto she held, watched as it caught the light and reflected it back at her. "Does being sorry mean I shouldn't kill you?"

Slicer laughed, but there was no amusement in the sound. "I know you better than that, Vixen. Always figured I was a dead man if you ever found out...but hell, I'd rather you kill me than Hawthorne." A look slid across his face and he shook his head. "Better you than him."

"Maybe the better thing to do would be let him know you told me."

Slicer blanched and a soft moan escaped him. But he didn't even seem to realize he'd made a sound. "Shit, Vixen. Please...please don't."

People had pled with her before. It never made a difference. Why on earth it did now, she wasn't sure. Slicer wasn't responsible for what she'd done, but he'd facilitated things. He'd made it that much easier for Hawthorne to use her. The bastard.

Staring at him, though, she realized he was just too pitiful. Killing him wasn't going to change what she'd done, wasn't going to bring Graeme any justice, it wouldn't ease her guilt...it was her own gullibility, or her own inability to trust that had led to this.

That—and Hawthorne. Hawthorne was going to die. There was no doubt about that. She closed the distance between them, watched as Slicer tracked her with his eyes until she stood just inches away and then he squeezed his eyes closed as though he just couldn't watch. She stood there, close enough that she could smell the buffalo wings he'd eaten recently, close enough that she could see the mad beat of his pulse throbbing in his neck. She stood there until he popped open first one eye, then the other.

Their gazes locked and she swung out. Vixen was strong, but she was short, slender and she didn't have the power in her body that most people in her line of work could claim. She made up for it with skill and just pure meanness. She struck at his throat and watched as he went down, clutching at his scrawny neck while his face turned a queer shade of reddish purple. Seconds ticked away and eventually, he managed to drag in a deep breath. Tears leaked out of his eyes but he made no move to wipe them away. He didn't even try to get to his feet.

Blowing out a ragged breath, Vixen said, "Get off the floor, Slicer." Weary, she turned away and went to stare out his window. Through the iron bars he'd had placed to help protect his gear, she could see down on the street. It was dirty, dismal and gray, just like the past she'd managed to escape eight years earlier. She spent too much time in places like this. Graeme had helped her get away from it, and if she hadn't let Hawthorne draw her into it, she could have stayed away.

She could have lived some sort of normal life with Graeme. Maybe she could have even figured out if she loved him or not.

Glancing back over her shoulder, she saw that Slicer was still on the floor, rubbing at his throat and eying her warily. "Get up. If I were you, I'd grab whatever you have to have and get the hell out of town."

He blinked. "Out of town?"

"Yeah. Out of town. I'm going to pay Hawthorne a visit, but being the slimy bastard he is, he's going to know something's up. Hell, he's probably got people watching your place. You really don't want him knowing that I talked with you, right?"

Slicer shook his head so hard it was a miracle his brain didn't start rattling. He licked his lips and slowly climbed to his feet. "Why you letting me go, Vixen?"

"Because I'm too damn tired to mess with you. And because if I'd trusted Graeme, even a little, this wouldn't have happened."

"What are you going to do?"

She gave him a hard smile. "I'm going to pay Hawthorne a visit," she repeated. She didn't bother mentioning that she had no intention of letting Hawthorne see another sunrise. Or that she really didn't care if she ever saw one either. Turning her back on him, she headed for the door, determined to get away before the storm of memories brewing inside her broke.

⊂Ӡ℘⊃

When the door opened, Graeme was standing in a recessed doorway. His view of Vixen was unobstructed but the shadows kept her from seeing him. Although going by the look on her face, unless he stood right in front of her and grabbed her, she wouldn't even notice him.

She knew the truth now.

He'd heard the entire conversation as though he'd been standing next to her while Slicer spilled his guts. Hell, Graeme wished he *had* been standing next to her, close enough to hold her, close enough to try and ease the pain inside her. Graeme could feel the echo of her misery and her guilt. In some distant part of his mind, he wondered if he shouldn't be reveling in the pain he felt coming from her. He'd stood in the hallway outside Slicer's place but it was like he'd been standing beside her, like she'd whispered every emotion and thought that passed through her as she watched the disc and figured out that she'd been used. That she'd been used to kill her lover and it was a lie that had pushed her to it.

But all he felt was his own misery at her pain. The need to soothe, stroke and kiss away all the doubts and shadows and guilt. The pain.

Any vindication he might have felt was lost in the face of what he felt coming from her as she left Slicer's apartment.

"Why you letting me go, Vixen?"

"Because I'm too damn tired to mess with you. And because if I'd trusted Graeme, even a little, this wouldn't have happened."

"What are you going to do?"

"I'm going to pay Hawthorne a visit."

It was the unspoken words after that had a cold chill racing through Graeme. A chill that had nothing to do with the frigid air of early spring, and everything to do with what Vixen was planning on doing.

He won't see another sunrise.

And I don't really give a damn if I do either.

Even now, as the echo of her footsteps died away, he was still shaken by what he'd heard echo from within her mind.

Graeme swallowed through a throat gone tight with fear and emotion and then pushed off the wall to follow her. The door to Slicer's apartment cracked open as he passed by and he stopped in his tracks, sent Slicer a narrow look. No, he couldn't feel any sort of vindication over Vixen's pain, but he could sure as hell feel violent inclinations towards the sniveling, pathetic coward who had helped Hawthorne.

"Get out of town," he said, his voice low and rough. "Before I kill you. Hawthorne won't have the chance."

Slicer's eyes went wide. "Who the fuck are you?"

"The man who'll sign your death warrant if you aren't gone in an hour. And don't make any phone calls, Slicer. I'll know."

He aimed a glance at the sky, wondered if his voyeuristic buddy was listening in, but since he'd spoken his piece without freezing up, he guessed not. Giving Slicer one more look, he hit the stairs.

CRSO

Vixen was an organized soul.

She'd come to hate loose ends over the past few years, and not just because loose ends could end up putting somebody like her in jail. They just bothered her. On the long, cold walk back to her apartment, she thought about all the loose ends she needed to tie up and wondered which ones were vital and which ones didn't really matter all that much.

The conclusion she came to was that not much of anything in her life mattered—at least not without Graeme. But there was one vital loose end. And if she failed with Hawthorne, somebody else would pay the price.

The mayor's daughter.

It bothered her that some silly debutante might die on one of Hawthorne's whims. Life shouldn't be cut short because somebody else determined just that—like Graeme.

She couldn't quite understand why it bothered her so much, but it did. Enough that she knew she'd have to do something to keep it from happening. Or at least try.

With that thought in mind, she reached for her phone. In some distant part of her mind, she wondered about who she had become. Her gut was clenched with guilt, her hands shook so badly she almost dropped the phone and she had to wonder what had happened to the blasé, unemotional woman she'd seen in the mirror a day or two earlier.

But the answer came even before the question formed.

Graeme.

Three years after she'd killed him, he'd finally managed to get through to her. It was the only thing that made sense as she made an anonymous phone call to the mayor. She didn't bother disguising her voice as she waited for him to answer the one personal phone he used for "unofficial" business. She knew the number from previous dealings with him and expected he'd know who it was without asking. Hopefully, for his daughter's sake, he'd also know she wasn't the type to bullshit.

"Hawthorne's gunning for your daughter. You pissed him off. You probably need to get her out of town for a while." That was all she said before she disconnected, and when he called back, she ignored him. She left the rundown streets of the West Side for her relatively safe apartment on the North Side. Relatively safe. Sooner or later, one of Hawthorne's goons would track the place down, but she planned on vacating the premises by the end of the day.

Once she dealt with Hawthorne.

That was her objective now.

Dealing with him. Shit, that seemed so…simple. So matter-of-fact. Like all the other men and women she'd dealt with, following the orders Hawthorne had given her. As long as it didn't push her past her own lines, she hadn't cared. She'd dealt with them all.

It had been business. Even to her, that sounded cold, but she couldn't think about that now. Couldn't think about what she'd become. Not now.

Not yet.

After Hawthorne.

She wasn't going to *deal* with him. This wasn't business. It was personal.

"You're not going to deal with him," she muttered as she let herself into the apartment. Over her shoulder, she shot a glance at her new neighbor's door. Her new neighbor with eyes that had managed to send her back three years.

Scowling, she slammed the door shut and threw the locks. She didn't need to think about those blue eyes. If she did, she'd think about Graeme and right now, she couldn't think about anything but what she needed to do.

Hawthorne. He was what she had to think about.

Deal with him. She snorted as she dug into the sparse closet, pulling out the clothes she wore when she had an assignment. "Drop the doublespeak, Vix," she muttered, stripping down to her skin and grabbing the black clothes. She never did a job without showering before or after. She wasn't going to change that now.

"You're not on an assignment. You're going to kill him. You're not going to deal with him. You're going to kill him." She'd really prefer slow and painful, but she doubted she'd have the option. Getting him alone, away from his goons, wasn't going to happen. So she'd go for quick. Get it over with so he was dead before anybody had a chance to help him.

And then... She cut that thought off and stepped into the shower, turning the water up as hot as it would go. The sting of it on her flesh was almost distracting enough to keep her mind from wandering down that dreaded path. She already had an idea of *"and then"* forming anyway, something that went against everything she'd ever thought about herself.

That's no answer.

The voice all but echoed in the small room and she jumped, reached out and slammed the shower door open.

The bathroom was empty.

Nobody was there.

But...hell. She'd heard somebody, right?

Shaking her head, she said, "You've finally gone and lost it, Vix." She shut the door and reached for the shampoo, scrubbing her scalp ruthlessly. She treated her body to the same treatment, scouring it with a mesh body sponge until it felt like she'd removed the first layer of skin.

Skin flushed red and sensitive, she climbed out of the shower. She stood naked in front of the mirror as she dragged a comb through her wet hair and used a towel to sop up most of the water. Without bothering to dry off the rest of the way, she quickly braided her hair to hang down her back in a thick cable.

Once she started getting dressed, she focused on her strategy. She'd let him think she was there to talk business. He'd have Carlos with him, but she rarely talked when that mean bastard was around, so Hawthorne wouldn't blink twice if she waited until Carlos left.

That dreaded *and-then* question tried to make another appearance. She managed to hold it off as she got her bag, a small black duffel that held a clean pair of clothes, a garbage bag and a small toiletry kit. Ideally, she tried to get someplace safe and anonymous when she cleaned up, but from time to time, it didn't happen. Even though she really didn't care if she walked away from this alive, she stuck with what she knew.

The shower. Securing her hair in a braid. The black clothes. Her bag. There was another piece of luggage, albeit an odd one—it was a velvet case, a larger version of the kind many women use to store jewelry.

Vixen's velvet held weapons. Long skinny stilettos, a black K-bar with a wicked curve, a matched pair of throwing knives, a garrote. If she had the choice, she'd use the garrote on Hawthorne, stand close to him as she choked the life out of him. But she was prepared to use any of the weapons—or the Browning that lay on the bed waiting for her.

She secured the weapons on her body with a speed and ease born of practice. Nobody looking at her would realize she was armed to the teeth. Well, Hawthorne might. A cold smile curled her lips.

Yeah, she hoped that all he needed was to take one look at her and he'd know she was on the hunt. One look, and know that he was her chosen target—not one assigned, but one she chose and one she'd pursue until one of them died. She wanted him to know it, and shudder with fear before she snuffed out his life.

What is that going to solve?

She stilled as a voice seemed to echo around her yet again. But there was nobody there. *Nobody*—and she damn well knew it wasn't self-doubts or recriminations.

"Insanity—that's what it is, babe," she muttered under her breath. Insane made a lot more sense than anything else.

Keeping that in mind, she jammed her feet into a pair of lace-up boots with thick, sturdy soles. Not quite as bulky as military-issue combat boots, but styled along similar lines, the boots had excellent traction and she could walk in them for hours if she had to. She tied them, putting a lot more care and thought into the task than it required, but if she was thinking about her damn feet, she wasn't going to think about the *and-then* or what she was pondering.

You won't do it, Vixen. You couldn't.

"Shit!" Now this was fucked up. She'd heard...something. Somebody. Spinning around, she searched the room and then stormed out, searching the apartment. It was empty, just as she'd expected. Nobody was there.

Besides, the voice she thought she'd heard, it couldn't be.

"You really are going crazy," she whispered,

Either that, or Graeme had waited three years to start haunting her.

CR80

Haunting you? Well, you're not too far off, baby, Graeme thought as he paced his apartment.

He wasn't haunting her—exactly. You had to be dead to haunt somebody, and he wasn't really dead. Although he wasn't exactly himself either. He didn't know what in the hell he was, except worried and determined to stop Vixen from what she was planning. Figuring out how was going to be the tricky part.

She wasn't wasting time either, which meant he couldn't waste it—shit.

Time's up.

He even heard a tinny little click, as though some unseen clock had just wound down on him. Like some fricking Hollywood special effect had intruded on his brain, he was staring through tunnel vision down at the street outside the apartment building as a car pulled up to the curb. He recognized the ugly face of the first man out of the vehicle and every protective instinct inside him started to scream.

Carlos.

That cruel, cunning SOB had been the brute strength to Graeme's more persuasive, if sometimes physical methods. Graeme used physical force when needed and Carlos used it because he wanted to. Because he liked it. He was, in the very basic sense of the phrase, a leg-breaker.

Graeme didn't remember leaving his cramped, confining apartment or crossing the hall to Vixen's. He didn't remember kicking the door down or stalking inside the apartment. What he remembered was finding her standing by the bed, a black duffel in one hand. In the other, she held a gun, ready and trained on the dead center of his chest. He strode forward, ignoring the gun. He figured whatever power had put him back on this earth would hopefully keep him from getting his chest plugged with lead. Wrapping his fingers around her upper arm, he said, "Come on."

She jerked, hard. Vixen was strong, but she was still a good six inches shorter than he was, probably a good sixty pounds lighter. He dragged her to the window and when she went to punch him, he deflected it, moved with her momentum and ended up circling her around so that her face was pressed to the glass. "You see that car?" he whispered against her ear. "You know who drives that car. You know why he's here."

Vixen went stiff. "Who the fuck are you?"

"Somebody who wants to save that pretty neck of yours," he replied and this time, when he tugged on her arm, she followed, still holding her gun and the duffel.

Not happily, though. If it had been anybody other than Carlos sent after her, she wouldn't have merrily followed along behind him, he knew it. And he didn't expect her acquiescence to last too long. Right now, he suspected she came because she wanted an answer and she figured following him was the best way to get it.

Graeme could give her answers, but they weren't any that she'd believe.

None of that mattered though, not right now. What mattered was that she came willingly enough as he led her out of the apartment and down the hallway towards the back stairwell. Somewhere between her apartment and the stairwell, she managed to put the gun away, although a quick glance over his shoulder didn't reveal where she could have put the weapon.

Her clothes were formfitting, black as midnight against her pale skin.

Hearing footsteps on the stairwell, he urged her against the wall, a little surprised when she let him. The man that cleared the landing was Rico, Carlos's cousin, and yet another knuckle-dragger. He glanced at Graeme with disinterested eyes and went to brush past him. When he saw Vixen, he stilled and gave her a fake smile.

Before he managed to say anything, Graeme slid up behind him and wrapped his forearm around the man's neck, jerked him off his feet. Wasn't as easy as he remembered, lacking the six inches he was used to from his previous life, but he managed and in a matter of seconds, Rico sagged limp in Graeme's grip. Graeme let go, watching as Rico hit the concrete floor of the stairwell. He reached inside Rico's jacket, pulled out the semi-automatic and used it to club Rico across the temple. Using a chokehold could put somebody out easily enough, but it never lasted. A quick knock to the head did a much better job. He tucked the gun into his waistband at the small of his back and looked up to find Vixen staring at him almost like she'd seen a ghost.

He wished he could say something to her. Tell her who he was. Reach for her and pull her up against him. Instead, he turned on his heel and continued down the stairs. Without looking, without even hearing her quiet footsteps, he knew she was following him.

Following him and watching with a suspicious, almost fearful gaze.

Everything, every person has a style. A rhythm that's unique to that creation. Music, dancing, singing, talking. Fighting. There could be two very similar styles, but something, no matter how small, sets one apart from the other. If Vixen wasn't as intimately acquainted with the style and methods of fighting, she probably wouldn't have noticed. If she wasn't intimately acquainted with violence, she might not feel like her heart was about to explode out of her chest.

But she knew the art of fighting, both defensive and offensive. She knew violence—and my, what a lovely thing to profess a knowledge of.

And she knew that when this as-yet-unknown man had slid behind Rico, snaking an arm around his neck and using a sleeper hold with minimal effort, it was like she'd seen it before. Exactly. The way he dropped Rico and then pulled Rico's gun, clubbing him to make sure his victim stayed out. The blank, dispassionate look in his eyes throughout the entire thing.

It was worse, or maybe better, that her heart couldn't tell

the difference when he lifted his head and focused that surreal, neon blue gaze on her face. When he looked away, she managed to suck in a desperate gulp of air. In the back of her mind, she had some half-formed notion of just turning her back on him, walking—no, scratch that—running away. Carlos might be looking for her, but she could evade him and if not evade, she could kill him.

But instead of doing that, as her would-be savior headed down the stairs at a fast clip, she fell in step behind him. Watched the way he moved, the way he slowed at the bottom of the stairs to glance through the narrow windowpane before moving onto the next flight. Watched the way he glanced back at her every few minutes, and once or twice, there was a softening to his features.

It was all wrong, seeing that smile on his face.

Seeing it warm those blue eyes.

Because it wasn't his smile.

It was...

"You're losing it," she whispered. She dug her nails into her palms, scoring her flesh and focusing on that small pain in hope of blocking out everything else. But no small pain was going to work. Hell, she could fall down and snap her leg in two and she'd still be staring at this guy, trying to see somebody who'd been dead for three years. Trying to see Graeme, even though there was no similarity, other than their eyes.

And the way he moved.

The way he handled himself as he grabbed Rico and dealt with him before Rico even knew what had hit him.

The way he glanced at her and smiled without even realizing it. Smiled like he had to, just because he was happy to see her. Looked at her as though he had to, just because he needed to see her.

Gee, two minutes with the guy and you're waxing poetic. You really have gone crazy, she told herself as they hit the street through a side exit, coming out into an alley. They took the back way so they could avoid the car parked in front of the apartment building, hopefully evading detection. A shiver ran down her spine as he waited for her to draw even with him. He kept his body placed just so, like he wanted to be between her and any threat. Men, before they realized how big a mistake it was, tended to stand too close to her, hovering in a way that drove her nuts. This guy was definitely standing way too much inside her personal space, but she didn't have the gut-deep instinct to step away, or an equally basic instinct to drive her elbow into his ribs to get him to back off a little.

That rhythm thing. Every creation has a rhythm.

When he reached out and took her duffel bag away and hefted it over his shoulder, there was something eerily familiar about that thoughtful gesture Moving down the crowded sidewalk along North Lake Shore Drive, she realized she'd found a rhythm that she'd thought was long gone. The rhythm she had had with Graeme.

Maybe you're not going crazy. Maybe you just need to get laid.

That thought popped up out of the back of her mind with the force of a kid throwing a rock through a window and it was about as unsettling. Unsettling enough that when he reached up to lay his hand on the small of her back as they wound through the tightly packed mess of bodies standing at the intersection, she jerked away.

Putting a few feet between them didn't help though.

A self-deprecating smirk curled his lips but he said nothing. As a matter of fact, he hadn't said much of anything since busting her door down, effectively deflecting her attack before showing her that she had unwanted company on its way to her door. Not a thing.

Apparently, if she wanted answers, she was going to have to ask some questions first.

"How do you know Carlos?"

He glanced behind them, back towards the alley and then at her. "I think we need to get a little farther away before we take time to chat."

Vixen narrowed her eyes. "No. I think now is a good time."

"You won't in about fifteen seconds." His voice was grim and this time when he reached for her, he didn't let her evade him. The nose of a car edged around the corner as he shoved her into the crowd of bodies. Just before he moved to block her from view, she saw Carlos' face, brows set low and scowling as he studied the street. Looking for her.

She knew Carlos would come chasing after her. But exactly when—*to the second*? Okay, a little too creepy.

But she didn't say or do anything to draw attention as her

nameless Samaritan urged her across the street as the light changed color. He moved quickly, herding her to the front of the crowd. Once across, the mass of bodies parted, some of the tourists continuing on north towards Navy Pier, the rest heading east or west. Instead of going north with the larger crowd, they headed east, once more losing themselves among the crowd. A quick glance over her shoulder revealed Carlos and his men slowly easing forward, heading north. Following the larger group.

They ended up on the Blue Line. He sat down, slouched in the seat with her duffel bag in his lap. Across from him, she settled on a vacant seat and studied him warily. All around them were bodies, most of them heading home after work, but some looking like they were either out for an evening or on their way to their jobs. Nobody was really paying any attention to them, but it probably wasn't the ideal time for that chat, either.

"Where are we going?"

He quirked a brow at her. "Easy as that? Don't you want to know who I am or anything?"

"Yes. Most especially the 'or anything' but now doesn't seem the time." Glancing around the car, she slid him a look and asked, "Do you have a place in mind or not?"

Not, was the answer that formed on his tongue. But what came out of his mouth was yes.

Graeme resisted the urge to scowl, knowing it wasn't going to do any good to get irritated. He didn't understand how he never exactly knew what he was doing until some unseen angel or whatever it was dropped the information into his head. Besides, it seemed a better alternative to have some place to go as opposed to riding around town until he figured out some other plan of action.

"Yeah, I have a place in mind." He leaned back in his seat, or at least as far as it would allow him to and hooked one ankle over his knee. From the corner of his eye, he watched her face and waited for some sort of response. But he didn't get one.

All she did was sigh and settle a little more comfortably into the seat.

Chapter Seven

When her phone started to ring, she ignored it.

It was the funeral dirge she'd programmed to play when Hawthorne called and considering she'd just managed to evade his men, she really didn't want to talk to him.

"You probably should pitch the phone."

She glanced at the man walking beside her. "Why?"

"How do you think he figured out where you were?"

She shrugged. "Either through the phone or because I didn't manage to lose his men as effectively as I used to." She really wanted to know who in the hell this guy was. More, she really wanted to know why she was following him without knowing where in the hell they were going or why it didn't matter all that much to her.

Because it didn't. Even though some rational part of her was telling her she needed to cut loose, and quick, she didn't do it. She didn't want to. She tugged the phone off her belt clip and studied it for a minute. Then she dropped it on the ground and brought up her heel, smashing it down on the phone three times in quick succession. Last thing she wanted was for some kid to find the thing. If Hawthorne was tracking her through the phone, she didn't want him sending Carlos in for her and having that thug find a couple of teenagers.

She scooped up pieces of shattered black plastic and electronic guts and tossed them into the trash can. Slipping her hands back into her pockets, she made herself meet the man's blue eyes. "Can you give me a name to call you?"

He hesitated and then responded, "Just call me Mac."

"Mac." She repeated it slowly and then asked, "And is that your real name?"

His only answer was a faint smile before he resumed his slow, unhurried walk, her duffel bag tossed over his shoulder. They were in a mostly residential area. A mile back, they'd climbed off the Blue Line and she wasn't entirely sure where they were. She'd spent the past eight years in Chicago but most of the time she was either uptown or out in the West Side. Hawthorne really didn't have much use for the quiet, family-type neighborhoods and that's exactly what this was.

She could hear kids laughing.

Music playing too loud.

A mother calling out for her son, her voice rising until he finally appeared on the third call. The slam of a car door and then a baby crying.

Normal life.

That's where she was. In suburbia, surrounded by something unfamiliar and alien.

"Taking me home to meet your folks?" she asked sardonically. "Kind of early for that, isn't it?"

Another enigmatic glance. "Kind of late for that. My mother died having me. Don't really remember my father."

He came to a halt in front of a small brick house with a neatly manicured lawn. Dipping his hands into his pockets, he studied the windows, the play of light behind the curtains. "We're here."

"I figured. So are we going inside or are we just here to stand on the sidewalk?"

"Inside." He sighed, but didn't sound happy about it. He ran a long-fingered hand through shaggy, gold-streaked hair and Vixen got distracted as she thought about doing the same thing. When he spoke, it took a minute to focus on the words instead of her very-much-out-of-character urge to touch him. He shifted, rolled his neck a little, kind of like a man getting ready to step into a boxing ring.

He looked awful damn tense.

But it didn't stop him from heading up the sidewalk and even the nerves in her belly couldn't keep her from falling in step beside him once more.

CR&O

When Graeme told Vixen he had a place in mind, he hadn't realized it was this place. He felt like a participant in some unknown script with his lines being dropped into his head on a sporadic basis and he really wished he could backtrack some and get the hell away from this house.

He knew where he was.

Vixen didn't.

He hadn't ever brought her here.

He hadn't ever mentioned Gus to her.

He hadn't ever mentioned that once upon a time somebody had cared enough about him to try and guide him away from the life he'd chosen, much as Graeme had tried to convince Vixen to keep out of Hawthorne's business.

He hadn't lied to her when he said he didn't remember his parents. He didn't.

But he remembered Gus Cramer.

He'd been fifteen when he ended up with Gus. Then, Gus's wife Charli had still been alive and the two of them were the closest thing to normal that Graeme had seen in his short, rough live. In and out of a series of foster homes, group homes and even two stints in different detention centers, coming into the house of the retired accountant and his wife had been a major shock to Graeme.

There were rules, which he hated.

Curfews, which he hated.

Regular, sit-down meals where he either had to sit with them...or he didn't eat. Another thing he hated.

But he put up with the rules because his case worker had told him that if he violated his parole, he was going to serve out the rest of his sentence. The original sentence for assault, battery, theft and possession had been for ten years, but he'd been released on parole after a year. Come hell or high water, he'd been determined to play it cool for a while. At least until he was eighteen and then the system wouldn't care so much and he could disappear.

After a couple of months with the Cramer's, though, he got used to halfway regular meals. Clean clothes. Somebody that gave a damn if he was around or not. Then Charli got sick.

The first time he'd ever really let himself maybe care about people and then he ended up losing one of them way too soon.

She got sick—Charli never took the time to go to the doctor when she woke up one morning with a sky-high fever. She just figured it was the flu and it would clear up on its own. It might have.

But then pneumonia settled in and she ended up in the hospital where she slipped into a coma. A week later, she was dead.

Graeme went from recovering juvenile delinquent to hardcore delinquent, uncaring that he was adding to Gus's grief, uncaring of the hell he caused. He ended up running away from Gus Cramer's house six months after Charli died. He'd had fifteen months of something resembling normalcy and he ran from it. Even as he ran, he'd wanted it back.

When he made the decision to get out, made the decision that he was done, the one person he'd known he could trust was Gus. Approaching the old man, though, had taken a lot more courage than anything else in Graeme's life. He didn't have to worry that something had changed in the past three years, that maybe the information that Gus was keeping safe for him wasn't here, or that Gus had died, or moved.

If Gus wasn't here, if the evidence Graeme had collected so painstakingly over the years wouldn't have been there, Graeme wouldn't have been lead here. He mounted the steps, remembered how he'd sat on the porch, smoking just to piss Gus off and watching while the old man painstakingly built a porch swing for Charli. It was still there, and it gleamed with a fresh coat of paint. Charli had only gotten to enjoy it for a while before she died so suddenly.

After knocking, he met Vixen's curious gaze.

"Who lives here?"

He couldn't tell her the truth. Because in a few minutes he was going to have bluster his way through convincing Gus that he needed the information Gus had hidden somewhere inside this house.

Only Graeme knew about it.

And Gus wasn't going to recognize the face Graeme was wearing now.

So instead of telling the truth, instead of lying, he simply replied, "Somebody that has information that might help you."

Vixen snorted. "Somebody living here can help me?"

He touched her. There was no way he could keep from

doing it any more. Reaching out, he trailed a finger down the smooth curve of her cheek, brushing a loose strand of hair back behind her ear. Her long, silken hair was still secured in a braid hanging down her back, but a few strands had worked free. "Does it matter where the help comes from?"

She sneered. "You're implying that I need help."

"Don't you?"

Whatever her response might have been was cut short as the door opened. Gus stood there, looking a little older, a little more frail. His big, barrel chest was still covered by the red flannel shirts he favored and he wore a pair of blue jeans that Charli would have long since thrown away. He squinted at Graeme and then at Vixen before focusing on Graeme again.

"Can I help you?"

"I'm here about Graeme McIntyre." McIntyre wasn't a name he'd claimed as his own since he was eighteen. He'd reinvented himself and Graeme McIntyre didn't even exist any more.

Vixen had too much self-control to show much reaction. He could sense her surprise, but no sign showed on her face.

Gus was easier to read. A shutter fell across his features, his eyes went distant and he shook his head. "I can't help you. Haven't seen him since he was a boy."

He went to shut the door and Graeme caught the door with his hand. "You saw him three and half years ago, at the pub where you and Charli liked to eat every Thursday."

Gus's faded blue eyes narrowed. "Son, you must be mistaken."

Hell, old man. He angled his chin towards the living room. "A couple months after Graeme moved in with you, he spilled a Big Red on the carpet. It was a new carpet and you came home to find him on his hands and knees scrubbing the stain out."

Gus blinked. He stopped trying to shut the door and instead leaned against the doorjamb, looking a little suspicious, a lot curious. "How do you know that?"

"The same way I know that Graeme gave you some information to keep safe."

Gus snorted. "Fat lot of good it did anybody. He went and got himself killed." His voice roughened and he heaved out a sigh. "I didn't even know about it until a month later." Passing a hand over his face, he looked at the floor for a minute and then lifted his head and met Graeme's gaze.

The grief Graeme saw there hit him like a sledgehammer.

"You know, I haven't thought about that stupid Big Red stain in years. Moved the furniture around a while back and it's covered by the couch now. Damn kid. You should have seen the look on his face. It was like he thought I'd toss him out on his ass over a stupid drink."

Graeme had half-expected just that, and when it hadn't happened, he'd been a little stunned. Almost as stunned as he was now as he recognized Gus's grief. He'd been missed, and not just by Vixen. He opened his mouth, uncertain of what he was going to say. *I'm sorry. For a lot of things. I missed you too.* But in the end, he didn't say any of that. He just glanced at Vixen and then back at Gus. "I'm here about the stuff Graeme left with you."

Gus scratched his chin and said, "Well, I don't see why you think I still have it."

Just barely, he suppressed a laugh. "Graeme told you it was important. You wouldn't have gotten rid of it." And even if it wasn't important, Graeme knew how the old man was. When it came to paperwork, Gus Cramer never got rid of anything.

Off to the side, Vixen continued to stand in silence, but he could see the curious, measuring look in her eyes. Graeme hunched his shoulders, more than a little uncomfortable. The two of them didn't realize it but he was getting ready to introduce the woman he loved to the only father he'd really ever known. "I need that information...Mr. Cramer." He glanced at Vixen and then back at Gus. "She needs it. Graeme was caught in a dangerous situation. That information was his way out. Now it's her only way out."

"Well, hell."

Gus stepped aside and let them brush past him, closing the door behind them. The hallway was a long expanse of polished hardwood. Close to the door was a narrow bench and he left Vixen's bag there before trailing after Gus into the living room.

Very little had changed. The couch was the same, just placed in a different spot—right over the Big Red stain. The carpet. The walls. The pictures. There was a picture of Graeme, one of a select few. In it, he was standing by the lake, staring at the fish in his hand with a surprised, vaguely disgusted look on his face. He looked younger than he could remember looking, but even at sixteen, he had been jaded.

Standing next to him in the picture was Charli, smiling, trying not to laugh at the look on his face. Three weeks after that was when she had gotten sick.

He saw the moment Vixen caught sight of the picture and he watched as her eyes went wide, her lower lip trembled just a little. Almost as though she was caught in a daze, she walked to the mantle and reached for the picture, staring at it. Her fingers shook as she touched his image.

Graeme... For a minute, Vixen couldn't do anything but stare at his face and wonder. It was Graeme, she had no doubt of that, but it was a Graeme a lot of people wouldn't have recognized. He looked younger. Happier. Less jaded. She shot the older man a look, searching for some sort of similarity. Graeme had always told her that his parents were dead, but this guy had a picture of him as a kid?

"Are you Graeme's father?"

He gave her a faint smile. "Sort of. I guess I was the closest thing he had. He was a foster child, came to live with me and my wife when he was fifteen. He was with me for about two years. Charli got sick and after she died, things got pretty rough around here. Graeme, eh, I guess on my own, I wasn't enough for him."

His voice cracked on the end and Vixen's heart broke a little. But not for him. Whoever he was. For Graeme. "You loved him."

"Yes." He gave her a tired smile and made his way to a big, cushy chair nestled up close besides the blazing fire. "Yes, ma'am, I did. He wasn't an easy boy to love, but me and Charli...that's my wife. Me and Charli, we loved him. I don't know how much good it did him."

He settled back in the chair and reached for a thick, simple white mug on a nearby table. Beside it was a book and a plate that held a half-eaten sandwich. "We're interrupting your dinner, Mr.... I'm sorry, I don't remember your name." She glanced at Mac and then back at the older man, her mind going blank.

"Just call me Gus. And no, you're not interrupting my dinner. That sandwich has been sitting there a good hour." He shrugged, disinterested. "Eating alone doesn't do much for my appetite. I don't believe I caught a name. For either of you."

"Vixen. This is Mac."

"Vixen..." Gus's eyes narrowed on her face. "You're Graeme's lady."

She blinked and fell back a step, caught off-guard. "How..." Then she snapped her mouth closed. No point in asking how he knew about her. Graeme had told him. And apparently told him enough that Gus knew they'd been together. Shame flooded her belly and she wondered what the man would do, say, if she told him the truth. That she'd killed his son. Foster son, the cynical bitch in her clarified. But the bitch's clarification didn't matter. Gus had loved Graeme, mourned him. She'd killed him.

"Graeme told you about me?" she asked, her voice just a little husky, but steady, thank God, not revealing any of the turmoil raging inside her.

Gus shrugged. "Not a great deal. But a bit. I talked to the officer investigating his death, but to be honest, I don't think they expended a lot of effort trying to find his killer." He lowered his coffee cup down and shoved up from the chair. "I don't suppose you know..."

Mac pushed between them. "I'm sorry, Gus, but we don't have a lot of time."

Vixen turned away, unsure if she should be thankful or what.

Gus tucked his hands into his pockets and met Mac's stare. "Son, I don't see what the rush is about. Whatever information Graeme gave me, what good can it do you? It didn't do him any good."

"All I need to do is get it into the right hands, Gus. Trust me."

Gus scratched his chin, studied Mac. Vixen wished she knew what he was looking for, wished she could understand why she had the urge to tell the older man it was okay to trust him. But she wasn't entirely sure it *was* okay to trust him. She didn't know that she wanted to—or that she deserved to. She sure as hell didn't deserve to have some white knight appear out of nowhere and try to help her. She'd had a white knight in her life once, one with rather tarnished armor, but still, that's what Graeme had been. He'd helped her, cared for her, loved her, saved her more than once...and tried to save her again but she'd betrayed him.

No, she certainly didn't deserve a white knight.

But it appeared she suddenly had two of them.

"So are you in trouble with these people the way Graeme was?"

She felt Gus's gaze on her and she fought the urge to squirm, fought the urge to turn away and hide from that insightful, gentle stare. Why hadn't Graeme ever told her about Gus? She'd thought he didn't have any family. He'd told her more than once that he didn't, and it was better that way. Nobody that Hawthorne could use against him.

"It's nothing I can't—"

"Yes," Mac interjected loudly.

Gus chuckled. "I guess that makes it clear enough." He sighed and returned to his chair, reaching for his coffee. This time, he took a drink before setting it back down. "I still have the information. But I can't get to it tonight. Graeme wanted it safe and secure...safe and secure to me means a safe-deposit box. Or in this case, a couple of safe-deposit boxes."

Mac looked a little nonplussed, as though he wasn't sure where to go from there. It was actually a bit of a relief to see that look on his face, since Vixen had been trying to figure out what she should do. She forced herself to smile at Gus. It felt odd. She was doing it to be polite. Polite was something she barely had a passing acquaintance with. "That will be fine. Will it be okay if we meet you here in the morning?"

Gus shrugged. "Be fine with me. But I have to ask, before you leave, do you have a place to go? These people, you don't want them finding you, I'm guessing. Do you have any place safe?"

Safe. It was harder to smile now, because all she wanted to do was sneer. She hadn't felt safe in three years. *Liar.* From the corner of her eye, she looked at Mac and saw that he was watching her from behind those dark tinted glasses. She couldn't see his eyes, but she knew he was watching her...the warmth of his gaze was almost as intimate as a touch. Guilt, self-directed fury and yearning swamped her. It didn't reassure her at all that she'd felt a little bit safe when he was next to her. Hell, even when he busted her door down, she hadn't felt threatened or even wary.

Tearing her gaze away from Mac, she looked at Gus and forced one more smile. "We'll be fine."

Gus laughed. "If you think I believe that, then you aren't giving me credit for having much of a brain." He jabbed a thumb over his shoulder and said, "I got a spare room. Used to be Charli's sewing room. It's not much, but it's clean. And it's safe."

Kindness wasn't something Vixen was used to. Even from Graeme, it had made her uncomfortable and she'd had five years to get used to it before she had killed him. From a total stranger, it was harder. Disgust, doubt, disbelief made her voice harsh as she demanded, "You got any idea how stupid it is to offer a room to a couple of people you don't know? Worse, when those people are anything like me, it's not just stupid. It could be fatal."

Gus smiled. "Again, you're not giving me much credit." He lifted one shoulder in a shrug. "You're not the easiest woman to read, but I have an idea that I know what you're thinking. You think I'm some foolish old man who doesn't realize it's a dangerous world. Or maybe you think that I don't see a woman being a threat." He slid his eyes back and forth between Mac and Vixen and smirked. "I can honestly say that if either of you posed a threat, it would be you. But that's not why you're here."

She bared her teeth at him and said, "You can't know that."

Gus laughed. "Yes. I can." He shoved out of the chair and shrugged. "It's your choice. Stay or go. But the room's there and as I said, it's safe, it's clean."

"That's kind of you," Mac said, moving to block her when she would have walked past him. "We'd definitely appreciate it."

Vixen gaped at him as Gus nodded and headed out of the room. "Are you nuts?" she demanded, her voice a bare whisper. "I'm not staying here."

Mac pushed his glasses up on top of his head and for a moment, she was struck dumb, staring into his eyes. Her mouth went dry, her heartbeat kicked up and all thought in her head stumbled to a dead stop. By the time she was able to think again, he cupped his hand over her elbow and guided her out of the room. In the small foyer right inside the front door, he said quietly, "Yes, you are. Both of us are. This is the safest place we're going to find. None of Hawthorne's men know about Gus."

Jerking away from him, she said, "You can't know that. For all we know, he's got people watching this place and being here is putting that old man at risk." She went cold inside thinking about that.

This was messed up.

Death didn't bother her—it never had. She wouldn't actively take an innocent person's life but innocent people died all the time. As long as she wasn't party to it, it wouldn't cost her any sleep.

This was somebody from Graeme's past. A past she knew nothing about. She even knew why she knew nothing about it. Graeme would have cared about this guy. If he hadn't, he wouldn't have worked to bury it. He cared—so he eradicated any and all traceable connections, the only way he could protect Gus.

"Nobody knows about him," Mac said. "It isn't possible."

"You can't know that."

Actually, he could, Graeme thought, but there was no way he could tell her that. Graeme Lawson didn't really even exist. He was nothing but smoke and shadows. Graeme McIntyre existed but he couldn't be connected with Graeme Lawson.

"Yes. I can."

She glanced over his shoulder, her eyes cold and hard. When she looked back at him, it was with that irresistible sneer and he had to fight to keep from reaching for her.

"Somehow, I don't know how, but somehow you knew Graeme. He had to have trusted you, otherwise you wouldn't know about this place, or that old man," she said, her voice low, almost brittle. "He put his faith in you—are you ready to bet that old man's life on being right?"

Shit. He had to touch her. When she glared at him like that, how could he not touch her? Graeme reached up and hooked a hand around the back of her neck, dragging her close. He didn't kiss her, although he wanted to. Her hands were fisted against his chest but when his lips slid over her temple, she jerked one down. He caught her wrist just as she went for the knife at the small of her back. Squeezing, he spun them around, pressing her against the door as he disarmed her. After tucking the knife into his belt, he lifted a hand and pressed it to her throat.

Under his fingers, he could feel the mad beat of her pulse. In her eyes, he could see the surprise, quickly veiled, followed by heat as he leaned in and pressed his body against hers. "I am right," he whispered.

She blinked, startled. "Huh?" Then she jerked her head

away from his as far as she could and sneered at him. "Arrogant bastard."

Dropping his gaze to her lips, he stared at her mouth until the sneer faded away and she started to squirm as nerves settled in. Then he made himself look into her eyes. Under his hand, the skin of her throat was satiny soft and it felt so damn fragile. Involuntarily, he squeezed lightly and then shifted his grip so he could cup her chin in his hand. "You keep sneering at me like that, keep challenging me, and I'm going to take you up on it, Vixen."

She swallowed. He felt it. Then she licked her lips and Graeme bit back a groan as he thought about the times she'd put that pretty pink tongue on him and licked him.

"Get away from me," she said, her hard-edged voice cutting through the memories.

But it didn't quell the heat raging inside him.

Leaning against her the way he was, he knew the heat was mutual. Her body reacted to his and he knew if he stripped her naked, he'd find her wet and soft, her nipples hard and swollen. Knew that if he touched her just so, he could have her climaxing in under a minute. He teased himself with that thought and leaned, pressed his mouth to hers. "Do you really want me to get away, Vixen?" he asked, tracing her lips with his tongue.

She didn't respond and he took advantage of her silence to deepen the kiss, pushing his tongue inside her mouth. He closed his hands around her narrow waist, stroked upward until he could cup the slight weight of her breasts in his hands. Rubbing his thumbs over her nipples, he trailed a line of kisses from her mouth to her ear. "Do you?"

Still no answer.

Playing with fire, he knew it, but he couldn't stop. Hoping like hell that Gus didn't come to investigate, Graeme slid a hand down her torso, undid the belt cinched at her waist. He lifted his head and stared into her eyes as he touched her, slipping the tips of his fingers inside her panties, down over curls and slick wet flesh until he could plunge them inside her pussy. "You're so soft...so wet. I think you want to get fucked— not left alone."

Daring her—

Her eyes, gone black with desire, burned into his. She

reached down and wrapped a hand around his wrist, tugging on him, but he had no intention of stopping just yet.

"You don't want to do this with me," she said, her voice stark, icy.

"Don't I?" He leaned into her harder, the aching ridge of his cock pressing against her and leaving no doubt about what he wanted.

"The last man I slept with?" She arched her head forward. Graeme met her lips, let her kiss him. Then she sank her teeth into his lip, hard enough to draw blood.

He didn't make a sound as he pulled away and when she reached down and stroked him through his jeans, he had no thoughts of caution or self-preservation. Nothing but her existed for him.

"The last man I slept with was Graeme," she said against his mouth. She slipped her fingers inside his jeans, cool and agile, seeking out the hard column of his dick and stroking him.

"I slept with him, let him tell me he loved me, let him fuck me and feed me and care for me. I even cared for him. Maybe I even loved him."

The shock of that, actually hearing her say it, had him jerking his head up. And as though that was what she'd been waiting for, she smiled at him. An ugly, angry smile that froze him through, one that warned him. Still, he didn't move away and when she slipped her hand farther down and caught his balls, squeezing until the pain was a brilliant, sickening wave inside him, he continued to stand there.

"And then I killed him."

She let go and this time, when she went to move around him, he didn't stop her. Sweat beaded on his brow and he sagged against the wall, wondering if he'd puke.

But already the pain was fading—fading until in a matter of seconds, it was gone. The pain in his heart remained though and it threatened to do what no physical pain could do. It almost sent him to his knees as she turned and stared at him.

"That poor old man." She continued to speak quietly, so quietly nobody more than two feet away could hear her. "He wants to know who killed the boy he loved like a son. And it was me. I'm a vicious, vindictive, cold-hearted bitch, Mac. I'll bite any hand that comes too close." Her gaze dropped lower. "And anything else."

Despite the threat in her eyes, he reacted with need, felt it swamp him completely and utterly, so completely that his body had already forgotten the pain she'd purposely inflicted on him. "Bite me all you want," he offered. "Just let me bite back."

Vixen jerked away, as though he'd physically assaulted her instead of flirted. "What are you? Stupid? Or are you just plain sick?"

"Both." Taking a step towards her, he brought his fingers to his nose. The scent of her body clung to his flesh and the need for more had every muscle in his body going tight. That need, it was a vibrant, seductive song in his mind and it wasn't one that would be silenced by anything short of his next death. Slipping his fingers into his mouth, he licked them clean.

She watched, frozen in place. In her gaze, he could see hunger but it was mingled with guilt, self-disgust and shame.

"I killed the man I loved. You really want to hop into the sack with me?"

"Yes."

Her nostrils flared as she dragged in a harsh, gulping breath of air. "Sick or stupid," she muttered. Turning on her heel, she strode away from him.

Chapter Eight

Graeme held the door for her and she slid past him, careful not to touch him at all. He closed his eyes, breathing in her scent before she moved too far away. Then he entered the room and shut the door behind him.

As he tossed her duffel bag onto the bed, she gave it a disinterested look and settled in the window seat.

It gave him a jolt to see Vixen sitting there. The room itself was different, but he could easily picture Charli sitting just like that, her head bent over some wooden hoop while she patiently counted stitches, pushing a needle back and forth through the cloth.

Vixen wasn't the sewing type.

But he could easily picture her sitting there, focused on a book, drinking coffee that was far too sweet and far too strong.

Tearing himself away from something that was just a fantasy, he glanced at the bed. "Get some rest. If I get tired, I'll bed down on the floor."

Without looking at him, she said, "I'm fine."

"Like hell."

Her gaze cut to him and he closed the distance between them. She had huge, dark circles under her eyes and her ivory skin had taken on a translucent cast. She was so fucking beautiful to him, but if he focused, he could see beyond that to the exhausted woman. "When was the last time you had a decent night's sleep?"

Leaning her head back against the wall, she shrugged. "I don't know. I don't sleep much."

"How much is not much?" he asked sardonically. "A few hours a night? Less?"

A pale, silvery-blonde brow lifted. "Depends on the night." With a restless shrug, she repeated, "I am fine."

"In less than twelve hours, we're going to leave here and go get evidence that could land Hawthorne in jail for the next two hundred years. He's made a lot of enemies—he gets his ass in jail, he might not even live until the trial. By now, he's figured out that something is up and you know what a suspicious bastard he is. He'll be looking for you. So will his men. You need to be ready."

A smile curled her lips—a cat's smile. A particularly mean cat that had its paw on the throat of a mouse, teasing it. "Oh, trust me. I am ready."

"You need to rest." If he concentrated, Graeme could even feel the weight of her exhaustion slamming into him.

He hadn't slept once since he'd returned, hadn't needed to eat, had barely even drank more than a few sips of water and that was more out of habit than need. He was no longer mortal and his body no longer had mortal needs.

But Vixen did.

Right now, she needed to sleep, she needed a decent meal inside her, and she needed room to grieve. He could feel the pain and it went deeper than the hunger, deeper than the exhaustion. If she gave into that now, it might break her, so he could understand why she fought it.

The sleep, though, she needed it. Not getting some rest now, while they were safe, was a damn fool move in his opinion. Crossing the floor, he crouched down beside her and waited until she looked away from the window and met his gaze. "You need to get some rest." He touched her. Huh. Apparently, he did have some needs and the need to touch her was one that he was helpless against.

Vixen reached up and batted his hand away. "No. I just need to be left the hell alone."

"Stubborn little bitch," he muttered, straightening and moving away from her.

Stubborn, but exhausted.

Thirty minutes later, while he flipped through an old fishing magazine, half out of his mind with boredom, he realized his awareness of her had become muffled. Looking up, he saw that she was still sitting in the window seat.

Sound asleep.

CRSO

Vaguely, Graeme could recall that he'd spent a decent amount of time over the past three years, trapped in that way station, wondering whether or not Vixen ever regretted what she'd done.

Wondered whether she even missed him.

Upon his return to life, he'd been faced with irrefutable evidence that she did indeed regret her actions, that she did miss him.

But it hadn't ever been driven home quite so hard. As he lay on the floor and listened to her cry silently in her sleep, he had to wonder if hell could possibly be any worse than this. It had been three hours since he'd lifted her in his arms and carried her from the window seat to the neatly made double bed. Up until fifteen minutes ago, the entire night had passed in silence.

But then she took a deep, shuddering breath. Sighed. Sniffled. The tears started to flow, seeping out from under her closed lids to saturate her pillow.

Finally, he could take no more of it and he rose from the floor and sat on the bed beside her. Laying a hand on her shoulder, he whispered, "Vixen."

At first, she didn't react.

When she did, it took him a minute to realize she wasn't entirely awake. She came to him in a rush of heat and hunger, her hair falling around them in a cloak as she crawled into his lap and kissed him, whispering to him in a broken voice.

I love you.

I'm so sorry.

Come back to me.

Forgive me.

Some of the words were spoken, others remained unsaid, but he heard every single one of them. He was no more a gentleman in this life than he had been in his previous one and when she started to work at the zipper of his jeans, he did little to slow her, little to stop her. He said nothing for fear that she would stop. For fear that she'd wake.

But in his mind, he told her, *I love you too.*

Please don't cry.

I'd come back for you if I could—but he wasn't back. Not really. He was back only for as long as it would take to save her, and then he would be gone again. That stark, unyielding knowledge struck him like an icy-cold fist and he reached for her hips, stopping her just before she would have impaled herself on his cock.

She didn't need any more pain brought upon her.

"Make love to me," she begged, fighting to break free from his hold. "Make me forget. I want to forget—I have to." She started to sob, even as she rocked, wiggled and fought to break free from his hands. She cried. "I have to forget, Graeme. It's killing me."

And her grief was killing him.

This death was so much more painful than the time she'd pushed a blade into his heart. He couldn't pull away from her, he realized. He couldn't pull away and leave her alone, all but sick with need and loneliness.

Wrapping his arms around her, he took her to the bed. Against her lips, he whispered, "I'll make you forget. I'll make you think of nothing but me."

Then he set about making that promise a reality. He stroked her, teased her, kissed her until she stopped crying and began to moan and reach for him. Then he pulled away and knelt between her thighs. He wanted to worship her. Wanted to cherish and protect and adore her.

For always.

Always... A cynical voice inside him laughed, mocked him. *You don't have always. You have until she's safe. Then it's done.*

Out loud, he swore, "Then damn it, it's going to be worth it." He sprawled between her thighs and pressed his mouth against the mound of her sex. Her folds were slick, wet, swollen—when he used his tongue to open her, she shrieked and reached down, fisting her hands in his hair. Graeme was a man starved—one more time, he could feast. One more time.

Growling against her flesh, he slid his hands under her bottom and lifted her closer. Circling her entrance, he rolled his eyes upward, staring at her over the pale, slender lines of her torso. Her eyes met his blindly—blind, yet he saw recognition in her gaze. Somehow, she knew him. That knowledge shook him to the core and in some part of his heart there was a despair unlike anything he'd ever known. If they had enough time, maybe she could have come to love him. Or perhaps she already had and she'd just needed time to admit it.

Then she whispered his name, rocked against his mouth and thought ceased. Starving—he alternated between suckling on her clit and lapping at her with his tongue. He couldn't possibly get enough of her, would never ease the hunger that burned through him. Could some eternity of fire and brimstone be any worse than never making love to Vixen again?

She whimpered, came with a hard, sudden jolt. As she started to scream, he covered her body with his, slanted his lips across her and swallowed the sound. Her body still shuddered as he wedged his hips between her thighs. Her body resisted him, her pussy still clenching and convulsing from her climax as he pushed inside. Deep, deep. She was tight, fist-tight, almost virgin-tight.

Three years—she hadn't been with another man, not even once.

If he had any sort of decency, he would take it slow, give her body time to adjust.

Even as she arched upward, a pained breath hissing out from between her teeth, he pressed onward. Vixen forced her hands between their bodies and shoved but Graeme didn't stop. He caught her hands, forced them down to the mattress, sank another inch of his aching length into her wet depths. "Everything," he muttered, pressing his lips to her temple, breathing in the scent of her. "Give me everything."

She jerked against his hold, struggled to free herself. He could feel her trying to retreat, her hips pressing back into the mattress. Graeme shifted her wrists so that he held both in one hand and then he reached down, between their bodies. He touched one finger to the erect bud of her clit. Circled it. Once. Twice.

On the third, her lashes fluttered down, her mouth parting as she gasped for air. Her body relaxed under his—not completely. He had to work his cock inside. By the time he was done, when he had every last inch of his dick buried inside her, wrapped in her silken, wet pussy, sweat was gleaming on his flesh and the need to come was nearly painful.

He wanted to plunge, deep, hard, fast. Over and over, until he came in a hot rush, while she screamed out his name.

But her body still resisted him, even as she melted under him, her body resisted his invasion. She wanted him, wanted this, he had no doubt of that. She was wet and hot, her nipples tight and hard, and her dark eyes glittered with arousal. Yet the hunger inside her was more hesitant and Graeme knew if he wasn't careful, he'd hurt her. If he didn't work to bring that hunger back to a blaze, it could flicker and die.

So instead of yielding to his body's demands, instead of letting his dick dictate, he let go of her wrists and guided her hands to his shoulders. He sank against her, slowly, shuddering at the feel of her soft, subtle curves cradling him. Threading his fingers through her hair, he angled her face to his and took her mouth.

It wasn't until he felt her softening under him, it wasn't until she moaned into his mouth and arched against him, that he started to move. And still, he forced himself to remain in control. Held tight to the reins of that control as he withdrew and slowly surged back in.

When her hips rose to meet his, he didn't lose it.

When she brought her legs up and wrapped them around his hips, he didn't lose it.

Even when she tore her mouth from his and buried her face against his shoulder, muffling a scream, he didn't lose it.

But then she whispered his name. Caught one of his hands and guided it upward until he cupped her cheek in his hand. Her face turned into his palm and she kissed him—sweet, almost innocent—or as innocent as something could be considering they were wrapped around each other.

But that sweet little kiss, the way she rubbed her cheek against his palm, like a kitten seeking a stroke, it shattered him. Physically. Emotionally. His control fell around him in razor-sharp shards and he growled her name. He ran one hand down her side in a rough, impatient caress, palmed her ass and tucked her more completely against him, holding her steady as he withdrew and then slammed back into her.

Hard.

Fast.

Her eyes widened, a startled cry escaped her lips. Her nails tore into his shoulders. "Graeme—damn it, please," she whimpered. "Pleasepleaseplease..." The words trailed off into a high-pitched keen that bounced off the walls.

He muffled the sound with his lips and rode her, impaled her on the rigid stalk of his cock, again, again, again—

The skin of his balls drew tight and fire danced inside his veins. The world threatened to go black before him as the climax stormed ever closer. He held back, focused on her face—stared into her eyes. He held back until she bucked underneath him, arched, her body rigid, every muscle inside her tense—every muscle. Including those silk-drenched muscles in her sex that gripped at his cock as he withdrew, clutching at him and trying to keep him locked inside her.

Bliss.

Complete bliss.

He let it take them both.

When the world dimmed out on him for a few seconds, he never even noticed.

It was a dream.

But it wasn't one that left her reeling with grief and guilt like most.

It was one that had her burning and aching with hunger, hot and slick with need.

He lay behind her, his body a long, hard line—unfamiliar—at first. Then he slid one hand around her waist, cupped her breast in his hand. She could smell him. Glancing at him over her shoulder, she saw the surreal neon of his eyes—and she knew him.

A dream.

A sweet, sweet dream. When he urged her onto her hands and knees, she went easily. But then he pulled away, leaving her. Straightening, she turned to reach for him, tried to say his name. He was there before she managed, dipping his head and kissing her. "Shhh. Be still."

He urged her back down, slid a hand down her back, cupped her rump and squeezed. Then he was gone. In the dim light, she could see little of him and she hated it. Her dream, though, right? If she wanted light, maybe she could just wish for it...

"Better things to wish for than lights," he said from beside the bed. She could make out his shadow—something about it seemed wrong. The rasp of a zipper, loud and out of place. "Like something wet, slick..."

"Wet?" She licked her lips. Confused. Her brain felt all muzzy and fogged, her thoughts slow and stilted. Too little sleep. Too much misery. It weighed her down.

"Wet," he said again as he joined her on the bed. "Like that slippery, sexy lotion you like to rub into your skin after you shower."

A faint click, a familiar scent—her lotion, all right. What was he... Oh. Oh. She tensed as he touched lotion-slicked fingers to her bottom, pressing against the tight pucker of her ass. "Graeme..."

"Too fucking long. It's been too long," he muttered. He knelt behind her, reached down and gripped her thighs, spreading them farther apart and urging her body forward until her torso collapsed onto the bed. "It's been too long—and there's not enough time."

Shaking, she buried her flaming face against the mattress as he got more lotion, slicking it on his fingers and pumping them in, out, working past the tight ring of muscle, stroking deeper and deeper. "Next time you rub this lotion all over your body, Vixen, think about this, think about me rubbing it inside of you, and all over my cock right before I fucked your ass."

She moaned and shivered, the hot, wicked words every bit as erotic as the feel of his fingers moving in and out, preparing her. Remember—yeah, even if this wasn't one of those dreams she could remember, she'd take part of it with her. It felt so real—it was almost like he was there with her again.

Then he pressed against her—and it felt too real. Pain flared. Burned. Tore through her as he slowly pushed inside. She whimpered, cried in her throat, tried to pull away. He wouldn't let her, sliding his hand around and reaching between her thighs so he could toy with her clit. With firm, steady strokes, he teased her, worked her body until she forgot how much it hurt as he relentlessly forged his way inside.

She undulated against him, icy-hot chills of pleasure coursing through her. The burn of pain hadn't fully retreated and as he withdrew, she sucked in a desperate breath of air. Braced herself, unwittingly tensing up as he pushed back inside.

His hands cupped her hips, holding her steady. "Relax," he whispered. "You've done this before. Relax for me...push down...that's it, sweet girl. Fuck, yeah, that's it..."

He talked her through it, his raspy, velvet-and-whiskey voice wrapping around her, his fingers gliding over her clit and teasing the heat back to the surface until she thought it would devour her. Yes, she'd done this before—only once.

One night, after Hawthorne had tried to make a move on her, right in front of Graeme. When they got home, Graeme had stripped her naked, told her to kneel—he'd fucked her mouth and after he came, he'd knelt down and picked her up, carried her to the bedroom and placed her on the floor by the bed.

There, he had proceeded to touch, kiss, tease every last inch of her. He'd fucked her ass and made her come so hard, made her scream out his name, made her beg.

One night—

And now in one dream.

Just a dream—even though it seemed so real, too real. He spread the cheeks of her ass wide and she shuddered, tried to pull away as the pressure grew too massive. Big, hard hands held her steady. "Everything, Vixen. All of it."

Pain and pleasure sliced through her. Desperate, she reached down and started to stroke herself, rubbing her clit. As the pleasure edged past the pain, she clenched down around him. Behind her, he tensed. Stilled. The ridge of his cock throbbed inside her ass and she whimpered, instinctively bearing down on him.

His body shuddered against hers—that was the only warning she had before he fell atop her, crushing her into the mattress. Pinned beneath him, helpless, unable to move, she cried out as he reared back and plunged, back and forth, back—forth—harder and harder until she screamed and pleaded and begged. Every stroke was heaven. Every stroke was hell.

Her fingers busily massaged her clit and her hips started to rise and fall, shallow little motions but it was as though it just urged him on. Each second that passed seemed to make him hungrier, make him harder. When she climaxed the first time, he growled above her. Kept moving. When she climaxed the second time, he wrapped her hair around his fist and jerked her head to the side, baring her neck. He raked his teeth down the side of it, along her shoulder, bit her. Hard. Too hard. And she loved it.

Shoving back, she met his body thrust for thrust.

Above her, he muttered, saying her name over and over, whispered sexy and naughty words. "Damn it, Vix. Listen to you scream my name—fuck, your ass is so damned tight, so sweet. Tell me you like this, tell me you want it..."

She did. Vixen did every damn thing he asked of her.

"Fuck yourself with your fingers...are you hot? Are you tight? I feel it—I can feel it when you do that..."

She felt him. Through the fragile membrane, she could feel his cock, hard, driving, pumping back and forth—too close to pain now. The lubricating effects of the lotion had worn off and now the only thing that kept her wet and open was the sweat that flowed from them. It wasn't enough, but she didn't care. Even though it hurt as much as it pleasured, she didn't care. He could kill her with the pleasure and pain, she wouldn't care.

Even when he swore and shoved up onto his knees, lifting her hips and forcing his length deeper, harder—she moaned and begged for more. He caught her body, hauled her upright so that she straddled his thighs, her back pressed to his front, his cock spearing her so deep, so completely buried inside her. The desperate, driving speed slowed—he used his hands to lift and lower her onto his shaft. Sweat flowed downward, easing his way just a little bit more. One hand glided up over her thigh, across her hip. He reached between them.

"I'm hurting you," he whispered. His voice was raw. Tortured. "Why don't I care? Why don't you?"

She reached up, back, twining her arms around his head. "Because we need it too much."

His other hand came around her hip and slipped between her thighs. Two long fingers pushed inside her, stroking and teasing. "Tell me to stop," he whispered against her shoulder. "I swear, I'll make myself stop. I don't want to hurt you..."

"Don't stop. Hurt me, damn it. I need it, Graeme. I need you, however, whenever...damn it, I love you." Words she'd kept trapped inside her too long. And now, unless she said them inside this hot, wicked dream, it would be too late.

Tensing her thighs, she lifted herself up, and then sank back down.

Pleasure and pain.

It burned through her and she craved it. "Fuck me, Graeme. I need it."

They raced together this time—and this time, when she came, he did too.

Dazed. Drained. Replete. But she feared letting go of this dream, because she knew what it would mean.

She didn't want to wake up—

He slid off the bed, moved through the darkness with ridiculous ease as he sought out the small bathroom tucked off to the side. There was a second door in the bathroom and if he opened it, he could stare into the room where he'd lived back before he set off on a road that had led him straight to hell.

But it had also led him to Vixen.

Instead of opening the door, he climbed into the shower, scrubbing away her scent, scrubbing away the results of one hot, blissful night.

Staring stonily ahead, he soaped his skin, rinsed off, standing under a stream of icy-cold water. Icy-cold—because he didn't deserve the comfort of a warm shower.

Didn't deserve to go out there and lay beside her while she slept.

When she woke, she'd remember what had happened, although he doubted she'd remember everything. Would she remember she'd said his name? Would she remember how she'd said she loved him? That he'd said it back her?

Fuck.

Part of him hoped so—it was all he'd wanted from her for so damn long. But when she'd said it to him, it was in the dead of night and she was caught halfway between awareness and dreams. And in her mind, Graeme was dead.

If he'd been a stronger man, a better man, he would have held her until she calmed—or forced her to wake up. Then if she had needed some comfort of the physical persuasion, she could see the face of a stranger and he wouldn't have to feel like he had somehow betrayed her.

Taking a couple of rags, he wetted them down with warm water and went back to Vixen. She lay sprawled on her belly, sound asleep. Resting a hand on her calf, he quietly said, "Vixen."

But she didn't move.

Setting his jaw, he cleaned up the aftereffects of the past

few hours. She slept through the whole damn thing. Even when he poured some of that lotion into his hand and slicked it over her body, she slept. Tossing the tube in the general direction of her bag, he sat on the edge of the bed and stared into nothingness.

But then he felt a hand brush across his back. Turning his head, he saw her staring at him through sleepy, heavy-lidded eyes. "Hold me," she whispered.

The plea in her voice wasn't one he could ignore.

Any more than he could have ignored her pleas earlier when she begged him to make her forget, when she begged him to touch her, make love to her. Even her plea that he come back to her.

If it was within his power...

Blowing out a sigh, he lay on the bed and drew her against him. Like a child cuddling a needed toy, he laid his hand along her cheek and cradled her head against him, stroked his thumb across her lip. In her sleep, she turned her face into his palm, rubbing against his touch like a cat.

Come morning, she'd wake. She'd realize what had happened and she'd be furious. She might even hate him.

He couldn't find it in him to care.

Because she would hate Mac—somebody who was a stranger to her, somebody she'd assume had just fucked her for the hell of it. He couldn't find it in him to care.

He knew the truth. Half-lost to dreams, she'd recognized him. Had come to him. Whispered she loved him.

As long as he could remember that for the rest of eternity, whatever happened to him was worth it.

But what about what happens to her?

Try as he might, Graeme couldn't silence that ugly, insidious voice.

Chapter Nine

It was a strange thing for her to sleep past dawn.

Even stranger for her to go through a night without waking every hour or so. She was a light sleeper, always had been. Came in handy when one of her mom's johns would slip into her room, thinking he could get a piece from the sleeping kid without having to pay. For different reasons, it came in just as handy as she got older.

For a few years, she had slept a bit easier at night, but it had been with Graeme.

Once he was gone, that peace had been lost.

Not gone, selfish, cold bitch, a sly voice inside her head whispered. *Murdered. You murdered him.*

Don't need the reminder, thanks.

She didn't need much sleep under normal circumstances, but the past three years of her life had been far from normal— even for her. Each day seemed to crawl by and at night, she yearned for peace and oblivion, but it never came. Even in her dreams, perhaps worse in her dreams, her guilt haunted her.

Feeling rested and at peace wasn't her norm.

But for the past ten minutes, she had lain quietly awake and tried to account for why in the hell she felt—human. Alive, even.

In a strange bed, in a strange house, with a strange man somewhere very close by.

Very close—but not in the bed with her. Not any more. She didn't need to look to know he wasn't in the bed. Even if she wasn't always hyperaware of her surroundings, she was hyperaware of him. If he was still in the bed with her, she'd know.

She ached.

In a sweet, wicked way. The way a woman could only ache after good, hard sex.

Licking her lips, she tried to wrap her mind around that.

Vixen didn't remember much of the previous night. Flashes, vague, wispy memories—more like dreams than anything else, but the ache in her body, the lingering discomfort had nothing to do with dreams and everything to do with sex.

She'd had sex with a total stranger, but even though part of her was appalled—horrified—she couldn't find any kind of anger. She'd had sex with a total stranger, but she was pretty sure she'd been dreaming of Graeme when it happened. That should make it worse.

She should be furious, yet she wasn't. Not at herself. Not at him.

She should feel guilty. So what if she didn't remember anything beyond those flashes? So what that she hadn't planned on it happening?

Vixen should feel guilty. Graeme was the only man she'd been with up until last night, and she had preferred it that way. Granted, until a very short time ago, she'd lived under the illusion that he'd betrayed her. Vixen figured if she hadn't been able to trust him, there was nobody she would trust.

In general, men still either disgusted her, aggravated her, or just left her cold and she hadn't once found a man who had come close to touching her on any level.

Until last night.

She had yet to open her eyes and face the clear, harsh light of day and a huge part of it was because she didn't know what would happen when she looked at him.

Vixen didn't even know his name. Mac wasn't it. He'd lied, but that didn't bother her. She'd lied about her name plenty of times. Sometimes it was just necessary. It seemed like she should know his name though.

Behind her, she heard a quiet breath, a soft, sighing sound.

Forcing herself to open her eyes, she rolled around on the bed and faced him.

The mirrored sunglasses were once more shielding his eyes and for that much, she was grateful. She sat up, holding the sheet to her breasts. Still, even through the sheet she could feel the burn of his gaze as his eyes tracked over her body.

She said nothing.

A faint, humorless smile tugged at the corners of his mouth and he murmured, "Talk about the awkward morning after."

Vixen had no idea what to say to that. She didn't feel awkward—confused. Very confused. But not awkward. However, she didn't want him thinking she wanted a repeat, either, so she didn't bother mentioning it.

"Is this where I apologize?" Mac asked quietly.

Now that, she could respond to. False apologies meant about as much to her as any other false declaration. "Why should you apologize?"

Shoving off the wall, he came to stand before her. She had to crane her head back to see him and just then, she wished she wasn't still naked under that sheet, wished she could stand in front of him so he didn't so completely tower over her.

He lifted a hand to touch her and before he even made contact, his fingers brushing over her cheek, Vixen's skin was buzzing. Her heart skipped a beat and she felt a familiar heat settle low in her belly.

"If you had been awake last night, would it have happened?"

"Not in a million years." Unable to stay there any longer, she climbed out of the bed. At the foot of the bed, she paused, wrapping the sheet around her toga-style and holding it in place with one fist. Covered, feeling just slightly more steady, she faced him. Her heart jumped into her throat as she realized he was standing just inches away now, although he had been a good five feet away. She hadn't even heard him move.

"Last night happened. It's over. It's done." She paused, trying to think past the fog of dreams, but nothing she grabbed onto was anything resembling reality. Her body, her mind, was convinced she'd been with Graeme.

Only the logistical impossibility of that kept her from thinking otherwise.

"Do you remember any of it?"

It was eerie—too often, it was like he tracked her thoughts. Meeting his gaze, she shook her head. "Nothing real." She took a deep breath, tried to relax the weird tension that had settled deep inside. "You didn't hurt me or anything, and I get the feeling that you tried to stop it. Am I right?"

He nodded. A muscle jerked in his jaw and she realized how tense he was. It didn't show on his face, other than that involuntary reaction he couldn't control, but he was tense—probably even more than her. Tense—worried. Vixen wanted to ask him about last night. For some very odd reason, she wanted some concrete memory to hold on to and not just the wisps of dreams.

She couldn't ask him, though.

Dragging her eyes away from him, she searched the room for her bag. *Get dressed. Get some distance*—she'd feel better for it.

But her eyes landed on the bag and she glimpsed the tube of her lotion in it.

Vixen stiffened as one clear memory from last night surfaced. A voice.

His voice. Not Graeme, but Mac's.

"Next time you rub this lotion all over your body, Vixen, think about this, think about me rubbing it inside of you, and all over my cock right before I fuck your ass."

Then another memory separated itself. His voice again...but it couldn't have possibly been Mac.

"Relax. You've done this before. Relax for me...push down...that's it, sweet girl. Fuck, yeah, that's it..."

He couldn't know that. It just wasn't possible.

But that wasn't even the most disturbing memory. The longer she stood there, staring into his shielded gaze, the more memories emerged from the depths of her sleep-shrouded awareness.

"I'm hurting you. Why don't I care? Why don't you?"

"Because we need it too much."

"Tell me to stop. I swear, I'll make myself stop. I don't want to hurt you..."

"Don't stop. Hurt me, damn it. I need it, Graeme. I need you, however, whenever...damn it, I love you."

He didn't move. Didn't say a word. But it was like the temperature in the room suddenly shot up thirty degrees. Sweat bloomed on her flesh, her legs went weak and deep in her core, she ached. She would swear that the man knew every damned thought going through her mind, was aware of her need, aware of her confusion.

Confusion, hell. Confused didn't touch it. Didn't ever scrape the surface of what she was feeling.

Her throat tight, heart pounding inside her chest, she bent down and grabbed the duffel from the floor, taking care not to look at the lotion. Damn it, how in the hell was she going to be able to use it? Her voice harsh, she said, "I need to get dressed."

No. She needed her head examined. That was what she needed.

But she had to settle for a long hot shower.

⊂⊃

Hell.

The old man was thorough, Vixen had to give him that. During the three-hour stint, Vixen became edgier and edgier with every damn stop. And there were several stops—five in all. They hit those five banks and with each trip in and out, she took entirely too much comfort in the fact that she'd armed herself that morning. Most of her weapons, she hadn't been able to take, considering they were going into a bank—lovely thing, metal detectors.

Even more lovely—weapons made of materials other than metal. Like the clear Lexan knives she had stashed in various places. Her garrote. Most people wouldn't recognize the garrote for what it was, even if they saw it. It was, to all intents and purposes, just a custom-made silk scarf—it looked pretty, but in her hands, it was deadly. The Lexan blades were just that— knives, made of a clear, nearly unbreakable plastic. It had been designed to replace glass. It was expensive, but worth it—the clear material meant even the more advanced scanning techniques weren't likely to pick it up. Vixen rarely went anywhere unarmed, but the weapons were nothing more to her than tools—something she used when needed and paid little attention to beyond that. But today, they'd become a security blanket.

By the time they were done, the trunk of his car was so damn full, it wouldn't hold even one more file. As Mac slammed the trunk lid down, she met his gaze over the car. "Exactly what are we supposed to do with all of this?"

"You aren't going to do anything," he said, his voice flat, his face expressionless. "You're going to stay with Gus while I take this to the police."

Vixen blinked. At first, she didn't quite realize he was actually telling her what to do. Even Hawthorne "pretended" to ask. He phrased it in much politer terms than an outright order and he also seemed more than aware that if he pushed too hard, she'd refuse just for the hell of it. Only Graeme—

Oh, no. Don't think about Graeme.

She decided to focus on the order instead. Tucking a lock of hair behind her ear, she politely asked, "Could you repeat that?"

Mac didn't seem too fazed. "You heard me."

"Yes. I heard you. I'm just a little puzzled why you think I'd actually listen to you."

In a voice thick with self-mockery, he muttered, "Me too."

From by the other side of the car, Gus said, "I don't know about you, but I'm not too comfortable having all this crap with me. The kind of people Graeme was tangled up with, I get the feeling they won't be real happy once this information is turned over to the cops. I'll breathe a lot easier when that is done."

Graeme.

Tearing her eyes away from Mac, she looked at Gus. "All of this came from Graeme?"

"Yes." He sighed, smoothed a hand over his gunmetal gray hair. "I asked him why he didn't just turn it over to the cops. But he said he couldn't. Not yet. Wouldn't tell me why, but I had a feeling it was because he wanted some assurance from the police. You wouldn't believe how often I wondered if he died for all of this."

Guilt, nausea, they dropped down on her like a stone. Vomit boiled up her throat, a nasty, ugly miasma. Yes. Graeme had died because of this—Hawthorne had known one of his top men was going to turn on him, and he used his top woman to take care of the issue. God, how could she have done it? A hand cupped over the back of her neck. His breath whispered across her flesh as he dipped his head and murmured, "Put it away, Vixen."

Put it away. Shit, talk about callous.

But he was right.

She nodded jerkily and climbed into the back seat. She reached under the seat and pulled her Browning out, sliding it into place at the small of her back. Outside the car, Mac shut the back door and climbed into the front seat, folding his long legs to fit into the cramped space.

Vixen stared out the window. From the corner of her eye, she could see the streaked gold of his hair. As though from a distance, she heard the indistinct rumble of his voice as he spoke to Gus. The words made no sense though. Right now, nothing made sense.

Nothing seemed real.

Her mind circled back to the boxes of files, discs and tapes stowed in the trunk.

Now wasn't the time. They had to get back to Gus' so she could go through all of these boxes and figure out exactly what Graeme had been hiding from the police, from Hawthorne.

From her.

That was the burn. Buried deep inside, there was a world of pain. Even now that she knew that Graeme hadn't betrayed her, there was pain. Because he hadn't trusted her. Hadn't come to her and told her what he was doing. He had done it on his own, in the dark—part of her suspected she knew why. Graeme's inability to trust was probably as deep as her own.

How long had he been gathering all this supposed evidence?

What sort of evidence was it?

He had met with the police, that much she did believe. Slicer had no reason to lie about that, and she believed him. He'd met with the police, although thanks to Slicer's skills, she suspected she'd never know exactly what had taken place. But Graeme wouldn't have gone to the police unless he knew without a doubt he could give them something they'd want— want enough to overlook whatever crimes they might want to pin on him. And there were plenty of those.

But Vixen knew cops—so had Graeme. They'd want Hawthorne bad enough to focus on the big picture, even if it meant overlooking Graeme.

She sat in the back seat, her mind whirling, her heart aching, as Gus drove back to his quiet, slightly shabby house. Set in a quiet, slightly shabby neighborhood, something about it made her sad. Wistful.

A normal life.

There had been a time when she'd been so damned jealous

of anybody that had something even resembling a normal life. Back when she was a kid and saw other kids going to school while she watched from the window with her mom behind her sleeping off a drunk. As she got a little older, living on her own on the streets and damn proud of it, even while part of her wished she had parents who would come looking for her if she was out too late, a warm place to go on a cold night, a safe place to crash when she was tired and hungry.

A knot formed in her chest and she resolutely swallowed it back down. Whining about all the chances she hadn't ever had, or all the ones she'd walked away from wasn't going to do her a damn bit of good.

No, what she needed to do was plan. There was no way in hell Mac was leaving her with Gus while he rode off to play white knight. Her inner bitch sneered at her.

What makes you think he's going to play white knight? Maybe he wants that mountain of paper for some other reason. But Vixen silenced her with ease. Ignored her completely. She didn't know Mac. She had no reason to trust him except for the quiet voice in her heart that whispered she could—that she *needed* to.

That voice had told her the same thing about Graeme and she hadn't listened.

It wasn't a mistake she was going to make again.

Although Mac seemed pretty damned convinced none of Hawthorne's men knew about Gus, Vixen wasn't ready to take that chance. They needed to get away from him, and fast. Needed to convince the old man to take a nice long trip, a few days, maybe a few weeks out of town where nobody could find him while Mac and Vixen dealt with Hawthorne.

Deal with—her thoughts came to a screeching halt.

Deal with.

Kill.

She didn't want to turn Hawthorne over to the police, she wanted the bastard dead. Wanted to see blood flow and life fade from his eyes.

Deal with—

She had to suppress the urge to smile.

There was no need for some complicated plan, she realized. She'd let Mac do whatever he wanted to do with all the junk in the trunk. He could turn it over to the cops, he could wallpaper his house with it, he could use it for a bonfire. It didn't matter. Because what Vixen wanted was Hawthorne dead.

She wanted nothing more than that—not even whatever freedom she might be able to buy using the information Graeme had collected.

Let Mac go to the police.

She'd handle Hawthorne on her own.

The look in her eyes would send chills down the spine of any man who had a half-functioning brain.

Graeme wasn't unaffected, but it had nothing to do with the fact that she was plotting out the death of Gerard Hawthorne in bloody, glorious detail. It had to do with an innate knowledge that if he didn't stop her, she would kill Hawthorne—and she'd end up dead as well.

Hawthorne wouldn't be a big loss. Graeme almost hoped the two of them ended up side by side in hell.

But he wasn't about to let Vixen throw away her life on this.

Not a fucking chance.

Damn it.

He had gone blank.

Graeme Mackenzie Lawson was the kind of soul that had a plan, a backup plan and an alternate backup plan, but he didn't know which way to turn from here. He desperately wanted to get Gus out of this. Get the old man safe and get out of his life. Maybe he should do that first but he'd have to be quick about it. Quick and watchful.

When her eyes met his in the mirror, he sensed her awareness of him—it was on a level that was almost eerie—almost an echo of his. Although she couldn't "feel" his thoughts the way he could feel hers, she sensed the direction all too clearly.

As her thoughts circled back to Hawthorne and her decision to just forget anything and everything else but handling the boss, he felt something ripple down his spine. Something cold, something ominous.

Something dark.

Death.

Utter. Complete. Final.

The cloud of it settled around them and Graeme knew without a shadow of a doubt that somebody was getting ready to die.

As Gus turned down the street that led to his house, Graeme's senses went on red alert, a wailing siren screeching through his head. Words of warning formed on his tongue, but his body locked down. He couldn't speak, couldn't move even as they pulled into Gus's drive and the warning wail turned into thunder.

Chapter Ten

Hawthorne—

Whether it was just shitty luck, karma or divine retribution, she didn't know. But even before they pulled into Gus' driveway, she felt it. An icy shiver ran down her spine. It swamped her, a sense of foreboding so strong it left her throat tight, her heart pounding and blood roaring in her ears. Slowly, as Gus slowed the car to a stop, she sat up straighter in the seat.

She couldn't see him yet.

But she had no doubt he was there.

Turned her head left, right, scanning the area around the car and beyond. She was aware of Mac, sitting oddly still, almost frozen, in the front seat. Of Gus, as he reached for the door handle and climbed out.

"Gus, wait," she said.

But he'd already climbed out.

From the corner of her eye, she saw movement.

Shit. There. Fuck. Carlos came sauntering around the corner, a mean smile on his ugly mug and a light in his eyes that Vixen didn't care for. She tensed her muscles, taking comfort in the press of cold steel against her body, the knife tucked inside her boot, the silk of her favored garrote, draped around her neck like a pretty, simple scarf, the Browning in its custom-fitted holster at the small of her back. She had her other weapons, well-balanced Lexan throwing knives—all easily accessible, and deadly accurate. Her fingers itched. She wanted to grab one—Vixen hadn't had itchy trigger fingers in years, but the need to bury the lethal plastic blade inside Carlos' body was a strong one.

"Mac."

He moved. A fleeting thought danced through her mind—the way he moved, first his body sagged, then tensed—he said nothing, but she got the weirdest idea that until that moment, Mac hadn't been able to move.

"Is it too much to ask that you stay in the car?" he asked, his voice grim as he opened the door.

She did the same, sliding outside and walking next to him as they moved around the car to stand by Gus. "Yes. Way too much." Staying in the car wouldn't do a damn bit of good anyway. It's not like it would keep her safe, not like it would make her feel safe. She edged a little closer to him, aligned herself so close that her shoulder was pressed against his arm. That light touch shouldn't make her feel comforted—Vixen didn't believe in false comfort.

But he made her feel better.

Safer.

As Carlos moved away from the garage, watching her with that evil, awful smile, her inner bitch told her it was just ridiculous to feel safe no matter what. She glanced at Gus. Tough old bastard. He knew what was going on. She could see it in his eyes. But all he did was hook his thumbs in his pockets and watch Carlos with unreadable eyes.

Some semblance of normalcy tried to rear its ugly head. *Don't worry about him—you've got your own neck to worry about.*

"Vixen."

"Carlos." She sneered at him—typical greeting for her, as far as he was concerned. She didn't like the bastard, never had. Although she wasn't exactly *afraid* of him, she had a woman's instinctive knowledge—not quite a fear, but close—that Carlos was a man who loved to hurt women. She hated uncomfortable, how nervous he made her feel. Worse he knew it. Knew it, liked it and if he got his hands on her, he was going to play on that almost-fear in ways that would have her begging for death. Easier, as far as she was concerned, to just bite the bullet now. "To what do I owe this pleasure?"

He smiled at her. "The boss, he's been looking for you. But you already know that, don't you?"

Vixen didn't bother answering.

"Whaddya say we go see him now." He glanced at Mac and

Gus, his gaze disinterested. He was focused on her—good. That was good.

Right?

Maybe she could just go with him—Mac was a smart guy. He'd get the mess of paperwork to the police and that much would be taken care of. All she really wanted was five seconds with Hawthorne anyway. Five seconds and he'd be dead and if she ended up the same way, she didn't care all that much.

But Carlos shattered those hopes too quick. "Your friends, they can come with us."

"I'm not going anywhere just yet, Carlos. Give Hawthorne my regrets."

With a smirk, Carlos kicked at the ground and shrugged. "I had a feeling you'd say that. But don't worry. He came with us."

Hawthorne stepped out from behind the house.

The sight of him had a cold fist settling her gut. His black eyes, cold and emotionless, met hers. He smiled, but it was an empty smile, one that meant nothing.

"Vixen. You've become a hard woman to find at times," he said, shaking his head. "If I hadn't had a few people on the watch for you, I may never have been able to track you down."

"Since when did I require watching, Hawthorne?"

Her question was nothing more than an attempt to buy some time while her brain furiously spun in circles trying to figure a way out of this mess.

"Since you started ignoring orders."

With mock innocence, she blinked and said, "Orders? I wasn't aware I'd been given any orders. There was a job offered, but I thought I was allowed to make my own decisions on that."

"Hmm." His eyes narrowed on her face. "Don't play the fool, Vixen. It doesn't suit you."

"I hadn't realized I was." Deliberately obtuse, maybe, but that wasn't the same thing as playing a fool.

"You disappoint me." Cocking his head, he turned to look at Mac. "I don't believe I know you."

"You might be surprised."

"Would I?" He stroked a hand over his jaw, smoothing down the neatly trimmed goatee as he studied Mac. "I don't care for it when I can't see a man's eyes."

Mac smiled. It wasn't a pleasant smile. "They are the

gateway to the soul," he quoted as he pushed his mirrored sunglasses up on his head. His lashes were low, still shielding his eyes. He looked at Vixen and slowly, the golden fringe of his lashes lifted and she found herself staring into those eerie, disturbingly familiar eyes. A sad smile tugged at his lips and then he reached up, cupped her face, stroked his thumb along her lower lip.

The shocking familiarity of that had her legs quivering and her heart slamming away inside her rib cage. With a knot in her throat that threatened to choke her, she watched as he looked away from her and focused on Hawthorne.

The impact of that neon-blue gaze affected Hawthorne with similar intensity from what she could tell.

Dazed, Vixen watched as Hawthorne retreated one small step. Under his perfect tan, his features went white and his Adam's apple bobbed as he swallowed. At his side, one hand clenched into a fist.

Save for the eyes, this man looked nothing like Graeme. But considering that Hawthorne looked like he'd seen a ghost, Vixen knew she wasn't the only one who looked at Mac and saw Graeme.

"Who are you?"

Mac didn't respond.

Reaching for some measure of control, Vixen offered a flippant answer. "He's my guardian angel, aren't you, Mac?"

He slid a hand down her back, rested it just above the base of her spine. Only a few inches away from the butt of her gun. "I don't qualify as anybody's angel, Vixen."

"Get away from him, bitch," Carlos said, his eyes narrowing suspiciously. He didn't seem fazed by Mac at all.

"You know, I've told you a hundred times I don't care for it when you call me a bitch."

He smiled evilly. "How about *puta*? Is that better?"

Drawing one of her throwing knives, she tossed it up, caught it, twirled it in her fingers and gave Carlos her own version of an evil smile. "No. You only wish I was a *puta*—it's the only way you would have ever had a chance with me."

"Oh, I'm going to get that chance."

"Children. Children." Hawthorne seemed to have recovered his composure. With a patently false, patently pacifying smile, he gestured towards them. "Behave now. Vixen, you really should put that away before somebody gets hurt."

He glanced at Gus—the first time he'd bothered to even pay any attention to the old man.

Something foreign rose inside her—unprepared to handle it, Vixen couldn't stop the instinctive urge she had to shift so that she was closer to the older man. And it was the biggest mistake she could have made. She didn't know how to handle feeling protective over people she barely knew. She barely understood a protective instinct at all, unless it was one borne out of self-protection.

But Hawthorne did understand those urges and he zeroed it on it like the hyena he was. "Vixen. Drop the knife—and any other weapons you have."

"I don't think so."

"Carlos."

Without blinking an eye, without batting an eyelash, Carlos drew his gun, pointed it at Gus and took out the older man's knee. One of Hawthorne's goons emerged from the background, caught the older man and clapped a hand over his mouth to smother the scream. The gun itself had a silencer and the only sound, other than Gus's strangled cry, was a muffled pop.

"Vixen. Drop your weapons or he dies."

"I drop my weapons, we all die anyway," she gritted out, her teeth clenched.

It was Owen Crites holding Gus and as the old man's body buckled, blood still spurting from his shattered knee, the bastard said, "Shut the fuck up." He shoved Gus to the ground and stooped beside him, wrapping thick, cruel fingers around Gus's neck. "Keep your mouth shut, or we'll take out the other one."

Hawthorne paid no attention to Owen. "Vixen." Drop your weapons now."

She bared her teeth at him. "Then what? You have Carlos shoot out my kneecaps?"

Carlos smiled. But Hawthorne reached over and pushed on Carlos' arm until the man lowered his weapon. "Hardly. I have plans for you that don't involve blood. I never did much care for blood in the bedroom."

Her gut went cold but it didn't come as a shock. She had known that was his intent. But it wasn't going to happen. She'd get her kneecaps shot out first. "I have no intention of joining you in the bedroom, Hawthorne."

"You will if you want to live. Now, drop the weapons and get in the car."

She didn't need to ask which one—at that moment, a sleek, shiny black limo pulled up. Tinted windows, bulletproof glass— the car *de rigueur* for all stylish, well-appointed criminals. "I'm not going anywhere with you."

"So stubborn."

Cocking a brow, Vixen said, "You know, it was a bad idea to force this here, Hawthorne. Nosy neighbors, quiet suburb. You really don't think you can force me into that car, do you?"

"I'm quite certain I can. You see, if you get in the car, I'll leave your guardian angel and the old man alone. Otherwise, I'll have Carlos shoot Lancelot—in the balls, I believe. I never would have expected it, but you fucked him, didn't you? All these years, you stayed celibate, quietly mourning Graeme even though he betrayed you—"

"He didn't betray me."

"No. No, he didn't." Hawthorne smiled. "Yes, I know you had a chat with Slicer. Carlos did too. Sometime in the next few days, his body is going to probably wash up on the shore and there's enough evidence planted in his apartment to frame you for his murder. Even if you try to get away from me now, you won't outrun the police, darling. However, cooperate and all that evidence will disappear."

"Cooperate. As in fuck you? No thanks, I'd rather go to jail."

"You still don't get it. I'm not giving you an option, Vixen. Get in the car—or I'll kill these men right in front of you, then Carlos will put you in the car and the harder you fight him, the worse it will go for you—and when I'm done, he'll have his turn with you. And you know what he likes to do in the bedroom. Blood isn't my style. But he enjoys it."

He closed the distance between them, standing close, so close she could smell the scent of his custom-designed cologne. The stink of it made her stomach roil as he dipped his head and murmured, "Just know this, Vixen, I'm not going to kill you. Carlos isn't going to kill you. Not yet. No matter what you do. What you say. Whether you try to run. You won't get away from me by dying—I don't give up that easily."

Dying would be easy. Swallowing the bile churning in her

throat, she averted her head and tried to breathe past the nausea. Shaking, half-sick, she glanced at the car. Shit. The possibility of being turned over to Carlos was something she'd do damn near anything to avoid. But she wasn't going to walk away from the two men who'd gotten sucked into the disaster of her life.

With the instinct of a shark scenting blood in the water, Hawthorne glanced at Mac then Gus. Smiled. "I'll let them live, Vixen. They mean nothing to me. I don't know who they are and I don't care."

Fucking liar. If he knew what was in the trunk of Gus's car, there was no way he wouldn't care.

Her eyes narrowed. Maybe he didn't know...what had he said, he'd had people watching out for her. She didn't have to fake the fear in her voice as she said, "They were just trying to help me get out of this life, Gerard. They didn't do anything wrong."

Did he know?

"As I said, I don't care about them. For all I care, Lancelot can put the old man in the car, drive him to the hospital. They can just disappear." With a charming smile, he said, "We can even follow them—and I'll allow you to hold onto your gun. I know you have one. We can follow them to the hospital and once they go inside, you'll turn over your gun. We can put this ugly mess behind us." He reached up, traced his fingers along her cheekbone, across her jaw, down her neck. "You won't have to know a moment of pain with me, Vixen. Not ever."

His fingers trailed lower, lower. He brushed the tips across one nipple and then cupped the weight of her breast in his hand. His touch was gentle—almost skilled. Still, nausea churned and roiled through her and she had to fight not to knock his hand away.

Then he fell back. "Carlos."

When Carlos came at her, she feinted to the side but two more men came up behind her and caught her arms, one clamping a hand over her mouth. Carlos drew a knife and cut her shirt open so that it lay open across her chest. He did the same to the sturdy black sport bra she wore and then he dipped his head and bit her.

Hard.

Bringing up her knee, she rammed it into his balls. As he

keeled over, one of the men holding her brought up a hand and clubbed her across the back of her head. Her vision went dark and she braced herself, expecting worse.

But nothing worse happened. When her eyes cleared, she realized she was still being held between the two men and although Carlos was red in the face and panting with pain, standing by the house and holding himself, he was nowhere even close to her.

Hawthorne was.

"You have a choice here, Vixen. Him. Or me."

From the corner of her eye, she saw Mac moving, quick as the wind. Seconds later, Hawthorne went flying through the air. A silvery flash—the sunlight reflecting off one of her throwing knives—she must have dropped it when they grabbed her.

Now it was buried in Carlos' neck.

His eyes went wide.

Blood bubbled on his lips, spurted from the injury and then he sagged and went down.

The man at her right demanded, "What the—"

It was as far as he got. Then next noise he made was a strange gurgling sound as Mac struck out, catching him in the neck with a well-placed strike. As Mac turned to focus on the other man, Vixen jerked away, determined to get the fuck away—

But cold metal pressed against her neck. Owen snarled, "I'll shoot the bitch."

Mac smiled. "No, you won't. Hawthorne wants her alive." Then his smile changed—it was the face of death. A shiver ran down her spine and it was like looking into the depths of hell. "Does he really want you alive?"

Apparently, her captor didn't think so. The gun swung away from her and towards Mac. She didn't waste time. Drawing the second throwing knife, she shifted her grip and buried the blade in Owen's side. He let go with a bellow and the gun once more swung her way, but Mac was already there. After quickly disarming Owen, he used the same technique she'd seen him use before—too eerie, too familiar—and used the gun to club him on the head.

As yet another fell, Mac turned and faced those still standing.

This time, armed. He reached out for Vixen's arm, drew her close. She needed no encouragement and remained close, although she focused on Gus instead. Her eyes went wide at his color. Deathly gray.

Eyes glassy—getting that fixed, unfocused stare too close to shock for her liking.

What in the hell do you expect? He's not exactly a spring chicken.

She knelt by him, focusing on his face. Reaching out, she tapped his cheek. "Gus. Hang in there. We'll get you out of this."

His eyes swung her way and he smiled weakly. "Don't think so, pretty lady. I'm sorry I couldn't help you do right by Graeme."

Guilt, even now, punched through her. Taking his hand, she did the one thing she hated—offered false comfort. "You'll be okay. We'll see this through—all of us."

"Not...me. Heart. Fuck, hurts."

"Vixen."

She heard Mac's low voice but didn't look at him as she laid her fingers on Gus's neck. The heartbeat was erratic. Thready. The skin around his lips was going blue. "I think he's having a heart attack, Mac."

For a moment, time stopped.

Then she felt something punch through the air, a tidal wave of fury. It was gone, almost as quickly as it came and then Mac was at her side. Still holding the gun, keeping it level, he knelt down beside her. Urging it into her hands, he said, "Move."

Heart attack—

Fuck, no. Not this. Death—that ugly shroud that Graeme had sensed closing around them. It had been coming for Gus? Why?

"Graeme..."

"Hey, old man..." So caught up in the darkness of his thoughts, he barely realized what Gus had said.

Or his response.

Not until Gus wheezed out, "My boy."

Fuck—how did he know...?

Of course, it didn't really matter, did it? Gus was dying.

Tears stung his eyes. He laid a hand on Gus' chest, felt the ever-weakening beat of the heart. He knew the basics of first aid—or at least he had, back in his old life. But he didn't bother doing it now. He could feel them—the asexual beings that had guided him into death—now they were reaching for Gus.

But there was a beauty this time, a light that had been lacking for Graeme. Gus had nothing to fear.

And he seemed to realize it, too. "Don't...don't look so miserable, Graeme. Going to be with Charli now. All I've wanted since I lost her. All I wanted..."

Then he was gone.

Woodenly, Graeme straightened. Back to everybody, he stared down at Gus' face and felt the burn of tears. The sudden, complete silence was almost comical when he made himself turn to face the others.

Vixen was staring at him slack-jawed.

Hawthorne looked at him with suspicion.

"Graeme—what the fuck are you talking about, old man?"

He came stalking close but stopped a few feet away, snarling in disgust as he caught sight of Gus' lifeless face. Cutting his eyes to Mac, he said, "What the fuck was he talking about?"

"Souls." He smiled and reached for his sunglasses, threw them on the ground at Hawthorne's feet. "Eyes. They're the window to the soul, aren't they, Gerard? You looked in her eyes one too many times and saw that she was mine—and you hated it. You looked into my eyes, and saw that you couldn't control me—and you hated it."

"Are you crazy?"

"Possibly." *No, most likely yes.* "Tell me something, when did you decide to have her kill me?"

Vixen's startled gasp hit him like a bucket of ice water, but it would have been like expecting a bucket of water to quench the fires of hell. He glanced at her, wished he could say something, wished he could explain—but the rage, it was too strong. After what he'd seen Hawthorne do—Carlos, what they would have done to her...

It was a miracle he could even speak coherently, for all he wanted to do was roar with rage as he tore these men apart until everything around them was painted red with blood. Instead, he smiled at Hawthorne as the man fell back one, two, three steps.

One of Hawthorne's men came up and grabbed his arm. "Boss, we gotta get out of here. We been here too long. Somebody's going to have seen us. Heard us."

"He's not going anywhere." Graeme didn't bother looking away from Hawthorne. "If you want to run, you better do it while you still can."

After a quick look at his boss, that's exactly what the guy did, headed for the long, sleek limo.

Hawthorne fumbled for his own gun, but his hands had gotten slow—too much telling his thugs who to kill, not enough killing of his own.

"The gun's pointless, Gerard. You can't kill me." A smile curled his lips and he whispered, "I'm already dead—you can't kill me twice."

You can't kill me.
I'm already dead.

The way he touched her, so oddly familiar. So gentle— nobody had ever touched her with that odd mix of gentleness and possessiveness.

The way he moved.

His eyes—

Vixen swallowed, watched as Hawthorne tensed on the trigger. Sweat rolled down his face and his hand shook. "Who in the fuck are you?"

He was terrified—Vixen couldn't blame him. *She* was terrified, even though it was caught in an odd mix of disbelief and hope. She looked at Mac, but it wasn't really Mac she saw. Or not entirely. His body kept changing, like some weird image-morphing program come to life. One minute she saw the lean man with sun-streaked hair, wide shoulders, narrow hips, beautiful hands—then she blinked and she saw a bigger man, one built like a football player, tall, wide, broad, with big hands and short dark hair.

Graeme—then not.

Her own hands were shaking something awful as she reached for her gun. Shaking so bad, she could barely focus enough to aim. Gritting her teeth, she dug deep and found some measure of calm, some measure of strength. Her hands steadied. One breath in. One breath out. The insanity around her faded away. She stared at Hawthorne, took aim—

Then somebody stepped between them just as she stared to squeeze the trigger. Hissing, she jerked the gun up only a half-second before she would have fired. "Get out of the way."

"You can't kill him, my pretty little Vixen. I'm sorry." He spoke without looking at her. The sound of his voice, those words sent another jolt of surprise through her. *My pretty little Vixen...*

Graeme...

How is this possible?

Her voice shook, wobbled, came out as faint as a whisper. "Graeme?"

He heard her nonetheless. Stilling, he turned his head, just a little, never completely taking his eyes from Hawthorne. "Yes." He sighed and once more his body did that morph thing, so that she was actually seeing Graeme—*Graeme.*

Alive.

Big shoulders rose as he took a breath, then as he blew it out, his body shifted again. Damn it, it was like trying to focus on a mirage.

What the hell did it matter? It was Graeme—he'd come back.

His voice quiet, mournful, he murmured, "No. I'm sorry—I'd give anything if I could, but no, I haven't come back. Once this is done, I'll be gone again."

There would be no time for a sweet, tender reunion. Not with Hawthorne so close.

"What sort of trick is this, Vixen?" Hawthorne asked.

Edging out from behind Graeme, she took a quick look at that ever-changing face and then at Hawthorne. She swore silently as she realized she'd distracted Graeme just enough so that Hawthorne had steadied himself out. His face no longer had that mottled, panicked look and the gun in his hand was level, completely level, and aimed dead center at Graeme's chest.

He sneered derisively at her and said, "I've got to give you credit, you had me going there for a minute. He almost sounds like Graeme—how long have you been coaching him?"

Hawthorne might be steady. But she wasn't. She couldn't

think of a damn thing to say, couldn't even get her brain to work.

Sirens started to wail in the distance and the sound of them came as a complete surprise to Hawthorne. He flinched as though he'd been hit and then he swore. "Damn it." He made as though to leave.

Graeme blocked him, shoving him back with a force that sent him sprawling.

Hawthorne's men were all but useless. Those who hadn't already taken off were either dead or injured and useless on the ground. Snarling, he came to his feet, the gun once more pointed at Graeme. "I don't know who in the fuck you are, but get out of my way."

Voice taunting, Graeme challenged, "Make me." He didn't seem to give a damn about the gun pointed at him, didn't seem to care that Hawthorne's finger was already squeezing tight on the trigger.

He didn't care—she couldn't *not* care.

She didn't even think. There was no time for it.

Her body moved of its own volition, her feet swift, silent, certain as she came between Hawthorne and Graeme.

Time slowed to a crawl.

She heard the quiet click as Hawthorne squeezed the trigger.

The muffled blast as the gun fired.

Seemed she could even see the bullet as it came flying towards her. She heard Graeme scream her name just as it tore into her flesh. The impact sent her stumbling back and if Graeme hadn't caught her, she would have fallen.

"No."

His voice came as though from a great distance and opening her eyes took too much strength, far too much considering she could feel it flowing out of her in red-hot, fiery waves. But she had to look at him. Had to. He crouched over her. His body and face continued in its illusive dance— Graeme's face, melting away into Mac's, then back.

But his eyes stayed the same—those amazing, perfect eyes, so intensely blue, gleaming behind a sheen of tears.

"No," he gritted out. "Damn it, this isn't how it was supposed to happen."

"Yeah. It...is." She gasped for breath, made herself force the words out, even though that sapped even more of her dwindling strength. "I took your life—only fair I give you mine."

Cold swamped her. Deep, bone-chilling cold, unlike anything she'd ever felt. But she smiled past it, smiled through the pain as she stared up at him. "It's really you."

"Shhh...stop talking, Vix. Just be quiet, be still. I hear sirens. Help will be here soon."

"I don't need help." She licked her lips—they were almost painfully dry. She was shaking, freezing, despite the hot flow of blood that was rapidly soaking her clothes, despite the fiery heat of his body. "I just need you."

She dragged her hand upward, touched his face. But she was so damn weak, she couldn't keep her hand up. As it fell away, she cried out. A muscle jerked in his jaw as he caught her wrist and laid her palm against his cheek. With a satisfied sigh, she smiled again. "Just you."

"I'm here." His voice was raw, broken. "Stay with me, okay, baby? Just stay with me."

She wanted to—in an unconscious echo of his earlier words, she whispered, "I'm sorry. I'd give anything if I could."

Darkness swarmed in on her and she fought it back. She had to tell him something—what was it...

She remembered—yeah, that. Needed to tell him that. Her lids had drifted down without her realizing it and she dragged them upward, stared at his face, into his eyes. "I love you, Graeme. I always did. I'm sorry I never told you."

He said something.

Screamed it.

But Vixen was already past hearing anything he had to say—it didn't matter though. He'd already told her, so many times.

Now, she finally had the courage to tell him.

Her body went limp in his arms and Graeme threw back his head, screamed.

"NO!"

Hawthorne had disappeared. Some part of him was vaguely aware of it as the bastard left, running away like there was a monster at his heels.

Graeme didn't care—right now, he couldn't care. Nothing existed beyond the pain. It tore at him, ate at him, destroyed him.

"No." His head dropped and he pressed his brow to hers. "Don't do this. Damn it, Vix. I love you, baby. Come on...hang in there."

It was too late. Even though he didn't want to admit it, he knew.

It was too late.

He was soaked with her blood, even though he'd pressed down on the ragged hole in her chest, tried to staunch the flow. "This wasn't how it was supposed to happen."

"This is exactly as it should have happened." The disembodied voice was all too damn familiar.

Lifting his eyes, Graeme watched as life, the world, everything but Vixen's still body in his arms, spun away. Round and round until everything dissolved. When the spinning stopped, the world reformed, and once more, he was back in the way station.

Caught once more between life and death—except Graeme's life lay dead in his arms. He had no life—not even here. Even if by some miracle he'd passed their tests, nothing existed for him now.

He'd failed her.

"Why did you let this happen?" he whispered, lifting his head and staring at the shrouded, androgynous form in front of him.

"Because this was how it was meant to happen—she took your life. Then she gave hers. You passed the test—as did she. Redemption. Salvation. Forgiveness."

"So she had to fucking sacrifice herself?" Surging to his feet, he cradled her against him, clutching her tight. She'd fade soon. If he'd succeeded, then she wouldn't be trapped here—and she wouldn't spend the rest of eternity trapped in hell, either.

She'd move on. Maybe he would too. Some part of him wanted to take comfort in that, but he couldn't. He just couldn't. It just wasn't enough. He'd wanted her to live, to have some sort of life. Know some happiness—

"You want a sacrifice, damn it?" he demanded. He looked down at her. Her eyes were open, fixed—blank as a doll's. He wanted to see life burning there. Wanted to see her reluctant smile, hear her laugh, even if it was for somebody else. "I'll give you a sacrifice. Let her go back. Change this. And you can do whatever you want with me. I don't care."

"I haven't the power to change time. I have no power over life or death. Only He does."

"Then ask Him," Graeme snarled. Tears burned his eyes. It never even dawned on him how odd it was that he could feel the tears—here, in this void where he had felt nothing for three years. "I'll ask Him. Let her go back. And I'll take whatever He sees fit to give me. Willingly. Anything."

"Anything?"

Lowering his head, Graeme stared at the cloaked figure. "Anything. I just...she's never had a chance at anything normal, never had a chance to be happy. That's all I ever wanted for her. I just wanted her to be happy."

Warmth.

It came from everywhere.

Peace.

Like the rays of the sun, he felt it shining down on him.

There was a whisper—but it resounded like a clap of thunder. Words spoken, but they rang through him like a song.

"There was one last test, Graeme. Sacrifice...true sacrifice."

A moment of utter silence, utter stillness. Then an overwhelming sense of pride, satisfaction. Pleasure. It radiated through him. Around him. Sang inside his heart, his blood, inside his very bones.

"Well done," the words whispered around him. He felt the brush of something against his cheek—and then...nothing.

Chapter Eleven

"You want a sacrifice, damn it? I'll give you a sacrifice. Let her go back. Change this. And you can do whatever you want with me. I don't care."

"I haven't the power to change time. I have no power over life or death. Only He does."

"Then ask Him. I'll ask Him. Let her go back. And I'll take whatever He sees fit to give me. Willingly. Anything."

"Anything?"

"Anything. I just...she's never had a chance at anything normal. That's all I ever wanted for her. I just wanted her to be happy."

"There was one last test, Graeme. Sacrifice...true sacrifice. Well done."

How his rage, his desolation could fade away so quickly, he didn't know. It was as though it had been washed away by something too powerful for the mortal mind to explain, or even comprehend. But then the darkness came—

Darkness.

Life ceased.

Time stopped.

Pain disappeared.

But so did joy.

So did pleasure.

So did hope.

But love...even here, trapped in the dark void, Graeme could feel love.

Had He listened, then? Had Graeme's last, final plea been answered? Vixen...as long as she was happy...

In his sleep, he sighed, shifted. Cool hands stroked over him. Unconsciously, he caught one, squeezed gently, laced their fingers.

Happy—as long as she was...

Awareness came on him slowly. Gradually. The dream became less and less real, fading into that surreal plane where things seemed both possible and impossible.

Things like one life traded out for another, because of one decent choice.

Where one more chance was given—because a willing sacrifice was offered.

Then, as the hands on his body grew more demanding, he let go of the odd dream and let himself waken.

If there was a better way to wake up, Graeme wasn't so sure he wanted to know. Her mouth was already cruising down over his chest as he pushed through the foggy place between slumber and waking. When he opened his eyes, she already had her hand wrapped around his cock, holding him steady as she took him in her mouth.

It was slow and sleepy, sweet and easy. One of the miracles of this woman he loved. Sometimes it was like this, like some sweet dream that couldn't possibly be real. Then other times it was heat and fire and raw power, something that had to be real, because the intensity of it could never exist within dreams.

Sweat bloomed on their bodies as she moved up and straddled his hips, taking him deep inside. She was hot, hot as fire, wet and silky soft around him, her pussy wrapping around his aching flesh in a slick, snug grasp. Her pale hair fell around her shoulders, down her back. Graeme reached up and fisted his hands in the long strands, pulling her down and covering her smiling mouth with his.

"I love you," he muttered.

Vixen sighed against his mouth and whispered, "I love you, Graeme."

It was slow, sweet, infinitely perfect, infinitely right. His slid his hands down, cupped her breasts in his palms, squeezing the smooth, pale flesh, pinched her nipples. His hands looked so dark against her skin—so rough against her soft perfection. She reached up, covered his hands with her own. Light flashed off the diamond in her wedding set.

For a second, the sight of it unsettled him—*wedding ring?*

That's not right...

Yes. Yes, it was. The memory of her standing at his side in front of a justice of the peace, promising to love, to honor...

Those vague half-formed memories faded away as she tugged on his hands and twined their fingers, urging his arms up over his head. As early morning sun filtered in through the curtains, painting her body a pale gold, he let her take him. As she moved closer and closer to orgasm, the slick wet satin of her pussy got tighter, hotter. He felt his body's reaction, hot chills racing down his spine, the sac of his balls drawing tight. Tearing his hands away from her, he flipped them over and drove into her.

The lazy, sweet lust blistered away, obliterated by the hotter burn of need. He couldn't lose himself inside her fast enough, couldn't do it often enough—not to make up for how long he'd been without—no. Not right. He'd never been without her, had he?

Yes—yes, he had. He'd lost her. Not just once. But twice—

Confused, torn apart inside with love and need, Graeme snarled and crushed his mouth to hers. He drowned in her taste, desperate to lose the weird thoughts, strange sensations of helplessness and loss plaguing him. Vixen whimpered into his mouth, her nails raking down his skin.

Guilt lit into him. Too rough, too hard. He tore his mouth away, whispered, "I'm sorry." His body shuddered as he tried to get control.

Her eyes flashed at him and she reached up, fisted her hands in his hair, pulled his mouth to hers. "You will be if you stop..."

He grinned against her lips. "Tough girl." But the smile faded as quickly as it formed, lost to the need. "Vixen..."

Shoving up onto his knees, he cupped her ass in his hands, tucked her in close against him. Staring down into her face, he rolled his hips, pushing, deep, deep, deep. But he could disappear inside her and still not have enough. "I love you."

Would she say it...

A slow, sexy smile curled her lips. "I love you too."

Then her lashes fluttered low and she stroked a hand down her torso, her fingertips sliding through the pale curls until she could circle them around her clit. The sight of her slender fingers working the tight, hard bud had his cock jerking in demand.

Deeper.

Harder.

Catching her knees, he hooked them over his arms and reared forward, slammed into her. Deeper. Harder. More. More.

It was a litany in his brain, and it fueled the need he couldn't really control. Losing himself to it, he fucked her hard and when she came screaming his name, he growled in satisfaction and let himself climax.

More. More. More. Even as his heart slowed and his breathing calmed, he needed more.

Rolling to his side, he caught her hand, pulled it up to his chest. "I love you."

And she smiled. He felt it against his neck just before she kissed him right above his rapidly beating pulse. "I love you."

CR&O

Vixen came out of the shower to find her husband sitting at his desk and staring out the window.

The window faced out over Lake Michigan. Today, it was placid, reflecting the perfect blue of the early summer sky. But she suspected he wasn't seeing the water. Knowing how his mind worked when he was focused on a story, she didn't bother saying his name, just went up and laid a hand on his shoulder. He covered it with his.

"You okay?"

"Yeah. Just had this weird dream last night."

She combed her fingers through his hair, the short dark waves winding around her fingers. He'd get it cut again. He never let it get much longer than this. The curls drove him nuts. But she liked them. She traced her fingers down his neck, along his shoulder, unconsciously seeking out the weird scar on his back. It was just above his heart—whatever had stabbed him should have killed him.

That was how they met.

She'd been walking down the street and there he was— laying facedown at her feet. Like he'd dropped down out of the sky. Dark, hot blood pumped out of his chest, staining the back of his shirt. The startled shout that had been forming in her throat died as something overtook her body—that was the only way she could explain how she knew what to do, how she knew she needed to kneel beside him and cover the wound, pressing hard against it with one hand as she dug into her pocket—looking for God only knew what.

Plastic wrap?

Why she'd had a 12-inch square of plastic wrap in her pocket, she had no idea. But she knelt by the man, covered the wound with the plastic, allowed just a bit of air to escape. Later, at the hospital, she'd been complimented on her quick thinking and a doctor had asked her if she was a nurse or something.

A nurse? Hell, no, she'd told him.

That had startled him, but nowhere near as much as it had startled her. Whatever she'd done had saved Graeme's life. She'd left the hospital covered in his blood, shaking, edgy, nervous—determined to put that very weird night behind her. Determined to forget about him.

But four weeks later, he showed up on her doorstep.

It was like…looking into the eyes of destiny.

She hadn't seen his face the night he'd almost died, but for some reason, staring at him as he stood on her front porch had been like looking into the eyes of destiny. She had known how he would look, that he'd have eyes an impossible shade of blue—even before he pushed his sunglasses up off his head, she'd known his eyes would be a surreal, unearthly blue.

She'd known how he would smell before she opened the door to let him come inside.

When he lifted a hand to cup her cheek, she'd known how his touch would feel.

When he kissed her, moving in and gathering her up close, it was like they'd done it a thousand times. She knew how he would taste before he kissed her.

But they'd never met—hadn't even said a word to each other until after he lifted his lips from hers.

It sounded so incredibly fucked up, but it felt so incredibly right.

When he'd asked her out to dinner that night, she'd accepted.

When she'd invited him inside afterwards, he'd accepted.

He'd never really left either.

Less than six weeks later, he proposed and even as she said yes, she'd wondered why he'd waited so long.

That had been three years ago. To this day, she didn't know who had stabbed him. But if she hadn't been there, in that exact moment, he would have died.

Chicago's West Side wasn't the place for nightly strolls. If duty hadn't pulled her there, she never would have gone there that late at night. Vixen had never been the type to take unnecessary risks. The necessary ones were fine. She'd been there on one of the necessary ones, tracking down one of her kids before the boy made a mistake that would lead straight to hell.

It had been a useless expedition because a uniform had picked up her client a few hours earlier. The kid ended back up in a detention center, so it might seem like a lost battle to some.

But if Vixen hadn't gone looking for her kid, then Graeme would have died.

He couldn't tell anybody what had happened to him, who'd stabbed him, or why. It was a case that remained unsolved—yet somehow, she knew he didn't even care. She did, but only because she wanted whoever had hurt him to suffer. And suffer. And suffer more.

Bending over, she draped her arms around his shoulders and pressed her cheek to his, staring at the computer screen. As she read what he had written on the screen, a shiver ran through her.

Strong.

Powerful—a sense of déjà vu so overwhelming that it weakened her knees for the briefest moment. Then it was gone. Must come from seeing her name on the screen—that was all.

Right? She laughed, feeling a little self-conscious. A little embarrassed. "Vicious Vixen? Should I be insulted or flattered?"

He shrugged, but it lacked his normal grace.

Concerned, she forgot the eerie feeling creeping through her and focused on Graeme. Walking around the chair, she stood in front of him, laid her hand on his cheek. He lifted his gaze to hers and her heart clenched at the sight of his troubled eyes. "Baby, are you okay?"

He forced a smile, but it wasn't reflected in his eyes. "Yeah. It's just this dream. It was about us—or at least, it seemed like it. Seemed like memory, something that really happened. Or maybe...I dunno, something that could have been. It's just weird, staying with me, you know?"

Seemed like memory—

Shaking it off, she made herself look at the screen. It was just words. That was all. Words on a screen. Words he might spin into a story—imagination, nothing else. "Trying to write it down?"

"I dunno. Yeah. Maybe. Shit. I really don't know."

She bent down, pressed her lips to his, lingered. Then straightening, she moved to stand behind and wrest his chair around until he was fully facing the computer. "Write it down."

Then she left him to it. He might write for a living, but she had to go out there and brave the concrete canyons. She was just now scrapping her way into the district attorney's office, and today she was going to start trying her first case—well, not completely hers. She was co-chair, but damn, what a case to start out on.

Gerard Hawthorne, long-time blight on Chicago's society, had finally gotten caught in a mess he couldn't wrangle out of— and Vixen was going to be one of the ones who helped put him away.

The job wasn't the glamorous one sometimes portrayed on TV, but it was a worthwhile one. Especially right now.

On her way out the door, she paused and looked back, frowning at the computer. Again, she shivered. A second later, she made herself turn away, made herself focus on her job— instead of Graeme's.

When she got back home, she'd read what he had written and no doubt, be amazed. It happened every time she read something he wrote.

But it would still be nothing more than words. Just a story.

As she started getting dressed, she heard the familiar clatter of fingers moving across a keyboard.

A story. Just a story, she told herself. But even as she finished getting ready and left, she found herself turning those first few lines over in her mind. Found herself thinking of the weird dream that had woken her, a dream that had tears burning in her eyes, a lingering, icy-hot pain in her chest—and a need to hold onto Graeme tight—so tight nothing could separate them.

Distantly, Graeme heard her leave but he was already lost to the scenes playing out through his mind.

He heard the phone ring—vaguely heard his foster father's voice, reminding him they were supposed to go fishing tomorrow.

But the story—he was lost to it.

The beginning wasn't right, not yet...but he'd work on it.

The names, he'd have to change them. In the back of his mind, he knew that and while part of him didn't want to change the names, he knew he'd have to.

If he wrote himself and his wife into a book, his readers would probably think he'd gone off the deep end.

Or worse—somebody might think it actually happened.

A story—nothing more. Even if it did feel like a memory.

Yeah, he definitely needed to change the names when he was done—he could do that. Even if nobody else knew, he'd know who the characters were—he'd know. Vixen would know. It was enough for him.

The beginning—shit, need to fix that. Something wasn't right. That wasn't where it all started, was it?

Dragging his mind away from that, he made himself focus.

He could fix the beginning later. That's what rewrites were for.

For now...

Vicious Vixen

Chapter One

They called her vicious.

They called her vindictive.

They called her violent, volatile...

But Graeme Lawson, arrogant bastard that he was, he had simply called her his...

About the Author

To learn more about Shiloh, please visit http://shilohwalker.com. Send an email to Shiloh at shiloh_@shilohwalker.com or join her Yahoo! group to join in the fun with other readers as well as Shiloh. http://groups.yahoo.com/group/SHI_nenigans/.

Some love can last a lifetime—
their love was destined to last longer.

Hunter's Edge
© 2008 Shiloh Walker

Angel's first words to Kel were I'm going to marry you. She was seven at the time. He was eight. And he didn't laugh when she spoke the words. Best friends as children, lovers as young adults, they had an unexplainable bond. Their future looked set. Until the night they were attacked by a creature that couldn't exist.

Angel survived the attack—barely. But Kel didn't. Or at least, nobody thought he did. His body was never found and Angel's life would never be the same.

The attack might not have killed Kel's body, but it sure as hell killed his heart. Twelve years later, there's one part of his former life that he can't move past. Angel. He can't let her go, but he can't have her either. She doesn't even realize he is still alive.

But when a threat surfaces, Kel's willing to do whatever it takes to protect Angel. Even if it drives them both to the edge of insanity and back.

Available now in ebook and print from Samhain Publishing.

She's his match—but he's not in her business plan.

Byte Marks
© *2008 Mardi Ballou*
A Fangly, My Dear story.

Hereditary witch Dominique LaPierre has always refused to use her powers, especially when it comes to business. Until now. Her new company, a computer dating service that hooks up the San Francisco human and para communities, thrives on crossing that boundary. Business is great despite opposition from the arrogant and conceited Antoine Thierry, a leader in the vampire community. And, to her irritation, she finds she's got the hots for him.

Antoine doesn't like or trust witches. Nor does he like the growing power of technology; real vampires, in his view, don't need it to have a social life. Besides, if he can't control the game, he doesn't want to play—except with Dominique. The heat between them could melt down any hard drive. She pushes his buttons on every level, from the board room to the bedroom. But he's holding out, especially when she looks to him to support her new business.

Antoine wants it all. His way—and his woman.

Available now in ebook from Samhain Publishing.

GET IT NOW